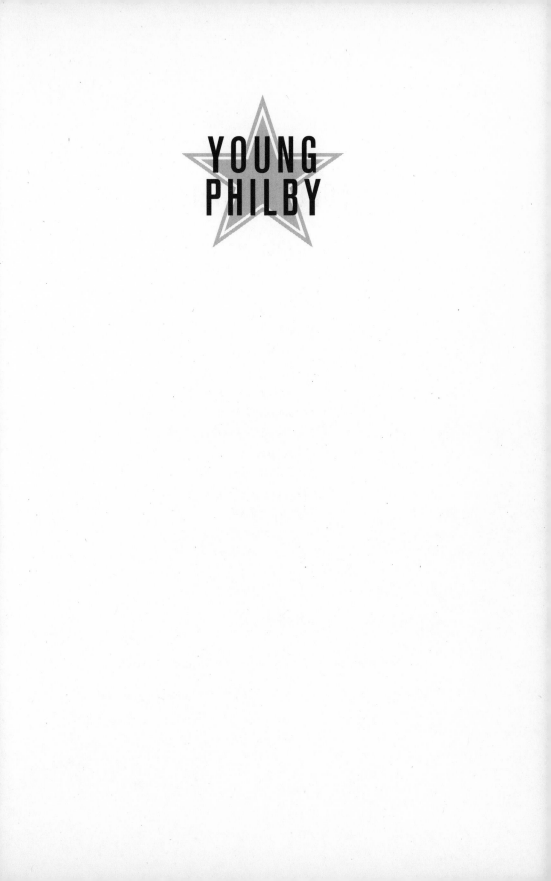

YOUNG
PHILBY

ALSO BY
ROBERT LITTELL

FICTION

Vicious Circle
Legends
The Company
Walking Back the Cat
The Visiting Professor
An Agent in Place
The Once and Future Spy
The Revolutionist
The Amateur
The Sisters
The Debriefing
Mother Russia
The October Circle
Sweet Reason
The Defection of A.J. Lewinter

NON-FICTION

For the Future of Israel (with Shimon Peres)

YOUNG PHILBY

ROBERT LITTELL

DUCKWORTH OVERLOOK

This impression 2013
First published in the UK in 2012 by
Duckworth Overlook
30 Calvin Street
London E1 6NW
Tel: 020 7490 7300
Fax: 020 7490 0080
info@duckworth-publishers.co.uk
www.ducknet.co.uk

First published in the USA in 2012 by
Thomas Dunne Books, an imprint of
St. Martin's Press, New York

This is a work c … events
portrayed in thi … tion or

A

ISBNs
Hardback: 978-0-7156-4328-0
Mobipocket: 978-0-7156-4452-2
ePub: 978-0-7156-4451-5
Library PDF: 978-0-7156-4450-8

Printed and bound in the UK by
CPI Group (UK) Ltd, Croydon Surrey

For Pita

PRINCIPAL PERSONAGES IN THIS BOOK

Yelina Modinskaya: Soviet intelligence analyst charged with reviewing the Englishman's dossier, *Committee for State Security case file no. 5581.*

Litzi Friedman: Hungarian-born Communist activist, agent for Moscow Centre in Vienna at the time Austrian Chancellor Dollfuss crushed the Austrian Socialists and Communists in 1934.

Harold Adrian Russell Philby: Young Cambridge University Marxist—nicknamed Kim after Kipling's legendary fictional spy—who turned up in Vienna in 1933 looking for adventure, a cause to believe in, comradeship, affection, love, sex.

Guy Burgess: Kim's brilliant, unconventional leftist classmate at Trinity College, Cambridge, who took a visceral pleasure in flaunting his homosexuality.

Teodor Stepanovich Maly: Moscow Centre's London *Rezident* who, using the pseudonym Otto, recruited the Englishman, offering him a clandestine alternative to calling out *Daily Worker* headlines to illiterate coal miners.

Miss Evelyn Sinclair: The Admiral's spinster daughter who knew the location of her father's dead letter boxes and was considered to be the institutional memory of His Majesty's Secret Intelligence Service.

Harry St John Bridger Philby: Kim Philby's eccentric father, nicknamed the Hajj, who converted to Islam and went to live in Arabia, but kept up with his old school chums in London.

Frances Doble: Bunny to her friends, Canadian film and theatre actress who starred in Nöel Coward's *Sirocco* but really came into her own at after-theatre champagne parties; an ardent royalist, she favoured Franco in the Spanish Civil War in the belief that he would restore her friend the exiled King Alfonso to the throne.

Miss Marjorie Maxse: Veteran recruiter for His Majesty's Secret Intelligence Service, spinster in her seventies who could whistle through her fingers to flag down a hackney carriage and was disconcertingly direct when vetting prospective espionage agents.

Anatoly Gorsky: the NKVD man who succeeded Otto as London *Rezident* and ran the Cambridge agents, including Kim Philby.

I suppose what one *should* be asking is whether an ideal becomes invalid because the people who hold it are betrayed. —Pat Barker in *The Ghost Road*

YOUNG
PHILBY

PROLOGUE: MOSCOW, AUGUST 1938

Where Teodor Stepanovich Maly is Refused a Last Cigarette

So: The Y in the *Y.* Modinskaya on my identification tag stands for Yelena, which was also the name of my late maternal grandmother, one of the first female commissars in the glorious Red Army at the time of the revolution. I am thirty-three years of age. Until my recent reassignment as an intelligence analyst I worked as a research assistant in the second chief directorate of the Peoples' Commissariat for Internal Affairs, better known by its initials NKVD. No, I am not married—unless of course you accept Senior Lieutenant Gusakov's formulation that I am married to my job.

Yes, yes, you are one of the few to grasp that it was an ordeal for me, too. It goes without saying it was an ordeal for the condemned man (that's the point, isn't it?), but I'd never even been down to the floors where they interrogate state criminals, much less interviewed one moments before his execution. I'd been given the seventeen cardboard boxes containing case file No. 5581 (each box stamped in red "Top Secret" and "Committee for State Security of the Council of Ministers of the USSR") one month, one and a half weeks earlier and had been poring over the contents for most of my waking hours since: reams of reports, typed on foolscap, from or about the Englishman; sheafs of telegrams that passed between the London *Rezidentura* and Moscow Centre, each month-worth bound by a thick elastic band; assessments of the Englishman's bona fides by the analysts who had worked on the case file before me. Despite putting in fifteen-hour days at my desk, I'd only managed to examine something like two-thirds of the documents. Concerning my conclusions, in theory my mind was still open, but I had already found inconsistencies in the précis prepared by my immediate predecessor before his deportation to a Siberian work camp. My section chief in the fifth department of the second chief directorate, Senior Lieutenant Gusakov, accompanied me as far as the door of the interrogation room. I have this memory of him throwing out a starched cuff and glancing impatiently at the watch strapped to the inside of his pudgy wrist. "You can have half an hour with him, Junior Lieutenant Modinskaya. Not a minute more. We must not keep the comrades in the crypt waiting."

A guard unlocked the door of what turned out to be a narrow, bare room with a high ceiling. I could hear him locking the door behind me once I was inside. The room reeked of a distinctly unpleasant odour. First light the colour of ash and the weight of lead oozed through a slit of a window high in the wall. I thought I caught the scream of friction brakes as trolley cars stopped in Dzerzhinsky Square outside the Lubyanka prison to take on workers coming off the night shift. As my eyes grew accustomed to the murkiness of the unlighted room, I made out the figure of a man sitting on a three-legged stool. He was tall, thin, gaunt even, unshaven, unkempt, dressed in a shapeless suit jacket worn over a soiled white shirt buttoned up to a skeletal neck. There was a wispy triangular moustache on his upper lip. The hair on his head appeared to be matted. He was wearing shoes without laces or stockings. I was relieved to see that his ankles and wrists were secured in irons.

I settled onto the only other piece of furniture in the room, a straight-backed wooden chair, the kind you might find in any honest Soviet kitchen. When the prisoner continued to stare off into space, I coughed discreetly. Taking note of my presence, he shuddered. His head twitched to one side in awkward salutation. I heard him murmur, "I ask you to excuse me."

"I beg your pardon?"

"The last thing I expected was to be interrogated by a woman. When they came to fetch me in my cell, I thought they were taking me to execution. I . . . I crapped in my trousers. I lost all olfactory sense when my nose was broken during the interrogation but I suspect, from the expressions on the faces of the comrade guards who led me through the corridors, that I must stink to high hell."

I sensed he was struggling to control his emotions. I saw him raise his manacled hands, but as his head was bowed I could not tell if he was wiping tears from his eyes or sweat from his brow or froth from a corner of his mouth.

"I am sorry to see you in these straits," I said, thinking an expression of sympathy would create a favourable atmosphere for the interview. "I notice you wear a wedding band. Did your wife accompany you when you were summoned back to Moscow."

"She was instructed to return with me. She did not anticipate . . ." The prisoner cleared his throat. "She considered the rumours of purges in the ranks of the NKVD to be capitalist propaganda. She said we in any case had nothing to fear as we were dedicated Communists, guiltless of any wrongdoing."

"Where is she now?"

"I hoped you would tell me."

"There was no mention made of her in the transcript of your trial."

"One night soon after my arrest I heard a woman calling my name from a distant cell. I thought I recognized my wife's voice." He looked up. "Please help me."

I turned away. "You have been condemned as an enemy of the people by a special tribunal. There is nothing I can do for you."

"Do you really think I am a Fascist agent?"

"I read the verdict—you confessed to working for the Abwehr Division of the Wehrmacht High Command."

"I was tortured. The confession was beaten out of me. I confessed when I could no longer support the pain." Speaking in a grating whisper, he said, "At least give me a cigarette."

Filling the room with tobacco smoke would have solved

one of my problems. It was unfortunately against the rules. "This is not permitted," I said.

"Every civilized country of the world provides a last cigarette to a condemned man," he said miserably.

I would have liked to cover my mouth and nose with a scented handkerchief and breathe through it. "We don't have much time," I told him.

"You mean, I don't have much time."

"You were the London *Rezident* when the Englishman was recruited," I said. I read from one of my index cards. " 'Cipher telegram number 2696 to Moscow Centre from London *Rezidentura* June 1934: *We have recruited the son of a distinguished British Arabist known to be an intimate of the Saudi Monarch ibn Saud and thought to have links to the highest echelon of the British Secret Intelligence Service.*' The telegram is signed with your cryptonym: *Mann.*"

The prisoner looked up quickly. The sockets of his eyes seemed to have receded into his skull, the eyes themselves were curiously lifeless, as if they had died in anticipation of execution. Was it conceivable that light went out of the eyes *before* life went out of the body? "Why does it always come back to the Englishman?" the condemned prisoner was saying. "I never put one foot in front of the other without the consent of the Centre."

"The Centre's consent to the recruitment was based on your assessment of the situation," I reminded him.

"My assessment of the situation was influenced by the Centre's eagerness to recruit agents in Great Britain."

"How many times did you meet with the Englishman?"

"I lost track of the count."

"The correct response is nine."

"Why do you pose a question to which you know the answer?" He shook his head angrily. "In my capacity as *Rezident*, not to mention as the Englishman's controller, it was routine procedure for me to meet with him at regular intervals."

"Describe him."

"The details are all in my reports to the Centre."

"I would like to hear it from your lips."

The prisoner sucked air noisily through his nostrils. "The Englishman was born into the wrong century. He was one of the last romantics. Naïve perhaps, but an idealist to the marrow of his bone. He was above all anti-Fascist. He considered Stalin to be the bulwark against Hitler, Communism to be the bulwark against Fascism."

"In your opinion was he first and foremost a Communist or an anti-Fascist?"

"It was the Centre's approach at the time—let's not forget the recruiting of the Englishman took place in 1934—to emphasize the anti-Fascist line of the international Communist movement, to call for a united front against the Hitlerian menace. So it is not astonishing that we recruited agents who were motivated predominantly by anti-Fascism."

"You were not put off by his background—his ultra-conservative father with contacts in Saudi Arabia, his upper-class roots, his elitist education at the university Cambridge?"

"Put off! On the contrary, it was his background that

first caught my eye. I saw the potential for a long-term penetration scheme. We had lorryloads of working-class Communists with East London accents, we had Newcastle miners who recited *The Communist Manifesto* at their daughters' weddings, but none of them could hold up his end of a conversation in a gentleman's club. How could they be expected to penetrate the government or the diplomatic corps or, better still, Britain's Secret Intelligence Service?"

"Surely the fact that he sought you out, as opposed to your seeking him out, must have raised suspicions that he was controlled by the British Intelligence Service, that he was sent by them to penetrate *our* intelligence service?"

"I don't contest that after he came back from Vienna he turned up at the London headquarters of the British Communist Party Central Committee—"

I glanced at one of the index cards on my lap. "At number 16 King Street."

He seemed taken aback by my familiarity with the case file. "At number 16 King Street, exactly. He declared that he wanted to join the Communist Party."

The prisoner had put his finger on one of the many inconsistencies in my predecessor's précis. I said, very quietly, "It defies credibility that someone who walks off the street into the central committee headquarters would not be photographed by British agents, would not then be put on a watch list. That being the case, the Englishman stood little chance of penetrating the British organs of state unless . . ."

The condemned prisoner finished the phrase. ". . . unless his ultimate goal was to penetrate *our* organs of state in order to feed us disinformation." He tried to cross his legs but the ankle irons restrained him. "The comrades at the London central committee informed him they had to check him out before he could become a member of the British Communist Party. They told him to come back in six weeks time. A report with the Englishman's name on it reached my desk. I ran a background check on him. At Cambridge he'd been a member of the infamous Socialist Society. His closest friends, his acquaintances were all, like him, fervent leftists. No sooner had he pocketed his diploma than he went off to Vienna to participate in the Communist-inspired uprising against the dictator Dollfuss. Surely you are aware that it was one of Moscow Centre's trusted agents in Vienna, Litzi Friedman, who first proposed his name to our organs? Her original report described him as a Marxist who considered the Soviet Union to be the inner fortress of the world liberation movement, who idolized *Homo Sovieticus*, who believed international Communism would lead to a healthier Britain, a better world. The Centre sent me to Vienna to sit in on one of the Friedman woman's semimonthly meetings with her Soviet controller. I personally heard her put forward his candidacy, I heard her suggest that he would make an excellent agent. I interviewed her in London after she fled Dollfuss and Vienna. Again she insisted on the Englishman's anti-Fascism, on his eagerness to join the Communist *internationale*. Moscow Centre weighed all of these particulars when it agreed the London *Rezidentura* should attempt to recruit him."

"According to the documentation in case file number 5581, you personally recruited the Englishman."

He nodded despairingly. "I organized a meeting on a bench in Regent's Park in broad daylight. The Friedman woman brought him to me after taking precautions to be sure they were not being followed."

"Then what?"

The prisoner managed a contorted smile. "At first he assumed it concerned his joining the Communist Party. The night before I'd written out what I would say as if it were a script for a radio drama. I played the role I had given myself to perfection. 'If you want to join the Party, of course they will accept you into its ranks with open arms,' I told him. 'You can spend your days selling the *Daily Worker* in working class neighbourhoods. But it would be a waste of your time and talents.' He appeared startled by my words. 'What are my talents?' he asked. 'You are, by background, by education, by appearance and manners, an intellectual. You are able to blend in with the bourgeoisie and pass yourself off as one. If you really want to make a significant contribution to the anti-Fascist movement, simple membership in the British Communist Party is not the ticket. The clandestine alternative I am proposing will not be without difficulty, without danger even. But the rewards in terms of personal achievement, in terms of actually bettering the lot of the world's working classes, will be immense. You came down from Cambridge—this alone will open doors for you in journalism, in the foreign service, even in His Majesty's Secret Intelligence Service. Will you join us in the struggle against Hitlerism and international Fascism?' "

Outside the Lubyanka, labourers had begun using pneumatic hammers to dig up the macadam roadway. I recalled a lecturer at training academy talking about the efficacy of long silences in an interrogation. At the time I hadn't been quite sure what he meant. Now I understood. Silences could be especially useful in the current situation, where the prisoner would be taken for execution once the interview terminated. It was in his interest to keep the conversation going. With this in mind, I held my tongue, my eyes fixed on the reels of the tape recording machine next to my chair. As the silence dragged on, he became anxious. He squirmed on the stool and raised his manacled wrists to thread the fingers of one hand through his hair. When I finally broke the silence, I could see he was grateful to me for resuming intercourse and impatient to respond.

"Did the Englishman know who you were when you made your proposition?" I asked.

"I told him only that he could call me Otto."

"Did he know for whom you worked? Let me rephrase the question: Did he know for whom you *pretended* to work?"

The prisoner winced at the word *pretended*. "I was not a novice at the delicate business of recruiting agents. I was appropriately vague—I talked about the anti-Fascist front, I talked about the workers of the world uniting against their exploiters. But the Englishman had brain cells between his ears. Although he was too discreet to say so, there can have been little doubt in his mind that I represented Moscow Centre and the Soviet Union."

"What happened after you invited him to work for you?"

"What happened was he agreed on the spot."

"Without hesitation?"

"Without hesitation, yes."

"Didn't it strike you as odd that he would not be uncertain, that he would not claim to need time to weigh the risks, to consider the consequences of his decision?"

"I appealed to the adventurer as well as the idealist in him. I invited him to hitch his star to the Bolshevik project of imposing proletarian order on capitalist chaos. I offered him a meaningful existence, which was one of the things that motivated me when I agreed to work for the Centre. Perhaps you signed on for similar reasons. Looking back on that first meeting in Regent's Park, it came as no surprise to me to find the Englishman nodding eagerly."

I decided to provoke the prisoner in the hope of making him depart from what was clearly a carefully prepared narrative. "From the point of view of the Centre, the recruitment of the Englishman must be seen in a more sinister light. How can he possibly be a bona fide agent when the person who recruited him is a convicted German spy?"

He retorted, "You are in much the same frame of mind as a dog chasing its tail."

"How dare you insult a Chekist!"

My outburst seemed to amuse him. "Someone minutes away from having a large-calibre bullet shot into the nape of his neck doesn't lose sleep over the insulting of a Chekist."

I concede I saw his point and decided there was nothing to be gained by taking offence. "You don't answer my question," I observed evenly. "Not only were you, the London NKVD *Rezident* and the Englishman's controller, a traitor to the motherland, your predecessor in the London

Residentura, Ignaty Reif, cryptonym Marr, who also vouched for the Englishman, betrayed the motherland and suffered execution. Still another of the Englishman's Soviet controllers—" I shuffled through my index cards until I came across the one I wanted—"Alexander Orlov, cryptonym the *Swede*, defected to the West last month—"

"The Swede *defected*!"

"His real name was Leon Lazarevich Feldbin—he is an Israelite. He vanished from his post in the south of France."

"Orlov was an honest Bolshevik. He fought in the revolution. He was with the twelfth Red Army on the Polish front after the revolution. Feliks Dzerzhinsky himself brought Alexander into the intelligence apparatus. If he appears to have defected, consider the possibility that he is part of a Centre operation to deceive the enemy services with disinformation."

"Needless to say, I have consulted my superiors. Orlov's defection was not an operation. He knew that the Englishman had been recruited by our NKVD—many of his reports from the field passed through Orlov's hands. Yet even as we speak, the Englishman has not been arrested. The facts speak for themselves."

The condemned prisoner slumped on his stool, shaking his head in disbelief. "You don't take into account the success of the Englishman's mission in Spain during the civil war."

"While he was supposedly working undercover in Spain as a British journalist, he was instructed to assassinate the Fascist leader Franco. Not surprisingly, he did not make the slightest attempt to carry out this order. Not surprisingly, given that you have been exposed as a German agent, given that Germany supported Franco and his Nationalist armies, you dispatched telegrams to the Centre defending the Englishman's failure to carry out the order."

"The order was preposterous. The Englishman was trained only in intelligence gathering. The instincts, the talents that are required for classic espionage do not prepare an agent for wet jobs. Beyond that there would have been no way for an armed foreigner to get close to Franco, no way to kill him and escape. The assassin, once caught, would have confessed to being a Soviet agent. It would have caused an international incident. Germany and Italy, both zealous supporters of Franco, might well have declared war on the Soviet Union. Only someone completely detached from reality could have issued such an order."

I had the appropriate index card in my hand but was able to quote the contents without looking at it. "The order originated with Comrade Stalin, who reasoned that the Nationalist armies and their Roman Catholic supporters would collapse and the Republicans triumph if the Fascist leader Franco could be eliminated."

By now the narrow room was filled with daylight. I could see the prisoner's lips trembling. After a moment he said, "In the years since he was recruited, the Englishman has provided us with a wealth of true information."

"Obviously he sent true information. Penetration agents are obliged to supply true information in order to establish their credibility and make you swallow the false information that they slip into their reports. You, an Abwehr agent, supplied the Centre with true information on the German order of battle and its armament priorities in order to make us swallow a certain amount of false information."

"I defy you to cite a single example of false information I provided."

I shrugged. The conversation was going nowhere. "You stood surety for the Englishman and passed on as true information what he wrote in his reports to you."

I gathered up the index cards on which I had written out questions. The prisoner noticed the gesture. "Don't go, for God's sake," he rasped. "I must talk to you as long as possible."

"I was given half an hour—"

He produced a book of matches from the pocket of his suit jacket. "I have written out a short note to Comrade Stalin on the inside cover. It is not too late for me if you can get this to him. He will surely remember Teodor Stepanovich Maly, he will recall my loyal service to the party during the revolution, my devotion to the state since. He will instruct the judges to reconsider their verdict."

"Pencils are forbidden to prisoners," I felt it was necessary to remind him. "This is a grave breach of rules and could have serious consequences for you."

I saw the condemned man holding out the book of matches as he shuffled towards me in his ankle irons. "You are my only hope," he whispered.

I am embarrassed to say I found myself stumbling across the room towards the door. I have a vague memory of rapping my knuckles on it. With relief I heard the key turn in the lock. The door opened. I filled my lungs with the stale air of the corridor. Senior Lieutenant Gusakov stood there with the comrades who had come up from the crypt, thick-set men wearing stained leather aprons over their NKVD uniforms and smoking fat hand-rolled cigarettes. The sight of a female emerging from the room took them by surprise.

"Take her away," one of them muttered. "This is no place for a woman."

Another comrade, a short man with a shaven skull, said with a snicker, "Unless of course she is the one sentenced to the highest measure of punishment." The other comrades looked away in discomfiture.

Senior Lieutenant Gusakov gestured with a snap of his head and started towards the elevator. "Was Maly able to shed light on the inconsistencies in your predecessor's précis?" he demanded as I fell in alongside him. He stopped in his tracks. "The Englishman—whose side is he on?"

"The evidence I have seen so far points to his being a British agent," I replied. "The condemned prisoner Maly said nothing to persuade me otherwise."

1: VIENNA, LATE SUMMER 1933

Where an Englishman Wanders into the Wrong Century

The Englishman came from another planet looking, no doubt, for adventure, a cause to believe in, comradeship, affection, love, sex. His luck, he found someone who dyed her hair so often she was no longer sure of the original colour: me. We were roughly the same age—he was twenty-one and fresh from university when he made his way to my flat in the centre of the city—but any resemblance between our life lines ended there. I was half Jewess and half not, with the two parts of my identity in constant conflict; I'd been a Zionist fighting for a distant Jewish homeland before I joined the Communists fighting for Austrian workers nearer to hand. I'd been married and divorced (when I discovered that my husband preferred to sleep *in* Palestine than *with* me). Once I'd even been thrown into an Austrian jail for two weeks for my Communist activities that came to the attention of the police;

I'd been caught letting my spare room to a certain Josip Broz, who turned out to be a Croatian Communist wanted in half a dozen Balkan countries. (He would hold party meetings in my apartment, pointing to one or another of the comrades and giving them assignments with the words *Ti, to—You, that*. He did this so regularly we nicknamed him *Tito*.) My stint in prison wasn't wasted; I discovered that, for want of a mirror, a girl could see her reflection in a cup of coffee well enough to apply lipstick, without which I feel unprotected. Despite my arrest, my clandestine work for Moscow Centre had fortunately gone undetected. You could make the case that I was at the opposite end of the spectrum from a vestal virgin. I had taken lovers when it pleased me to take lovers but I was careful to keep an emotional distance between us, which is why they invariably ended up becoming former lovers. The truth is, I'd never really been *intimate* with a male of the species before the Englishman. Intimate in the sense of taking pleasure from giving pleasure. Intimate in the sense of feeling that waking up in the morning next to a stark naked *Homo erectus* was an excellent way to begin the day.

Ah, the Englishman . . . You won't believe how innocent he was when he appeared on my doorstep: handsome in a timid sort of way, painfully unsure of himself, suffering (I later learned) from chronic indigestion, talking with an endearing stammer that became more pronounced when the subject turned to social or sexual intercourse. I could tell right off—girls are born with a sixth sense for body language—he'd never gotten laid, at least not by a female. Whether by a male is another matter entirely. Late one night, when we could hear artillery shells exploding in the workers' quarter across town, the Englishman downed a schnapps too many and told me he'd been b-b-b-b-b-buggered, as he put it. I never did discover if this initiation took place at one of those posh British boarding schools that don't light grate fires until water freezes in the faucets or later at Cambridge. I happened to have had enough intercourse with the King's English, not to mention the King's Englishmen, to know what *buggered* meant. Forgive me if I don't share the details. I'm rambling. Oh dear, I do ramble when I talk about the Englishman. Yes, I was saying that, sexually speaking, he was green behind the ears when he fell into my life. I would have been surprised to learn he'd ever set eyes on a young woman's breast, much less touched one. He certainly didn't know how to unfasten a brassiere. When we finally got around to sharing a bed, which was ten days after he moved into my spare room, it quickly became apparent he had only a theoretical notion of feminine anatomy. But, to his credit, in sex as in espionage, he was a quick study.

"Where did you learn to fuck like that?" I drowsily asked him the morning after that first night.

"You b-bloody well taught me," he said. "Your org-gasm is on my lips. I can taste it."

This, friends, turned out to be quintessential Philby, Kim to his mates, Harold Adrian Russell to the upper-crust English swells who happened by our table to sponge cigarettes when we took tea, as we did almost every afternoon, even in winter, on the terrace of the Café Herenhoff.

But I skip ahead—the tale is best told chronologically. Try to imagine my stupefaction when, responding to a knock so tentative it was almost inaudible, thinking it was the Negro come to deliver coal, I opened the door of my three-room flat to find a young gentleman shifting his weight from foot to foot in excruciating uncertainty, a rucksack hanging off one lean shoulder, a small but elegant leather valise on the floor next to his swanky albeit scuffed hiking boots. My first fleeting thought was that I was in the presence of someone who had wandered into the wrong century. He had the soft pink cheeks of an adolescent who almost never needed to shave; dishevelled hair with the remnant of a part in the middle; wrinkled flannel trousers with a suggestion of a crease; frayed trouser cuffs pinched by metal bicycle clips; a belted double-breasted leather motorcycle jacket with an oversized collar turned up; a beige silk scarf knotted around his throat; motorcycle goggles down around his neck; a worn leather motorcycle bonnet, the kind someone might have worn when motorcycles were first invented, hanging from a wrist. "There is no number on your door," he said, "but as you are b-between six and eight, I decided you must be seven."

I worked my fingers through my freshly minted blonde pageboy to see if the chemist's peroxide was still damp. "What were you hoping to find at number seven?" I demanded, laying the foundation for the emotional wall I meant to raise between us.

My visitor, speaking English with the barest curl to his upper lip, said, "I was led to b-believe I might be able to let a room at Latschgasse 9, ap-partment number seven."

The more he stammered, the more I saw my emotional wall crumble. "And who led you to believe that?"

"One of the comrades at the Rote Hilfe alliance that assists p-persecuted refugees."

"What brought you to Vienna?"

"My motorcycle brought me to Vienna. I took the liberty of p-parking it in your courtyard next to the rubbish b-bins."

"I am not inquiring about your mode of transportation. I am inquiring about your motivation."

"Ahhh. Motivation." I remember him shrugging in confusion. I was to discover that clichés irritated him, the more so when they spilled from his own lips. "Vienna is where the action is," he said. "Or will b-be. I came to do my p-part."

I thought about this. "Are you saying you rode a motorcycle all the way from England *to do your part*?"

"Not counting the channel, it's only nine hundred miles, give or take." He favoured me with a shy smile. "If I may be so b-bold, what about you?"

"What about me?"

"Why are you in Vienna?"

"I have a rendezvous with history." In those days, like these days, one couldn't be too vigilant. "Don't change the subject. How did you know about Rote Hilfe?"

"One of my professors at Cambridge is a wheel in the B-british Communist P-party—he gave me a letter of introduction to the Austrian Committee for Relief from German Fascism. I can show you the letter."

He started to reach into his rucksack but I waved him off. Anyone could produce a letter. "What is the address of Rote Hilfe? Which comrade gave you my address?" I stood ready to slam the door in his perplexed face if he answered incorrectly.

He produced a small spiral notebook from an inside breast pocket and, moistening the ball of a thumb on his tongue, started to leaf through the pages. I could see they were chock filled with neat, almost microscopic, handwriting. "Right. Rote Hilfe is situated at Lerchengasse 13, up three flights, right as you come off a very seedy stairwell indeed, down four doors and B-bob's your uncle." He looked up. "Oh dear, I don't suppose you're familiar with *B-bob's your uncle*."

"I am able to figure it out," I said. "Go on."

"Yes. Right. The Rote Hilfe office consists of four rooms, one of them with used clothing spilling from cartons p-piled to the ceiling, another crawling with shabby soaks whom I took for Communists hounded out of Germany by Herr Hitler after the Reichstag fire. The ones who weren't p-playing sixty-six were sleeping in their overcoats on mattresses set on the floor. The whole apartment stank of cooked cabbage, though I never saw a stove where cabbage might be cooked. As for the comrade who gave me your address, I only know his nom de guerre. His friends called him Axel Heiberg. They had a good laugh at my expense when they got around to explaining that Axel Heiberg was the name of an island in the Arctic Ocean."

"Do you always do that?"

"D-do what?"

"Mark down everything you see in a notebook?"

"Actually, yes. When I was eleven my sainted father

dragged me off on a grand tour of the Levant—Damascus, B-baalbek, B-beirut, Sidon, Tyre, Tiberias, Nazareth, Acre, Haifa, Jerusalem, you name it, I've been to the souk. He ob-bliged me to keep a journal. I've been more or less at it since." He held out a pale palm. "Philby," he said. "Harold Philby. Kim to my very few friends."

"Why very few?"

"In my experience *Homo sapiens* usually disappoints. Only *Homo Sovieticus* rises to the historical occasion—challenging industrial Capitalism, National Socialism and its *fuehrer*, and your dreadful Dollfuss here in Vienna."

I remember being so moved by this declaration that I clasped his hand in both of mine. "Litzi," I said, perhaps a bit more eagerly than I would have liked. "Litzi Friedman, Latschgasse 9, apartment number seven. I pried away the seven to throw off the police if they should come around looking for me again. Tickled."

"Tickled?"

"Tickled to make your acquaintance, of course. Do come in."

"Money."

"Money?"

"*Zahlungsmittel* in German. *Fizetőeszköz* in Hungarian. *Valuta* in Italian. *Argent* in French. *Money* in the King's English, which is a language you speak more or less fluently."

It will have been early in the evening of Kim's second day in Vienna, I'd been too tactful to raise the subject the first day. We'd just gotten back to Latschgasse 9 after picking up packets of leaflets at a secret albeit primitive underground printing press and delivering them to workers' militia headquarters in the great housing projects off the rim road. I will confess it was exhilarating to ride on the back of Kim's Daimler motorcycle. I became a bit giddy looking up at the church steeples and what the Americans call skyscrapers (some of them ten or twelve stories high) soaring over my head as we sped through the narrow streets of the Innere Stadt. A light rain had begun falling when we turned onto Latschgasse, plastering my shirt to my skin. I noticed that my Englishman (as I'd begun to think of him) didn't notice. Food for thought: Was the problem with his eyes or what our Viennese Doktor Sigismund Freud calls the libido? Back at my flat, I changed into a dry shirt and dried my hair on a towel, then set out sandwiches and some flat beer and raised the delicate matter of rent. "Yes, money. British pounds. Austrian schillings. German Reichmarks. How much do you have?"

"Are we talking c-cash?"

"We are not talking IOUs. Of course we're talking cash."

"Ahhh. Yes. Well. My sainted father paid me for typing up the manuscript of his b-book—he rode a bloody camel across the Arabian desert from the Persian Gulf to the Red Sea in forty-four d-days. Hell of an exploit—T. E. Lawrence thought only an airship could cross what the Saudis call *the empty quarter*. Make d-damn good reading if father could find a p-publisher who didn't think our *Lawrence of Arabia* owned the copyright to desert sagas. Didn't help that the footnotes were in Urdu, which my father speaks fluently.

Or was that Persian? Hmm. About the money, I have loose change left over from that odd job, plus the hundred quid he gave me for my b-birthday."

A hundred pounds was a fortune in working class Vienna. "You actually have one hundred pounds sterling?"

He nodded.

"Show it to me."

He was sitting on one of the kitchen chairs we'd carried into the parlour for the committee meeting later that night. Kim rested his left ankle on his right knee, unlaced the hiking boot and pulled it off. Then he produced the wedge of bills that had been taped to the underside of the tongue in the boot. He handed the money to me. I counted it. There was a hundred pounds sterling, all right, in crisp five and ten pound notes. The bills were so new I feared the ink would rub off on my fingers.

"How long did you plan on this lasting?"

"Actually, I thought, what with living on the proverbial shoestring, I m-might be able to stretch it to a year."

"Twelve months?"

"That's the usual length of a lunar year."

I snatched up a pencil and began doing sums on the back of an envelope, converting pounds to schillings, adding up what he would need for rent and board. "In Vienna you can eat for six schillings a day if you're a vegetarian." I looked up. "You are a vegetarian?"

"I am now."

"Good. I read an article in our Socialist newspaper *Arbeiter-Zeitung* suggesting the average person lives 2.4 years longer if you don't eat meat."

"Does your b-budget include cigarettes."

"How much do you smoke?"

"A pack a day."

"Haven't read anything suggesting cigarettes are bad for your health. But you'll have to cut back all the same to pinch pennies."

"If I smoke less than a pack a day I s-stutter more. You're also forgetting petrol for the motorcycle, assuming we continue to make use of it in Vienna."

"Oh, we will certainly use it. I'll get our transport committee to pay for the petrol." I tallied up the columns. "I think seventy-five quid will see you through the lunar year." I counted out seventy-five pounds and handed it back to him."

He looked down at the bills, then up at me. "What are you planning to do with the other twenty-five?"

"Congratulations. You have just joined the Vienna Relief Committee. By coincidence, annual membership for Englishmen on motorcycles happens to be twenty-five pounds."

"But I came here to join the International Organization for Aid to Fighters of the Revolution."

The moment had come to begin his education. "If you want to work for the Communist cause, you will have to do it discreetly. In time I can put in a good word for you in certain circles. Meanwhile you must play the role of a naïve young English idealist who has come to lend a hand with refugees. The Austrian Communist Party, along with the International Organization for Aid to Fighters of the Revolution, have been declared illegal by Dollfuss and his gang. We Communists work through the Relief Committee, which is legal. Your twenty-five pounds will get four or five of the German comrades you saw sleeping on mattresses to safety in France." I looked at him. "Can I interpret your silence as agreement to make this contribution?"

"D-do I have a choice?"

I scraped my chair closer to him until our knees were almost but not quite touching. (Didn't want him to panic.) "You always have a choice—that's what life is about. Choices. Not making a choice is a choice." I must have smiled, which is what I usually do when I am about to make a suggestion that I don't want the *suggestee* to accept. "You can keep the hundred pounds, pack your rucksack, and go back to England if you don't want to join us."

"I am very happy here in Vienna, thank you."

The comrades who turned up for the committee meeting were impressed when I told them the Englishman had contributed twenty-five pounds to the Relief Committee. The professor from Budapest, an illegal who was trying to stay one step ahead of the Austrian police, wasn't. "You gave him back seventy-five?" he asked me in Hungarian. "What the devil's wrong with you?"

Kim looked at me. "You speak Hungarian?"

"I *am* Hungarian," I told him. "I was raised by my grandparents in what was then the Austro-Hungarian empire."

"But I have heard you speak German."

"My grandparents sent me to *gymnasium* in Vienna. I've been here since. This is their apartment." I told the Hungarian professor, "The Englishman will be invaluable to us when the revolution starts. With his motorcycle and his British passport and his pale English face he will be able to pass police checkpoints. We got past two of them today, Dollfuss's Heimwehr militia bullies didn't even search our rucksacks." I translated what I'd said into German for the district committee comrades. One of them, his eyes fixed on Kim, asked me in German, "How can you be sure he is not a double agent?"

Kim, who spoke German the way English people speak any language other than English, which is to say with discomfort, said, "Sie k-können nie sicher sein." Turning to me he asked in English, "Would your friends feel m-more at ease if I were to repair to my room?"

The Hungarian professor said in Hungarian "If the short count"—he was referring to Chancellor Dollfuss, who was notoriously dwarflike—"wanted to spy on us, he wouldn't try to infiltrate a district committee, he'd try to infiltrate the Party's Central Committee."

"You can stay," I told Kim. To the others I said, "Right now he is too innocent to be a single agent."

"I'm not sure I should take that as a compliment," Kim remarked.

"The great advantage to innocence," I remember telling him with a suggestive smirk, "is that there is a certain amount of pleasure to be had in losing it."

"Our Litzi is being sexual," one of the comrades, a university student with long bushy sideburns named Dietrich, told the others in a mocking singsong voice. They all laughed. Except me. Dietrich was one of my former lovers.

A bit flustered, I turned to the professor and invited

him to begin his lecture. Removing his eyeglasses, rubbing the bridge of his nose with his thumb and third finger, speaking a German more imperfect than Kim's, he began. "Industrial capitalism rests on the pedestal of the theory of equilibrium, which holds that the process of producing something creates just enough purchasing power to buy it. The Great Depression and the subsequent distress of the world's working classes have demonstrated that this convenient theory of equilibrium no longer—"

Leaping to his feet, Dietrich cut off the professor in mid-sentence. "Your Marxist theories are boring me to death," he declared. "They have become irrelevant. The rise of Fascism has focused the attention of many of us on things other than economics. We should be talking about how to stop Hitler from annexing Austria—"

Dietrich in turn was interrupted by Sergius, at seventeen one of the youngest workers' militia delegates to a district committee. "Look at the glasses of tap water Litzi has set out on the low table," he said. "The glasses are still but the water in them is trembling, as if what's going on in this city—what's going on in Europe—is shaking the crust of the earth."

"The water is trembling because Dietrich leaped to his feet," one of the worker delegates said with a soft laugh.

"The water is trembling," I remember saying, "the way the ground trembles before an earthquake. Revolution will explode in Vienna. There is a good chance it will spread to the entire capitalist world."

Sonja, Dietrich's current girlfriend and the only other

woman in the room, raised her hand. She was, like me, in her early twenties; unlike me she was strikingly beautiful, with the high cheekbones and deep-set coal black eyes associated with Caucasus mountain tribes. I seem to remember that one of her grandparents was Uzbek. "For shit's sake, Sonja, we're not at the university," Dietrich snapped unpleasantly. "You can speak without raising a hand."

"I want to put a question," she announced.

"By all means pose your question, dear girl," the Hungarian professor said.

Sonja leaned forwards, her breasts swelling over her low-cut Austrian peasant blouse. Her cleavage was not lost on the voyeurs present. "I am, as you know, the Socialist party's representative on the district committee," she said. Unaccustomed to speaking publicly, she took a deep breath before plunging on with a fierce intensity. "I am a Marxist but not a Communist. And I ask the question that many of my Socialist comrades ask: Which is the greater evil, German Fascism or Soviet Communism?"

Dietrich, who was a die-hard Communist, rolled his eyes, which made me wonder what the two of them talked about in bed. Several of the district party comrades who held Communist Party cards turned away in disgust. And then a curious thing happened. My Englishman, who had been following the conversation attentively, looking from one speaker to the other as if he were at a country club tennis match, addressed himself directly to Sonja. Here, as best I can reconstruct it, is what he said: "When you say Soviet Communism, you of course mean Stalinism. I think we must distinguish between the two. Stalin's fastidious autocracy must be seen in historical p-perspective. The cadres that organized the B-bolshevik uprising lived as illegals for years, even decades, before the revolution thrust them into positions of power. Even then their grip on p-power was tenuous—they had to defend the revolution against foreign invaders and their White Russian lackeys in a b-brutal civil war. This surely explains, in p-part, the invasive role of the Soviet secret police and the disagreeable purging of the party ranks in the twenties, explains also Stalin's conviction that he is surrounded by enemies and must eliminate them before they eliminate him. In the pursuit of enemies, real or imagined, Stalin has undoubtedly d-distorted Communism. But Communism, as opposed to Stalinism, is another cup of tea entirely. Communism will carry on after Stalin and Stalinism. To answer your question: Hitler, who has the loyalty of the German military, and Fascism, which has captured the imagination of the German masses, are clearly the greater evil."

Blushing in embarrassment, Kim glanced quickly at me. "Our Englishman is less innocent than we thought," I said. "He has answered the question correctly. Those of us who have pledged allegiance to the Communist cause defend an ideal, not an individual."

"You're saying," Sonja said, looking intently at the Englishman in her eagerness to understand, "that Stalin is the lesser of two evils?"

"That's not exactly—"

"If Hitler is the greater of two evils, it follows that Stalin must be the lesser of two evils."

"It's more complicated than you're suggesting . . ."

"The lesser of two evils is still evil?"

"You're twisting my meaning . . ."

Sonja would not let go. "You're saying that Stalin's betrayal of Communism does not invalidate Communism?"

"Nobody said anything about Stalin *betraying* Communism," Dietrich declared heatedly. "There is a difference between *distorting* and *betraying. Distorting* is a tactical course change. It's trimming your sails to the wind. It's adapting to an evolving reality so the strategic objective, which is dictatorship of the proletariat, can be reached."

Sergius agreed. "It's Lenin's two steps forward, one step back."

The professor touched Sonja's shoulder blade. "Stalin *is* Communism, dear child. Whichever path he decides on, rest assured it is the right path."

"With or without Stalin, world revolution is inevitable," I said. "Talking eternally about it at Latschgasse 9, apartment number seven, won't speed it up. I propose we put the theoretical portion of our meeting behind us and move on to practical matters. Those in favour?"

All the members of the district committee except Sonja raised their hands. Seeing she was outvoted, she frowned at Dietrich, who seized her wrist and lifted it for her. The others laughed.

Dietrich brought up the question of acquiring arms for the workers' militia units, which skirmished nightly with the toughs in Dollfuss's militia. An important arms shipment hidden on one of the barges that plied the Danube, which flowed through Vienna's outer suburbs, had been discovered and confiscated by the police earlier in the week. The story had made headlines in the government-run newspapers. One of the militia delegates pointed out that we were starved for funds, which were desperately needed in order to purchase arms abroad. The district committees had been asked to impose a tax on neighbourhood merchants, who up to now had only been asked to contribute voluntarily. We discussed the matter at some length without reaching a consensus. The church bell down the block started ringing the hour. We all counted the rings in our heads. "Twelve," Dietrich announced. He stretched his shoulders and reached to rub the back of Sonja's neck. "Twelve," she agreed, resting her hand on his thigh.

All of a sudden I could imagine what they talked about in bed.

"Let's make revolution."

"Ahhh." I can picture Kim clearing his throat, a nervous tic that usually surfaced when he didn't quite know what to say. "Yes. Let's."

And we did. We smuggled seven Soviet Simonov rifles and four German Walther 41s, broken down into component parts and buried under garbage in collection trucks, to *Schutzbunders* (the workers' militia of the Austrian Social Democratic Party) in Karl-Marxhof, one of the fortresslike tenement blocks. We smuggled twenty-one German Bergmann pistols and a dozen Soviet Tula Tokarev automatics, concealed in a baby carriage, to a makeshift arsenal set up in the coal bin cellar of a toy factory. We brought in ammunition for all these weapons, four or five bullets at a time, hidden in my brassiere. We supplied gunpowder wrapped in small cornflower paper satchels to a clandestine munitions factory workers had set up on the top floor of a tenement. We slipped rucksacks filled with leaflets hidden under Hartmann's hygienic towelettes past checkpoints, with Kim blushing a shade redder than the teenage Fascist militiaman who waved a towelette aloft and cried out to his comrades, "Look what I found!" Carrying cartons lebelled as Austrian baby food, we delivered medical supplies to one of the makeshift infirmaries in the massive workers' housing projects. In the first days, Kim was bewildered by it all: the anxious faces of women and men who unpacked the weapons we brought, the preparations for violence in improvised factories, the cramped and airless cellar bins where meetings dragged on until the early hours of the morning. There were occasions when we were invited to vote and nobody could remember what we were voting on. Groggy from lack of sleep, we often got back to my apartment as Vienna was soaking up first light like a dry sponge.

I'll be candid: As the days sped past, I found myself waiting with growing impatience for Kim to make a move, the way men usually do when they want more from a woman than conversation. The back of a hand casually exploring your upper spine to see if you're wearing a brassiere is as good a place as any to begin. Massaging shoulder blades is always useful. Touching thighs when you're crammed into a café booth invariably takes the relationship to another level. A kiss on the cheek that, missing its mark like an errant arrow, grazes a corner of your lips must surely be seen as a hint of intimacies to come. The flat of a palm on your stomach daringly close to the undercurve of a breast can only be the seal on a done deal. Under ordinary circumstances all that remains to be decided is the venue: his bed or yours. But from *my* Englishman, nothing. Zero. He would offer me a cigarette (he smoked those dreadful French Gauloises Bleues) and even hold the flame of a matchstick to the end while I sucked it into life, or accept one of mine (a newfangled Czech cardboard filter tip) without so much as our fingertips touching. In the fullness of time I came to understand that I would have to lead this particular horse to water *and* make him drink if I hoped to quench *my* thirst.

"Let me ask you something," I blurted out the evening of his tenth day in my flat. "Are you . . ."

"Am I what?"

"Are you . . ." I grimaced and spit it out. "Queer?"

We were emptying ashtrays overflowing with cigarette ends into the garbage pail after a late night meeting of the district committee. Kim looked at me sharply. I thought I detected a blush on his English checks.

"*Queer* as in *homosexual*?"

I nodded weakly.

"What m-m-m-makes you ask?"

I settled onto the sofa next to him, our thighs touching. "Do you find me attractive? Do I *attract* you?"

"I find you . . . intensely 't-tract-tractive."

"Well, then?"

"Well, what?"

"Do I have to draw you a diagram?"

"Actually, I've b-b-been working up the nerve to ask you if we m-m-m-m-might—"

"For God's sake, Kim, you don't need to ask!"

"Ahhh."

At which point he did what he could bring himself to do—he grasped a fold of skirt above my knee as if he were staking a claim on the fabric and the body beneath it. "You have to understand, chaps like me are afraid to court b-beautiful girls like you."

"What are you afraid of?"

"We're afraid you'll say no, which would d-demolish the little b-bit of ego we have." He cleared his throat. "We're afraid you'll say yes and we won't rise to the occasion, which would also d-demolish the little b-bit of ego we have."

"I'm afraid, too," I whispered.

"What on earth would you be afraid of? You could have any man with a snap of your fingers."

"I'm afraid I'll snap my fingers and no one will hear. I'm afraid the rain will plaster my shirt against my breasts and no one will notice."

"I noticed," he said simply.

"That's a start. As for not rising to the occasion, I was married once, I have had experience helping men rise to the occasion."

"You make it sound so mechanical."

"There is a certain amount of mechanics involved. A woman who is not timid about using her hands and her mouth can make any man rise to the occasion."

He worked the fabric of my dress through his fingers

the way a Muslim manipulates worry beads. I slowly opened my thighs so he would understand he had been invited in. "Tickled," I murmured with an encouraging smile.

His lips trembled when we kissed—it was almost as if he were stammering. Then he said something quite memorable, and it sticks in my that mind he managed to say it without the faintest trace of a stammer. "If we have sex, knowing me, I am bound to take it seriously."

"Knowing me, I'm bound not to." I regretted the words the instant they passed my lips. Which I suppose explains why I quickly added, "Who can say I won't make an exception for you?"

As a child, I assumed everyone had a controller. In my case it was my maternal grandfather, Israël Kohlmann. I've lost count of how many delicious summers I spent at his country estate in Kerkaszentmiklós, a Hungarian village within hiking distance of the frontier with Croatia. Grandfather was the only Jewish landowner in the neighbourhood, but if there was anti-Semitism in the Hungarian air I was too young and too carefree to get a whiff of it. When I think back to those summers, I remember rope-skipping down the long poplar-lined gravel alley that led to grandfather's manor house; I remember hiding for days, with the rest of the family and the servants, in the dark cellars when the Reds, and later the Whites, pillaged the countryside during the dreadful years of the civil war that followed the Bolshevik Revolution; I remember swimming with my male cousins in the Kerka, the river that gave its name to the village. It was before I had breasts, I was stark naked and I was as fascinated by their genitals as they were by the absence of anything remarkable between my legs. My controller, which is to say my grandfather, must have learned about the nude swimming because one day I returned home to find a bathing costume set out on my bed. When I went swimming with the boys after that I wore it.

Sometimes.

Having been raised by a controller, I found it perfectly normal, when I was recruited by Moscow Centre, to be reporting to a controller. The first one called himself Dmitri. He had a theory that a female agent was best debriefed in a bed, so I used to whisper in his ear as he made love to me while loud American jazz played on the gramophone in case microphones had been concealed in the room. I told him whom I had observed talking to whom, I described the mood in the workers' tenements, I summarized what had been discussed at district meetings, I suggested who among the comrades might be pro-Soviet enough to be recruited by Moscow Centre as an agent. One day I turned up for my semi-monthly debriefing to discover Dmitri had been summoned back to Moscow so suddenly he'd left his treasured collection of American jazz behind, which seemed strange to me at the time, though I didn't put two and two together until years later when I read about the purge within the ranks of the NKVD.

His replacement, an overweight man in his fifties with tufts of hair pasted across his scabrous scalp, instructed me to call him Boris. He wore a monocle in the socket of his good eye, the other had been replaced by a glass eye after a grenade exploded in his face during General Frunze's conquest of the Soviet city that now bears the general's name. With a thumb hooked under one suspender, Boris would puff away on a cigar; from time to time he would wave his hand to create a porthole in the smoke and take long looks at my body with his good eye. I uncrossed and recrossed my legs, thinking the least I could do for a Red Army hero was reward him with a fleeting glimpse of thigh. In the end he would lose interest in my thighs, the porthole in the smoke would close and he would debrief me through the smoke.

Two weeks before my Englishman turned up in Vienna, Boris, too, was suddenly summoned back to Moscow; he departed so hastily he left a wife and a son behind, who promptly entrained for Italy and were never heard from again.

The third controller, whom I found waiting for me at the safe-apartment in the Judenplatz, a little square at the heart of Vienna's first Jewish ghetto at the end of an alleyway north of Schulhof, was, to my surprise, a woman, which supported the hunch I had that women were considered equal to men in the Soviet Socialist Republics and thus could rise to positions of importance. Depending on the time of day and the brightness of the light coming through the single window, she looked to be in her early forties or middle fifties. Her hair had been pulled back in a tight knot, her thin lips (without a trace of lipstick) looked as if they had never entertained a smile, her eyes were so heavy-lidded I could not make out the colour of her pupils. She instructed me to call her Arnold.

"But that's a man's name," I said.

"Precisely. That way if you are careless enough to refer to me, everyone will think your controller is male." She dipped the nib of her pen into a small jar of ink and looked up expectantly. I started to speak in German but she waved a forefinger the way my grandfather used to when he was cross with me. "Today we will speak in English so my colleague can follow the conversation," Arnold said.

Looking across the room, I could make out what appeared to be a tall, thin comrade sitting in a corner so shadowy his features were scarcely visible. He was wearing a dark suit and tie. He was obviously a chain-smoker because several times I noticed him lighting a cigarette on the burning end of one that had been smoked down to a stub. The embers glowed in the murkiness each time he sucked on the cigarette, creating just enough light to reveal a triangular moustache on his upper lip.

"Aren't you going to introduce us?" I asked Arnold.

"He knows who you are. You have no need to know who he is."

Laughing nervously, I mumbled something about her not being very polite.

"Politeness is for the captains of industry who exploit the proletarian classes. To the business at hand. Your report."

I launched into an account of my recent activities: the

smuggling of firearms into the workers' tenements and gunpowder to munitions factories.

"If civil war breaks out and the housing projects are attacked," my controller asked, "in your opinion how long can the workers hold out against Dollfuss's Heimwehr militias?"

"The workers' militias have a small number of rifles and pistols, perhaps one firearm for every twenty workers. They don't have much ammunition for the weapons they have, something like four or five rounds per weapon. They will be at a great disadvantage in a pitched battle with the Heimwehr."

"Describe the mood in the great housing projects?"

"The mood is revolutionary. A spark could ignite an uprising. Since Dollfuss disbanded parliament, he rules, like every tyrannical dictator, by decree. He has already outlawed the Communist Party. If he outlaws the Social Democrats, who still control the Vienna city council, it will be the last straw. There will be a storm of protests. Whether the protests turn violent will depend, in my opinion, on how Dollfuss and his militia ruffians react."

"I am told you have rented your spare room to an Englishman."

I fumbled in my handbag for a cigarette and a book of matches, lit the cigarette, and dragged on it to still my nerves. Was I in a pickle with Moscow Centre for bringing an Englishman into my circle of friends without my controller's permission? "He turned up at my door," I explained. "A British Communist vouched for him, the comrades at Rote Hilfe gave him my address."

"What is his name?"

"You surely know his name if you are aware he rents my spare room."

"What is his name?"

"Harold Philby. His friends call him Kim."

The gravelly voice of the man sitting in the shadows across the room reached me. "Are you sleeping with him?"

I glanced at him. A thin plume of his cigarette smoke drifted towards the ceiling. "Yes."

My controller asked, "What can you tell us about his political orientation?"

"He considers himself a Marxist and a Socialist and admits to being attracted to Communism. In any case he is an enemy of Hitler and an admirer of the Soviet Union, which he considers to be the rampart against the spread of Fascism. In his mind's eye, he sees himself as a foot soldier manning this rampart here in Vienna, working to thwart Dollfuss in the short term, to thwart Hitler's eventually annexing Austria."

"Is his family left-wing?"

"From what I could gather, I would suppose the opposite to be true. His father, Harry St John Philby, is something of a minor celebrity in England. Kim told me he'd been a member of one of the British expeditionary armies that drove the Ottoman Turks from Arabia. Since then he fancies himself an Arabist—he taught himself Arabic, converted to Islam, and went off to live in Jiddah, where he runs a modest business importing Ford motor cars. If Kim's father holds political views at all, they must surely reflect his establishment roots."

"What, then, accounts for his son's being a Marxist and a Socialist?"

"I am only guessing, of course, but it can be explained in part as a rebellion against a domineering father, rebellion, too, against the stifling social class in which he was raised. He speaks often of England's enormous unemployment in the wake of the Great War and the Great Depression, how nothing was done by Ramsay MacDonald's supposedly Socialist government to remedy this. Kim's worldview seems to have been formed during his undergraduate years at Cambridge University, where his closest friends were all leftists. Several had worked in the coal mines before obtaining scholarships to university. Kim himself joined the Cambridge Socialist Society. I don't know if there was a Communist cell in Cambridge; I don't know, assuming a cell existed, if he became a member. But there is absolutely no doubt about Kim's determination to take part in the struggle against Hitler and Fascism."

"From time to time you are on record as recommending Austrian or Hungarian comrades as potential recruits to Moscow Centre. Would you recommend your English roommate?"

"Intellectually and emotionally, there is no question whose side he is on. As he is fresh from university, he has had little field experience in organizing cells, in propaganda techniques, and none at all in living clandestinely. But I can say that he has a mental agility—"

The man sitting in the shadows interrupted. "What does that mean, *mental agility*?"

"He is a fast learner," I said.

I could hear the man in the shadows laughing under his breath. "Those of us who are still among the living are all fast learners."

My controller glanced at reminders she had jotted in ink on the palm of a hand. (I made a mental note of the technique—it was a good way to hide reminders, since they would wash off with soap and water.) "If we were to decide to recruit your Englishman," she said, "how do you think he would react?"

"Kim? Why, he would be flattered. He would be thrilled."

"Would he be able to keep his recruitment secret from his family and his Cambridge friends?"

"He would be bursting to tell *me*. But the answer to your question is yes, I believe he is capable of keeping secret things secret."

"In your opinion, would he more useful as a foot soldier manning the ramparts, as you put it, or as an agent operating covertly?"

"I do both."

The man in the shadows had a sense of humour. "She has a point," he said with a faint snicker.

My controller didn't have a sense of humour. "We are not scoring points," Arnold said with obvious irritation. "We are laying the foundation for world revolution."

"I quite agree," remarked the man across the room. "World revolution is our goal. But first we must recruit activists who can help us eradicate Fascism from the heart of Europe—comrades willing to put their lives at risk smuggling arms, informing on governments and their militias."

My controller turned back to me. "In your opinion, is your Mr. Philby capable of leading a double life?"

"He is certainly capable of compartmenting his life. I have seen him convince English chums on the terrace of the Café Herenhoff that he'd come to Vienna to see the sights and sample the *schnitzel*. He would have to be taught the ropes, of course. He was rather innocent, naïve even, when he arrived in Vienna. He has matured since."

"No doubt thanks to you."

"I don't deny I have played a role in advancing his maturity."

"What have you taught him?"

"To speak German more grammatically."

From the shadows, the man repeated the question. "What have you taught him?"

"I taught him . . ."

"Comrade Friedman," the man said, "we count on you to respond to our questions without hesitation. Collecting intelligence has a great deal in common with the assemblage of a jigsaw puzzle. The information you give us could assist us in filling in gaps in the puzzle."

"I taught him how to love a woman. He had no experience in this matter. I taught him how to deal with the police if he were to be arrested: to tell the truth as often as you can, to stay as close as possible to the truth when you are obliged to lie. I taught him some of what my previous controllers taught me: how to be sure you are not being followed, how to slip away if you are being followed, how to fabricate invisible ink using urine and write messages between the lines of a genuine letter, how to easily alter your appearance. I myself change the colour of my hair once or twice a month. I also taught him simple word substitution codes that can be used to communicate with people outside if he is arrested."

"Examples, if you please."

"I taught him *Send me a toothbrush and tooth powder* means *I have given them false names and false addresses.* The message *Send me a bar of soap* means *I have been forced to give them true names and true addresses.*"

"May I say, Comrade Friedman," the man in the shadows remarked, "that Moscow Centre is pleased with your work."

I will admit his words went through my body like an orgasm. My fingertips tingled with pleasure. I was almost speechless with gratitude. "I thank you," I managed to mumble.

We had our first fight, my Englishman and me, on our hundredth anniversary—a hundred days since we'd met, ninety since we'd begun to sleep in the same bed. I learned more about him from that first fight than I'd learned from the ninety-nine-day armistice preceding it. It began when I remarked, with extreme casualness, "I saw you looking at Sonja during the meeting tonight." We had reached my apartment, windblown from the motorcycle ride across Vienna. "Not that it matters," I quickly added, "but you were undressing her with your eyes, though I have to say, when she leans forwards there's not much undressing left to do."

"It obviously matters or you wouldn't have mentioned it." Kim tossed a shoulder. "Identify the crime? She is very p-p-pretty."

I threw his words back in his face. "'*If we have sex, I am bound to take it seriously.*'"

"But I do take our relationship seriously."

"Whatever happened to monogamy?"

"We are not m-m-married."

"We sleep together every night, which while it lasts is roughly the same thing as being"—here I made the blunder of imitating him—"m-m-married."

He reacted the way a bull does to a cape—figuratively speaking, he pawed the ground and charged. I had never seen him quite so livid. "You're flogging a dead horse, Litzi. I fantasize about Sonja when she leans forwards and I catch a glimpse of her b-breasts. Every b-bloke around the table fantasizes about her. That's why she leans forwards. I fantasized about you when the rain p-plastered your bloody shirt to your bloody b-body."

I was in a dark mood, too—before Sonja, all the boys around the table fantasized about *me*. So I flogged the dead horse at hand. "In the end you men are all the same," I said. "Anybody—*any body*—that inspires an erection becomes an object of fantasy. Tell me something, Kim, where does fantasy stop and reality begin? To put it another way: Does fantasy ever stop and reality ever begin?"

"Depends on the situation. Every situation, sexual or otherwise, has a bit of b-both, I suppose."

"So what you're saying is that every time you get an erection, you're responding to a bit of reality and a bit of fantasy?"

"Sounds to me as if you're suffering from erection envy." He shook his head in disgust. "Women are so b-bloody unfair."

"How unfair? Why unfair?"

"Look, in a heterosexual couple, it's the male of the species who has to supply the erection if there is going to be sex. All you girls have to do is spread your b-b-bloody legs. If your lips aren't lubricated by desire, we can fix that with saliva."

"You've certainly come a long way on the subject of sex."

"I owe it all to you."

"Fuck off, Kim."

"I did. I fucked off from Cambridge. I fucked off from England. I fucked off from my sainted father, though come to think of it he was the one who suggested Austria as the place to fuck off to. I wound up in Vienna. I wound up in your apartment. I wound up in your b-bloody b-bed. I'll fuck off from here, too, if it suits me."

I was flinging my clothing on the floor as I pulled them from my body. "Why are we unfair, for God's sake? Where do we get it wrong?"

Kim went around the room collecting my clothing and folding things over the back of a chair. "At the end of the day," he said, "you hold our erections against us because if we can get them with you, we can get them with anybody we fancy. *Through no fault of ours*, we p-produce serviceable erections when we are *attracted* to the b-body of the female in question. No attraction, no erection. Even with all your mechanical expertise, no attraction, no erection. Women hate the simple truth: Men may appreciate your intellect or your charm or your cooking or your p-political courage or your humour, but we can't come up with erections unless we appreciate your b-bloody b-body. I could find myself in b-bed with what's her name—the chairman of the philosophy department at the university . . ."

"You can't even remember her name, how could you find your way to her bed. It's Frau Voggel."

His voice turned hoarse and he paced the bedroom brandishing a cigarette he had neglected to light. "Frau Voggel, yes, right. I could be in b-bed with *the fat cow Frau Voggel*, chatting about that legendary celibate Immanuel Kant, which is what we talked about after the concert last week, but I couldn't get an erection if my b-bloody life depended on it."

"Come to the point."

"The p-point is, my fantasizing about Sonja should be seen as a sign of sexual health. It's like—like doing bloody pushups or running bloody laps. To stay in shape, to keep the b-bloody libido fit, men need to *fantasize*. Listen, Litzi, women have this enormous advantage. You are able to make love to an overweight soak of a man in his sixties who has a small p-pecker and a big bank account and an annual income that can keep you in the style to which you would like to become accustomed *whether or not you are attracted to him*."

The boil had been pierced. He needed three matches

before he succeeded in lighting the cigarette twitching between his lips. I could see his hand trembling as he held the flame to the end. Smoking took the edge off his anger. Settling onto the bed, he noticed that I was propped up against the pillows. Naked. "What was that all about?" he asked.

"Something tells me it was about your father."

He thought about this. "Sorry I went spare. My sainted father made the mistake of taking for lawful wedded wife someone who thought of marriage as a gilded cage. Talk about women being unfair, given half a chance she would have locked herself and her husband in and thrown away the key. It was so b-bloody Victorian. Her idea of happiness had something in common with rearranging deckchairs on the Titanic. She loathed everything my father loved—the endless empty quarter of Arabia, the B-bedouin camps in the middle of nowhere, the flatbread baked in the oven of the sand, the stench of humans who don't have enough water to waste it washing, the wells where the camels get first dibs and the chaps riding them come jolly second. Oh, Dora dipped her big toe into the desert once or twice, joining St John when he let a bit of air out of the tyres of his Ford estate and set off into the sand tracks towards a horizon that somehow remained out of reach. That's what horizons are about, isn't it? To lure you towards p-places you can't get to, to tease you with the unattainable. Ahhh, my sainted father has his faults—which of us doesn't?—but he appreciates b-beauty in all its forms: desert sunsets, blinding sandstorms, veiled women with mysterious eyes, handwoven silk that clings to the female b-body arousing fantasies of the body the silk clings to, B-bedouin warriors racing their camels to an oasis. Once St John came across a Bedouin racing his camel to an oasis—he turned out to be the Wahabi ruler of the Najd in Central Arabia named Abd al-Aziz ibn Saud. I've actually met the b-bloke, a six-footer who receives guests with princely hospitality. My tent is your tent sort of thing, except when he says it, he means it. St John once told me ibn Saud was the greatest Arab since the Prophet Mohammed. Mind you, doesn't say much for the other Arabs, but what the hell. When the Turks were driven from Baghdad, father persuaded the Foreign Office to put his p-pal on the throne of an invented entity called Saudi Arabia—the b-bugger was so grateful he rewarded St John with an Arab wife, by whom I expect to have half siblings in the not-too-distant future. As my father has converted to Islam, he can legally have two more wives. Why not? Four seems quite a sensible number to me. Whilst my sainted father gallivants around the Middle East trying to reach horizons that elude him, mother is at home in London, thank you, tending the tea roses in her gilded cage."

"Is that what brought you to Vienna, Kim? Trying to get to a horizon your father couldn't reach?"

While he was mulling this over I said, "Well, I don't see our relationship as a cage, gilded or otherwise. I certainly don't feel ambivalent about your erections. And you can look down Sonja's blouse till you're blue in the face."

Every day brought its ration of rumours: a friend of Dietrich's who worked at a frontier customs post reported that

Hitler's storm troopers had crossed the Bavarian Alps and were marching on Lintz (false), a woman who delivered eggs to the chef who cooked for Dollfuss heard he was counting on Italy's Mussolini to prevent an eventual German annexation of Austria (true), my Soviet controller had it from an unimpeachable source that the Socialist workers' militia had been secretly mobilized with orders to overthrow Dollfuss and create an Austrian Socialist Republic (false). "Keep your ear to the ground," Arnold instructed me. "Let me know if you hear anything."

All I heard was the falling snow muting the sound of traffic below my window. If you concentrated hard enough on the flakes drifting through the yellow light of the new electric streetlamps, it looked as if you were rising through the snow into the night sky. And then, ominously, one evening in February, the tap water in the drinking glasses stopped trembling. Kim and I exchanged looks. (When we compared notes much later, we discovered both of us had thought the same thing: that the earth might have somehow stopped rotating on is axis.) About the time we noticed the stillness of the water in the glasses, all the lights in the apartment, along with the shortwave radio tuned to the BBC foreign service, went out. Kim padded over to the window and peered up and down the street. "There's n-no electricity on the block," he said quietly. "Even the streetlamps have g-gone out."

"What do you think it means?"

"It m-means the generators have stopped generating electricity."

I should say here that electricity stoppages were the rule

in Vienna, not the exception, and we had candles ready at hand. I lit several. When the telephone rang Kim said, "I'll get it." He put the receiver to his ear and listened. "*Woher wissen Sie, dass?*" he demanded.

"How does *who* know *what*?" I asked impatiently.

"It's Dietrich," Kim told me. "He says the electricity has gone off in Karl-Marxhof. He says Dollfuss's Heimwehr gangs are stringing barbed wire across the streets leading to workers' tenements."

"The revolution has started," I whispered breathlessly. "The workers will rise up and sweep away the capitalists and the Fascists. Vienna will become the second Paris Commune. It's my rendezvous with history."

Kim, more levelheaded than me, said, "The Paris Commune was crushed in six weeks. If it's really revolution, the workers in Vienna won't last six d-days—the Heimwehr mob are armed to the teeth, our *Schutzbund* comrades will fall back into the tenement b-blocks but I don't see how they can hold out for very long."

I called the telephone number my controller had obliged me to memorize. A woman answered and said "If you're calling for roses, we don't deliver in winter." I said, "But we're already twelve February—the winter is almost over." Having exchanged pass-phrases, my controller said: "Report." I told her about the electricity going out, about the barbed wire.

"Is that all?"

"Isn't that enough?" I demanded.

The telephone line went dead in my ear.

"What was that all about?" Kim asked.

"I make reports," I explained.

"To whom?"

"To a woman with a man's name who doesn't deliver roses in winter."

Kim had the bright idea of telephoning Eric Gedye, the correspondent who covered Austria for the *Daily Telegraph*. He was a fixture at the Café Herenhoff, which is how we came to know him. "Electricity seems to have gone out in the city," he told Gedye. "Any idea what's up?"

I could see Kim shut his eyes as he pressed the telephone to his ear. "So it's b-begun," he murmured. He listened for a moment. "Don't know what we'll do. I suppose we'll wait for instructions."

He turned to me when he'd rung off. "The Dollfuss people are putting about that nonsense of an armed uprising by the *Schutzbunders*. Gedye says it's a p-provocation—Dollfuss is using it the way Hitler used the Reichstag fire—to purge Socialists and Communists. Your short count has b-banned the Social Democratic Party and declared marshal law. His soldiers have occupied the Social Democrats' headquarters in Lintz and started shooting up tenements in the city. The power plant workers here in Vienna have gone out on strike in p-protest. The army are bringing howitzers into Vienna to attack the tenement blocks."

The telephone rang again. Was it my imagination or had the ring become shriller, had the interval between rings grown shorter? I snatched the telephone off the hook before Kim could reach it. It was Dietrich. He was yelling in order to be heard over the bedlam in the background. "We'll go immediately," I yelled back, startled by my own voice, which seemed to reverberate through the apartment.

"Why are you yelling?" Kim asked when I'd hung down.

"Because Dietrich was yelling," I said. In my excitement I remember thinking this was a perfectly rational explanation. "He says we are to meet him at the Herenhoff and wait for orders."

We pulled on galoshes and coats and hurried downstairs. I wanted us to use Kim's motorcycle but he said it would attract too much attention, so we wound up going on foot. Walking through the falling snow, with the flakes melting on the skin of my face and muffling our footfalls on the sidewalk, it was hard to imagine that Vienna was on the brink of civil war. The Herenhoff was swarming with clients jammed onto benches reading newspapers by candlelight. Others were shouting at the top of their lungs to people who were immediately across the table from them. (I had always imagined people would whisper during a civil uprising. When I mentioned this to Kim, he actually burst out laughing. It was the last time he would laugh for weeks. Laughter, it seems, was the first victim of Dollfuss's small war.) Waiters in black Spencers threaded between the tables, the trays filled with mugs of beer balanced on palms high over their heads. Dietrich had managed to save two seats at a miniscule table at the back near the toilets. "Where is Sonja?" I shouted.

"She is helping to throw up barricades in the streets around the Karl-Marxhof tenements with her Social Democrat friends, who are having second thoughts about Stalin being a greater menace than Hitler, about Hitler being a greater menace than Dollfuss. Listen, Litzi, our cell leader has ordered us to set up a machine-gun post on a roof of the university off the Ringstrasse." Dietrich looked at Kim. "You are welcome to join us, Philby."

My Englishman never hesitated. "'Course I'll join you," he shouted. "P-puts me a game up on my sainted father. My first revolution and I'm only twenty-two. He didn't get to chuck the Turks out of Mesopotamia until he was thirty."

"Sergius is coming by to give us the key to a coal bin with guns and ammunition hidden in it," Dietrich said.

"Right. Does either of you know how to work a machine gun?"

Dietrich and I, we avoided each other's eye. "It isn't difficult," Dietrich said. "One of us will feed in the belt of bullets. The second will pull the trigger. The third will wet the burlap wrapped around the barrel to keep it cooled."

"You must have learned that from *All Quiet on the Western Front,*" Kim remarked. He plucked an indigestion tablet from a small tin and popped it into his mouth.

"I learned it at a field camp where Communist instructors showed us how to use firearms," Dietrich said.

The filaments in the overhead electric bulbs flickered, then went dark again before coming on full force. Conversation in the café died away and we all stared at the fixtures, holding our breaths as we waited to see if the lights would remain on. They did. Kim shrugged. "Feeding in bullets sounds like something I can do," he said in a normal conversational tone.

A fat Viennese gentleman at the next table said, "This is not the moment to be joking about bullets, young man."

Dietrich, suddenly emotional, reached across the table to wring Kim's hand. "I consider you to be one of us, Philby," he announced.

By the time Sergius turned up, we were each nursing a third cup of coffee. Out of breath, his eyes tearing from the cold outside, Sergius scraped over a chair and tried to get the attention of one of the waiters.

"You have the key?" Dietrich demanded.

"What key?" Sergius said.

I could see from the look on Sergius's face that he was finding the situation comical. Either that or he was trying to mask his nervousness. "The key to the coal bin," I said.

A waiter passed. Sergius plucked at his sleeve. "Beer," he said. He grinned at Dietrich. "Why do you need coal at a time like this?"

Dietrich leaned across the table. "This is not the moment to fool around. We're supposed to retrieve a machine gun and ammunition from the coal bin that you have the key to."

"I have the key to the coal bin on"—Sergius mentioned an address in a back street not far from the café. "The bad news is the only thing hidden there is coal. We don't own a machine gun."

"Why are you here?" I asked the comrade.

"I was sent to tell you there is no machine gun. You can go see for yourselves if you want. There were a few rifles and pistols hidden in the coal bin, along with some cartons of Italian fireworks, but they've already been distributed to workers."

"Who ordered you to set up the machine-gun p-post on the roof?" Kim asked Dietrich.

"Our cell leader."

"Telephone him."

"Can't. He's on a police wanted list. He never sleeps in the same bed two nights in a row."

"What do we do now?" I asked Kim.

He looked from Sergius to Dietrich to me. "We ought to head for the epicentre."

"The tenements?" I said.

My Englishman nodded.

We heard trucks rumbling down the cobblestones outside. Kim and I rushed to the door of the café. Half a dozen flatbed trucks loaded with coils of barbed wire were driving slowly past the Herenhoff, the headlights of one truck illuminating the cargo in the truck ahead of it. Several of the trucks towed howitzers, their muzzles covered in canvas. I will admit I was quite alarmed at the sight of field artillery. As for Kim, I never detected the faintest suggestion of fright on his face or in his voice. Under that boyish grin he had nerves of steel. In my mind's eye I see Kim, sensible as usual, counting the trucks passing in the street and nodding as if he had stored the information and understood its significance. The painfully shy *Homo erectus* who had washed up on my doorstep in a previous incarnation no longer existed.

What a difference a hundred days can make.

Even after Kim brought me to safety in London, flickering images of the next several days—which is how long it took for Dollfuss to eradicate Socialism in Austria—would haunt me. (Kim claims they are fragments shored up against my ruin. Lovely phrase. He says he swiped it from a poet. I forget his name. Fragments. Ruin. Why not?) I notice a baby carriage in Hyde Park and I see orderlies in soiled white laboratory coats ferrying the wounded to makeshift infirmaries in baby carriages. A pothole in Piccadilly Circus makes me think of shell craters pockmarking the streets around the Karl-Marxhof tenements when the Heimwehr thugs opened fire with their howitzers. I come across a discarded shoe in a Maida Vale rubbish bin and I *see* the small mountain of shoes in the alleyway behind the Karl-Marxhof infirmary. Some of the shoes—dear God in heaven!—some of the shoes still have human limbs in them. I spot Spanish tourists walking two abreast towards Harrods—the fragment that leaps to mind is an endless line of prisoners, their hands clasped behind their necks, being marched two abreast through the debris-strewn streets towards what the English during the Boer War called a concentration camp.

Oh, my eyes have seen horrors that my brain would give anything to stop remembering.

I'm working on it.

Sometimes the fragments join in a sludge of memories.

The night of the 12th of February: With the leadership arrested, with the revolutionist factions decapitated, our Socialist and Communist friends wandered the streets in confusion, not sure where to make a stand, not sure what form the stand should take if a stand were to be made. The armed *Schutzbund* militias retreated to the tenement blocks to defend the barricades. It must have been nearly midnight when Kim and Dietrich and I reached the epicentre. I remember scrambling over barricades thrown together with automobiles and delivery wagons and pushcarts and heaps of tyres and a mountain of furniture. Eventually we came to the fortresslike tenements at Karl-Marxhof. Dietrich found Sonja behind a second barricade. She and other girls were tearing sheets into bandage strips and folding them into cartons. A hundred or so young Communists, red ribbons tied around their upper arms, manned the barricade. A handful carried rifles, the others an assortment of clubs made from table legs. One young man wearing a greatcoat with a fur collar appeared to be armed with a carpet sweeper. Many of the Communists sprawled on couches that had been dragged down from apartments and formed part of the defence system thrown up to block the street. A young Communist with his pointed beard dyed bright red climbed onto a kitchen table and, using a megaphone fashioned out of cardboard, delivered a fiery speech. Only part of what he said reached my ears, something about how the first shots of the next great war were being fired here in Vienna. The Communists manning the barricade cheered him. Oh, yes, an absolutely indelible memory: Sergius began to pound out the *Internationale* on an upright piano wedged into the furniture that had been piled on the barricade. Several of the Communists began to sing the words. People watching from the tenement windows joined in. Soon the entire street resounded with the glorious words of the *Internationale*. To my amazement, I will say *to my delight*, tears sting my eyes now when I think of it, everyone was singing in Russian.

Vstavay, proklyat'yem zakleymyonniy
Ves' mir golodnykh i rabov
Kipit nash razum vozmushchonniy
I v smertniy boy vesti gotov.

My Englishman and I, we tried to warm ourselves at a furniture fire blazing in the middle of the street. I don't remember what time it was when the attack began, only that it was still too dark to make out the dials on the small wristwatch grandfather gave me for my fifteenth birthday. We heard a distant roar that sounded like motors coughing into life beyond the barricades. This next fragment—it is within the realm of possibility that I fantasized it, and repeated it to myself so often I began to think of it as something that really happened. In my fantasy, Dietrich, hearing the motors drawing closer, offers Kim a revolver. Kim looks down at it as if he's not sure what it is, then says, "I could not shoot a b-bullet at another human." "Even if the other human is shooting at you?" Dietrich asks. Kim shakes his head slowly and I hear him say "There must be another way to fight the good fight." Dietrich says, "Find it." Kim nods. "I will."

No, I never raised the subject of Dietrich's offer of a revolver with Kim. Perhaps I was afraid he would tell me I'd invented it. I had fallen for my Englishman and I wanted this particular fragment—this evidence of humanity—to be reality and not fantasy.

I can still reproduce in my brain the shrieks rising from the tenement windows when the giant bulldozers arrived at the first barricade and began punching gaps in it. Several young Communists shot fireworks that shrieked en route and exploded in sparkling circles when they slammed into the bulldozer cabs. We could hear rifle bullets ricocheting off the plows. Kim seized my hand and pulled me into a doorway. I remember a narrow staircase winding up and up, each floor smelling of garbage or urine or cooking kerosene. Then a blast of cold air hit my face. I was on the roof, peering over the parapet. Far below, as if in a sinkhole, I could see automobiles being lifted like toys and flung to one side. Thick black smoke rose from the tyres that had been soaked in kerosene and set afire. Tanks churned through the gaps opened by the bulldozers, their treads crushing furniture, the machine guns in their turrets spitting sparks in all directions. A figure raced towards one tank carrying a can of kerosene with an oil-lamp wick burning in its throat. As he raised his arm to throw it he was cut down by a scythe of bullets. A second figure appeared out of nowhere to pick up the can but it exploded in his hands before he could throw it. For an instant the explosion illuminated the street like a burst of lightning. I believe I recognized the comrade before he was engulfed in flames, it was my onetime lover, it was the Dietrich who had leaped to his feet to tell the Hungarian professor that his Marxist theories were boring him to death. And the crazy thought crossed my mind: *At least he didn't die of boredom.*

When the tanks broke through the second barricade,

shoving aside the upright piano and the mangled furniture, the Communists with us on the roof began throwing bricks down at the hunched shadows advancing behind the tanks. The comrades in the street fought heroically. For a brief moment it looked as if the attackers were hesitating, but perhaps that, too, was fantasy imposing itself on reality. Soldiers in helmets and greatcoats surged through the gaps in the barricade and spread out in the street, shooting at anything that moved in doorways or windows, smashing open the street doors of the tenements with rifle butts, launching what turned out to be a methodical search of the apartments. One of the comrades on the roof burst into sobs. Another shook him by the shoulders. "We must save ourselves," he yelled.

Kim pressed his lips to my ear. "We, too, must save ourselves."

I heard a voice I recognized as mine say, "Why must we?"

"To fight fascism."

I have a vague memory of being pushed over parapets to other roofs. White sheets were flying from chimneys in sign of surrender but the Heimwehr gangsters weren't taking prisoners. Howitzers started to shoot out the ground floors behind us so that the tenements would collapse into themselves. I remember spiral staircases, I remember clammy tunnels with large rusting sewage pipes running through them, I remember air passages that were so narrow you had to walk sideways, I remember cellars packed with doctors trying to staunch the flow of blood of wounded men, with women trying to staunch the flow of mucus from the noses of sobbing children. Kim found an English acquaintance, an artist of some sort, I think his name was Spender, we'd had a drink once on the terrace of the Herenhoff, drifting like a dazed soul in a cellar filled with dazed souls. Kim tried to shake him out of his stupor but Spender pulled his arm free and cried out, "*Sunt lacrimae rerum*—they weep for their houses, which are crashing down around their heads."

Shaking his head crossly, Kim murmured. "*Lacrimae rerum* gets it wrong—these are tears for events, not things."

After an eternity the cellars and the tunnels gave way to stingingly icy air, to a night sky brimming with stars, to alleyways filled with cartons of shoes, some of them with limbs attached, to streets rank with the stench of cordite, to checkpoints manned by nervous soldiers who aimed rifles and flashlights at us as my Englishman frantically waved his passport. *A British citizen and his girlfriend caught up in a war, let us through, for God's sake.* My apartment. The dull but not unpleasant thud of artillery shells exploding across town—it reminded me of the dry thunder over my grandfather's estate that brought no rain. I remember my Englishman gazing out the window at the low clouds on the horizon tinted blood red by fires burning out of control beneath them. He was drinking schnapps straight from the bottle when he turned his back on the fires and told me, out of the blue, that he'd once been b-b-b-b-b-buggered by a schoolmate.

What did that have to do with the thugs running riot in the workers' tenements across the city?

Kim forbade me to leave the apartment—the streets were crawling with Heimwehr patrols hunting down Socialists and Communists. He himself went outside two, sometimes three times a day. I could see him from my window, hunched over the handlebars of his motorcycle, waving his British passport to get past checkpoints or patrols. He had given himself a mission—scrounging old but serviceable overcoats and suits and ties from the journalist Gedye and the artist Spender and their English friends, delivering the clothing to the *Schutzbund* comrades trapped in cellars and sewers, many of them wounded; their only hope of fleeing was if they could pass themselves off as civilians caught in the crossfire, and for this they needed clothes that weren't battle worn and bloodstained.

After the three-day civil war, comrades, several of them with festering shrapnel wounds, all of them exhausted, made their way to my apartment. Some stayed only long enough to disinfect their wounds with alcohol, others (having no place else to go) camped. The Hungarian professor and three students occupied the spare room, two on the bed, two on the rug folded to make a mattress. Three young Communists who had crawled through sewers to escape the epicentre lived in the sitting room. Kim and I shared what food we had with the others as we clustered around the shortwave radio post trying to make sense of the BBC bulletins through the static. I translated the news into German for the comrades. According to the BBC, fifteen hundred had been killed and another five thousand had been wounded when Dollfuss crushed a Communist uprising in Vienna. (Some Communist uprising!) In what appeared to be a meticulously planned operation, Socialist and Communist leaders were being rounded up. Those who managed to avoid arrest were fleeing abroad. Opposition headquarters had been closed down. With the movement crushed, the workers' militias collapsed in disarray. The BBC correspondent reported seeing women frantically digging up the gardens at the Engelhof when word spread that weapons were buried there. The workers' tenements, long considered to be impregnable Socialist fortresses, had been occupied by the army and the government's Heimwehr militia. Workers' rest homes and holiday camps across Austria had been closed by the police. Terror gripped Vienna. Civilians caught with rifles or pistols were being shot out of hand.

In my apartment, we existed in a kind of suspended animation. Kim sat next to my phonograph, his head in his hands, listening to scratchy records of Beethoven sonatas, each of which, to the professor's dismay, he could identify by its opus number. When we ran out of coal, we started breaking up furniture and burning bits of it in the stove. First went the legs and backs of chairs. We burned the curtain rods, the drawers in the dressers, then the dressers themselves, even the wooden cooking spoons. We burned the frames of my grandfather's paintings I'd rolled up and pawned to raise money for German refugees flooding into Vienna after the Reichstag fire. We burned the frames of the two small charcoal designs I'd bought in Paris—I would have pawned these, too, but they were signed by someone the pawnbroker never heard of named Modigliani and had no value.

Sonja appeared late one night, her face stained with

dirt, her eyelids swollen from unshed tears. Because of the cold, she never removed her overcoat so the boys didn't get to see if she was still wearing her low-cut blouse. Pity. It might have warmed them a bit. When I told her how Kim and I, we'd watched the attack on the barricades from the roof, she said the comrade I'd seen throwing a can of kerosene at a tank wasn't Dietrich, the way I thought. Poor Dietrich, she said, along with the young Sergius, who never stopped taunting his executioners, had been dragged from a coal bin and taken to a city park and shot into a newly dug trench by a firing squad made up of Fascist women. When I asked how she knew that, she smiled a bizarre smile and said "Dietrich came to me in a dream and told me."

Late one night a week or so after the February events, Kim came to me in a dream—so I thought until I felt his breath in my hair. I couldn't see his face but I could feel the tension in his body. We could still hear sporadic rifle fire in the city and I supposed he was going to say something about being unable to sleep because of it. "We must leave," is what he said.

"Leave the apartment?"

"Leave the apartment. Leave Vienna. Leave Austria."

"With your British passport, you could leave. I would never make it past the frontier."

"We'll get you a British p-passport."

"How?"

"Wives of British citizens are given British p-passports. I stopped by the embassy this afternoon to verify this."

"We're not married."

"Things are calming down in Vienna. Shops, offices are starting to open for b-business. So is the town hall. I went there after I went to the embassy. I spoke to the clerk who does marriages. I slipped him five pounds, I said I would give him another fiver when he performed the ceremony. He said he c-can marry us in three minutes—matter of signing and stamping a piece of p-paper. We could be there when they open for business at eight. We could be at the embassy by eight-thirty. With a signed and stamped certificate of m-marriage, we could get you a British p-passport and be on the way to Italy by nine."

When I didn't immediately say anything, he said, "Right. Someone has just suggested m-marriage. You could have the d-decency to react."

"What about the professor and the others?"

"They have a better chance of surviving if you're not here when the police break in the door."

"I am not against marrying you, Kim, but I prefer to stick it out in Vienna."

"You can't, Litzi. You were arrested once so they know you're a Communist. They may even know you give reports to a woman with a man's name who doesn't deliver flowers in winter. Your name will be on lists. It's only a matter of time b-before they come around looking for you. On top of that you're Jewish. Everybody knows Hitler intends to annex Austria. Anschluss is only a question of time. He wants to get his pound of flesh from the Jews who refused to let him study in the Vienna Art Academy. Ah, if only they'd admitted him, he might be an artist starving in a garret in Vienna instead of Chancellor of Germany in B-berlin. Litzi, if Dollfuss doesn't kill you for being a Communist, Hitler will kill you for being Jewish."

In the darkness, Kim kissed me. I distinctly recall his lips were *not* trembling. Mine were. He had taken charge of his life and mine. We were married at eight-fifteen the next morning by a town hall clerk who badly needed the talents of a dentist. I signed the register identifying myself as a student without religious affiliation. Kim claimed to be a British tourist. Next to "Religion" he wrote, in English, "None that I am aware of." At nine the British Consul handed me a brand new British passport with an old photograph of me glued onto one page—I had dredged it up from the metal box under the bed, it was me before I'd seen piles of shoes with limbs still attached to them. There was no mistaking the innocence in my eighteen-year-old eyes. In the photograph my hair was shoulder length and sun-bleached. The consul, a kindly gentleman who was counting the days until he could return to Scotland, asked me if blonde was the original colour. I told him I had dyed my hair so often I wasn't sure. He said not to worry, if the frontier police noticed the discrepancy, they wouldn't find it remarkable that I had transformed myself into a redhead. All the girls were doing it these days, he said. He wished us good luck and Godspeed. I told him I didn't believe in God. Kim coughed up a laugh and said he did believe in speed. The Consul said he did, too. He saluted the newlyweds from the small balcony over the embassy's polished brass entrance as we saddled up in the courtyard below. Kim wore his rucksack on his chest, I wore mine on my back. It contained clothing and (in the hope they might one day be worth something) my two small rolled-up Modiglianis. I hung on to Kim's shoulder straps as he stomped the motorcycle into life.

Was it the air stream in my face that brought tears to my eyes as we headed through the achingly familiar boulevards of my beloved Vienna towards England, a country nine hundred miles away, give or take, that I could scarcely imagine?

2: LONDON, APRIL 1934

Where a Chap from Cambridge has the Bright Idea of Spying for the Reds

Bugger if I remember who came up with the idea of organizing a welcome home bash for Kim. The word spread that the sod was back in town with a Magyar wife in tow and suddenly the party was on the agenda. One of Philby's Cambridge chums offered his mother's Cadogan flat—she was said to be travelling on the continent with her husband and his lover at the time. At the appointed hour Don Maclean came round. Good fellow, Maclean. He'd put on weight since Cambridge, where he earned a first in foreign languages. Straight as a ramrod, sexually speaking, but I don't hold that against a chap. He and Kim had had a falling out at university, never did find out over what, think it had to do with Maclean's having joined the fledgling Communist cell at Cambridge whilst Kim, for reasons beknownst only to himself, never actually pocketed a party card. That asshole Anthony Blunt crashed the party. He was wearing a starched *col cassé*, you'd have thought the twit was the King of England; he wasn't bashful about claiming to be a distant cousin of the Queen, he certainly dressed to fit the role he'd assigned himself. Would have turned him away except he was clutching a bottle of half decent whisky. Anthony made something of a splash at Cambridge in French art and you could count on him to tone up the conversation if, as was often the case, I toned it down. Bob Wright, Kim's coal miner mate—Kim had lodged with Wright in Huthwaite when they were both reading economics—appeared with two Malthusian League ladies, one on each arm. He'd picked them up at a stationer's shop on Kensington High Street, they'd just come away from a forum on constipation, or was it contraception? With their little yellow badges, Malthusian Leaguers, like the suffragettes before them, were fair game if you were heterosexual. It was common knowledge they preached birth control in order to practise free love. (At the nightly poker games during our Cambridge undergraduate days, there had been a running argument over whether Malthusians wore knickers. As none of us had been able to offer eyewitness evidence, the question had never been resolved to anybody's satisfaction.) Two girls from Newnham, reeking of water closet (which is to say, *working class*) perfume, appeared on the threshold claiming to have been invited by someone whose name slipped their minds. Vaguely recognized the one who introduced herself as Mildred, she looked to be up the spout and got brassed off when one of the Malthusian ladies asked her when the baby was due. "Piss off, huh—I'm not *pregnant*," she snapped. "I'm starting the Hollywood grapefruit diet immediately breakfast tomorrow." I should say here that the mere sight of Newnham girls filled those of us from Cambridge with wistfulness for our misspent youth—wearing identical white blouses and pleated skirts, they had filled the front rows of lectures at Trinity on the dialectical idealism of Hegel. It was a time-honoured tradition in those hallowed halls that Newnham girls were duff and no Trinity boy who prized his reputation would deign to talk to one. As the welcome home bash in Cadogan was off campus both in terms of geography and time, I thought it would be tolerable to chat up Mildred before she transformed herself into a grapefruit.

Broke the ice with, "Don't you think it curious that men shake hands with the same hand they use to wipe their arses?"

"But surely that's the point," she said brightly.

I inquired as to whether she'd read Lawrence's *Pornography and Obscenity*.

"Lawrence of Arabia wrote a book on pornography?"

"That's D. H. Lawrence, love."

When she confessed she wasn't familiar with the book in question, I shared with her the theory making the rounds of London public houses that pornography was literature intended to be read with one hand. Encouraged by the blush spreading across Mildred's Midland cheeks—a reaction typical of girls with a modest university education—I confided my earnest conviction that Mussolini was queer. I suggested that if one really wanted to distract him from his lustful designs on Ethiopia, all one need do was parade some beautiful fairy across the steps of the Capitole in Rome. Mildred wanted to know if I would be willing to sacrifice myself. "I am as much a patriot as the next faggot," I said huffily.

"Jolly good show," she said. "I shall put forward your name if they call for volunteers. By the by, what is your name?"

"Guy Burgess."

"*The* Guy Burgess? Oh dear, I'm embarrassed to be seen talking to you. Whatever you have might rub off on me."

Whilst talking to Mildred, I'd noticed a most delectable boy climbing the spiral stairs to the sitting room. Anthony, who had already spoken to said boy downstairs, whispered in my ear that he was an unemployed actor working as an usher in the West End. The poor fellow looked to be lost in the shuffle. The usher-slash-actor, his hair slicked back with sweet-smelling pomade, eventually gravitated in my direction as if by inadvertence. We beat about the bush for a suitable interval.

"Guy," I said.

"Jeffrey," he said. "What do you do?"

"I do anybody who needs doing."

"I mean by way of work."

"Indeed, work. At the moment I am weighing several options. My hope is to snag something in the F.O. Like almost everyone at Trinity, I read economics but switched to politics when politics became fashionable. Where did you go to school?"

"I didn't. Never made it past Sixth Form."

"Blessing in disguise, I should think," I said. "Too much knowledge can bloat the brain."

"Surely carnal knowledge will be the exception to your rule."

"Depends on whom you're carnal with," I said. "Are you by any stretch of the imagination a Socialist?"

"I am more bleeding heart liberal than Socialist."

"I grasp the bleeding heart part of the equation," I said. "Pray tell what exactly do you mean by liberal?"

"Pretty straightforward. A liberal is someone who is not revolted when he discovers his closest friend is a closet heterosexual." He punched me playfully on the shoulder, which was more than enough encouragement to keep me focused on him despite his having spilt gin on the lapel of my new blazer.

"I myself don't disparage closet heterosexuality," I confessed. "Been known to shag the occasional female if the bloke she's with is pretty enough."

"Females bitch about men thinking with their dicks. Do you?"

"Obliged to. I'm twenty-three this month and I've already fucked my brains out."

Eventually I smiled a certain smile and he bared his teeth in agreement and trailed after me to the W.C. at the end of the hallway where I delivered on the smile's promise and gave him a blow job. I'd been so eager I'd forgotten to latch the lavatory door. We were at it in the shower stall when one of the Malthusian League ladies burst in. She didn't bat an eye when she spied me squatting back on my heels so as not to soil my trousers, my fingers wrapped around the cock in my mouth. (I belong to the school of fellatio that holds that good hand work is every bit as indispensable as good tongue work. Swallowing is an ineluctable part of my ethic.)

"You might have knocked," my usher-slash-actor said crossly to the suffragette.

"*Mea maxima culpa*," the girl said in a syrupy voice thickened by Anthony Blunt's whisky, "but I desperately need to piddle."

The usher-slash-actor, buttoning his fly, and I, patting dry my lips on a silk handkerchief, emerged from the shower stall and planted ourselves in front of the Malthusian Leaguer with the intention of monitoring her response to this particular call of nature.

"Don't pretend you have never seen a girl urinate," she exclaimed, flipping up the back hem of her skirt and parachuting onto the toilet seat.

"Need to settle an old argument," I explained.

"What argument?" she demanded, closing her eyes in bliss as the pressure eased on her bladder.

"Whether League stalwarts like yourself wear knickers."

"We are freethinkers in our deeds and the garments we choose not to wear reflect this," the girl allowed.

"No knickers?" concluded the usher-slash-actor.

"No knickers," confirmed the girl, snatching a fistful of toilet paper and blotting herself so deftly we never caught so much as a glimpse of her freethinking cunt. "No brassieres neither," she added, heading for the door without bothering to flush the toilet. She spun around with one hand on the knob. "Not that it changes anything for Nancy boys like yourselves but we Malthusian Leaguers make use of a revolutionary form of female contraception—a copy of Margaret Sanger's *What Every Girl Should Know* held firmly between the knees."

The usher-slash-actor tossed his head in admiration. "Now that's an exit line," he said.

I got to meet the famous Magyar Litzi Friedman when Kim finally showed up with her at the Cadogan flat, her clothing and short hair dishevelled from motorcycling in from Maida Vale, her eyelids puffed from having the wind in her face, her lips chapped beyond any repair lipstick could provide.

"Least you could do, old sod, is equip her with a pair of aviator goggles," I said.

"I did—she lost them somewhere between Vienna and the Italian frontier. I didn't feel it worth our while to turn b-back and look for them."

Anthony tried to elbow into the conversation. "Has anybody seen Gaspard Dughet's *Sacrifice of Abraham* at the National Gallery?"

But all ears were on the Magyar girl. "I say, does she speak English?" Don Maclean inquired of Kim.

"I speak it well enough to know what *buggered* means," the Friedman girl shot back.

Her spunk couldn't help but confound Kim's Cambridge mates. "As the actress said to the bishop," I exclaimed, "*buggered* is a splendid place to begin one's mastery of the vernacular spoken in this *scepter'd* isle."

Litzi ran her fingers through her hair, which was the colour of pitch. Gathering what little surplus there was at the nape of her neck, she slipped a rubber band from her wrist and deftly installed the tuft in it, passing the hair three times through the band. The gesture, so simple and at the same time so elegant no man could possibly pull it off, fascinated me. If she'd been a boy I would have been keen to let my hair go longish and ask her for a private lesson. I brought around two glasses of gin, neat, for Kim and his Hungarian. "Bloody decent of you to save a Jewish girl from the clutches of Fascism," I told him. "I myself would be quite prepared to marry one so long as I was not expected to consummate the union." I winked at Jeffrey. "Not against carnal knowledge per se if the individual being carnalled is fitted with a suitable anus."

"I wasn't saving a Jewish girl," Kim said, clearly irritated. "We happ-ppen to be in love."

"That explains everything," I observed drily.

"Indeed," Don Maclean agreed, completely missing my fling at irony.

As always in those days the conversation quickly turned to Germany's Fuehrer. "There's a story going round Hitler got syphilis from a Jewish whore in Vienna," Don Maclean remarked.

"I hope it's true," the Friedman girl said.

Blunt prowled the fringe of the group. "For my money, Dughet has more talent than Poussin, who happened to be his brother-in-law and teacher."

"Fuck off with your Dughet and Poussin, Anthony,"

Bob Wright told him. "Can't you see we're on to more important things than Frog art?"

Sipping at our chilled gin, we toured the ominous horizon as seen from the leaded windows of a flat in Knightsbridge. We all agreed that the Reichstag fire had been set on Herr Hitler's orders to give him a pretext to crush the great German Communist Party. But we were at a collective loss to come up with the name of the young Dutch Communist who had taken the rap for the crime.

"It's Marcus something or other," Don Maclean said.

"His name is Marinus, not Marcus," the Friedman girl said. "Marinus van der Lubbe."

"That's right," Bob agreed, eyeing Kim's Magyar spouse with newfound respect. "Marinus. Brave chap."

"Brave chap indeed," the Friedman girl said. "He was convicted in a kangaroo court and beheaded in the prison yard."

"That Bulgarian Communist who was accused with the Dutchman—" I said.

To Kim's manifest satisfaction, the Friedman girl supplied his name as well. "Dimitrov. Georgi Dimitrov."

"Read his speech to the judge in *The Times*," Don Maclean said. "Bloody miracle the Germans found him *not* guilty."

"The fix was in," Kim said. "Russians were holding two or three German aviators as hostages against Dimitrov's liberation."

"Could be Herr Hitler still doesn't control all the strings of the German body politic," Bob Wright said.

The Friedman girl said, "He controls the important strings. He had a plurality in the Budestag until he expelled the Socialist and Communist deputies, at which point he had an outright majority. Make no mistake, nothing will stop him short of war."

"Seems you've gone and married an Amazon," Don told Kim.

"Has she had one breast removed, the better to draw back the string on her bow?" I asked with mock innocence.

"Both my breasts are intact, thank you," the Friedman girl said. "Would you care to verify them?"

She actually put her fingers to the top button of her shirt. I do believe she would have opened it then and there, if only to discomfit me in front of my friends.

"Burgess doesn't fancy breasts," Don observed with a wry smile. "Do I have that right, Guy?"

The Friedman girl seemed quite exasperated by all of us. "You seem to take what's happening in Europe—what happened in Vienna—lightly. Kim takes it seriously. He was in Berlin five days after the Reichstag burned to the ground. With his own eyes he saw the monster rising from the ashes."

"Didn't know you'd been to Berlin, Kim," I said.

"I don't talk about it because I am not very p-proud of how I comported myself," he said.

"You have nothing to be ashamed of," the Friedman girl said with sudden passion. "If you could have seen him in Vienna—motorcycling through the city, bluffing his way past checkpoints, delivering false papers and clothing to

Schutzbund militiamen trapped in the sewers, some of them with festering wounds. Not a few who managed to escape the Fascist thugs owe their lives to Kim."

"She is greatly overstating my c-contribution," Kim said.

Bob looked at Kim. "What did happen in Berlin?" he asked quietly.

"Spill the beans, Kim," Don said.

"Go ahead and tell them," the Friedman woman said. (She clearly had more of an influence on him than any of us.) "It will give them a better appreciation of what Hitler and Germany have in store for the world."

Kim shrugged his lean shoulders. "At one point I found myself inside a chemist's shop. Truck p-pulled up filled with brownshirts. They jumped from the back and painted *Jude* on the store window. Posted themselves at the door and turned away customers. The chemist was a little man with a Jewish name. He stood there trying to catch his breath as if he had run a hundred yard dash. He was so humiliated he couldn't b-bring himself to look me in the eye. Whether humiliated for himself or for Germany, or for that matter both, I cannot say."

"Then what?" Bob Wright coaxed gently.

"Say the rest of it, Kim," the Friedman woman said.

Kim looked as if he, too, were trying to catch his breath. "As I quit the shop," he went on, his voice unsteady, "the brownshirts demanded to see my p-papers. When I produced my British p-passport, one of them asked what I'd been doing in a Jewish shop. I wanted to tell the b-bastards to go to hell. I'm ashamed to say I lost my nerve. I knew they would rough me up. I loathe violence. I get sick to my stomach at the sight of b-blood. I even dislike sports that involve physical contact. So I mumbled something about the Jews being their p-problem, not mine. And I went on my merry way. I left without so much as a b-backward glance at the chemist inside his shop."

The Magyar girl put an arm around Kim's waist and pulled him close to her. Bob said, "You are coming down too hard on yourself. Which of us could swear he would react differently?"

"You would," Kim said. "Whether in the coal mines or at Cambridge, you never b-backed away from a fight."

"You had the nerve to go to Vienna," Bob said. "You had the nerve to help the poor sods in the sewers."

"I d-didn't help the Jewish chemist in his shop."

Truth to tell, I found Kim's little story touching. Pushed one to look inside one's self, something I didn't often do for fear of what I might find. "You *couldn't* help the Jewish chemist in the shop," I said. "If you had butted in, you would have only made his situation worse than it was."

"I trust everyone here is taking note," Don said. "Guy Burgess has been caught out being serious."

"Appreciate it if you didn't spread this around," I said. "Ruin my reputation as a scapegrace."

A fortnight later I lunched with Kim at a pub in Holborn. He was working nearby for £4 a week as a subeditor for the *Review of Reviews*, a scruffy monthly stuffed with dreary articles pilfered from British and American journals. The one thing that made it halfway readable was the motoring page, that and the occasional letter to the editor which, as the *Review* received no letters addressed to its editors, were written by Kim under pseudonyms. "Ah, the things one does to p-put groceries on the table," he said with a sigh as we slid into a booth. A big-breasted female mopped up the spilt beer on the tabletop with a damp rag that, if you rang it out, could fill a mug. She produced a pad and a child's colouring crayon and looked from one to the other, her mouth drooping open. "What's your pleasure, gents?"

"You," I said.

She swallowed the weary laugh of someone who has heard it all before. "No call to be gettin' fresh, shall we."

"Let's order," Kim said.

"What do you offer by way of pot pie?" I inquired.

"We have the house pot pie, dearie. It's all up on the chalkboard in large upper-case letters."

We each settled for house pot pie and a pint of bitter.

"How's your Magyar Amazon surviving Maida Vale exile?" I asked.

"Life here is too damn humdrum to suit her," Kim said.

"After Vienna, she was bound to find London a bit tedious," I said. "Is she a Communist?"

"Very much so," he said. "That's what she misses, Guy. She feels she's been put out to p-pasture. In Vienna she was in the thick of things. She was a member of a district committee. Important comrades came to her flat for meetings. She collected leaflets from a secret printing press and delivered them to Communist cells in the workers' tenements."

"You ought to find something for her to do. She could

hand out leaflets in Hyde Park reminding the natives that the end is nigh."

"The both of us marched in the May Day p-parade yesterday. I have to say it was Vienna redux. Must have been thirty thousand in the streets. Litzi was radiantly happy. Today's her b-bloody b-birthday. Haven't found her a p-present yet."

"How old is she?"

"Twenty-four."

"Yes, well, her body might be twenty-four but her eyes are twice that."

"You're spot on—she's seen things she would p-prefer to put out of mind," Kim agreed.

"What's your old man up to these days?" St John's latest exploits were always good for a quarter hour of conversation.

"Ahhh, he's going to drive his Ford estate from Jiddah to Britain via Transjordan and North Africa. He's planning to cross over to Europe at the P-pillars of Hercules. I am trying to talk him into contributing a travelogue to the *Review*. I'm proposing to call it *Mecca to Maida Vale*. Snappy b-banner, don't you think?"

Our bitters arrived. The pot pies weren't far behind. We degusted in silence for a time.

"I say, Kim, does your father work for His Majesty's Secret Intelligence Service? Everyone says he must."

"Not that I know of. On a first name b-basis with one or two of the top chaps from his salad days, though he categorically refuses to name names. What makes you ask?"

"All that meandering the Saudi desert is certainly

suspicious. Seems as if he spends half his waking hours buttering up ibn Saud. Here's the thing, Kim, I have a wizard idea. We ought to become spies."

"Funny, I thought you said *spies*."

"I did say spies. Consider the advantages. You would get to get a stipend, don't you think? Help make ends meet, sort of thing. Drink real claret instead of the bilge water they serve here. And it would be damn glamorous. Think of all the sods you'd get to take to bed on the grounds you're fucking them for their secrets."

"For whom would we spy?"

"Adolf's out of the question. Ditto Benito. If worse came to worst, we could always spy for the home team." I had a sudden inspiration. "Or the Reds. What about the Reds?"

"The Russians? Surely you must be joking?"

"But Kim, they're on the side of the angels—dictatorship of the proletariat and all that twaddle. Holidayed in Moscow some weeks back. Must say I came away impressed."

"If something in Moscow impressed you, it will have been one of the fairies you p-picked up at the Metropole."

"You make the very serious mistake of reducing everything to sex, Kim. The economy is what impressed me. It works. No sign of the Great Depression having reached Mother Russia. No unemployment. No soup kitchens. Universal health care. No strikes. Well, no strikes because there are no labour unions, but no labour unions because the proletariat owns the means of production, whatever. Hell, Moscow's even building a tube. They say you'll be able to set your watch by the trains pulling into the stations every minute on the minute. They say the stations will make Covent Garden look like a cesspit. They say Joe Stalin's five-year plan will pull them even with Germany and Britain in, well, eh, five years."

"They'd bloody better p-pull even with Germany. Chances are they'll be at war with the Huns in five years."

"All the more reason to spy for them." Disregarding the stench of stale beer wafting from the tabletop, I leaned half across. "The NKVD is the aristocracy of the Soviet Union," I said, speaking in what theatrically would have been termed sotto voce. "Its spies are the aristocracy of the NKVD."

"Well and good to join an aristocracy, but what on earth could we tell them?"

"Well, for starters, we could beef up this conversation. *Lunch with a junior cabinet minister's principal assistant who said such and such*. That sort of drivel."

"You *are* joking?" The smile faded from Kim's face. "You *aren't* joking? Listen up, Guy, you're talking sheer nonsense. If we were to spy for the Reds, we'd be spying on Britain."

"Not at all. We would be helping out the only country in Europe that stands against Hitler. We would be contributing to the defeat of Fascism, thus saving Britain."

Kim laughed off my suggestion. "A spy could be tortured," he said. "Have you thought of that?"

"He'd have to be caught first. We would never be caught. Who would think a couple of Cambridge boys like us would spy for the Reds?"

"Who indeed? I suppose you've figured out how one goes about offering one's services. P-post a letter to the Soviet embassy, perhaps? Better still, buttonhole Ambassador Maisky on his morning constitutional in Kensington Gardens."

"That's where your father comes in," I told Kim. "If he really works for SIS as we all think, he will know the identity of the NKVD's man in London. You could pry it out of your paterfamilias somehow—tell him you're doing an article for your *Review* on Soviet spies in Britain. Christ, if we knew the name of the NKVD's man in London, be a bloody piece of cake to get in touch with him."

"You're mad, Guy."

"The very least you can do is agree to think about it."

"I most certainly will not think about it."

Kim waved a hand to get the attention of the serving girl and motioned for the bill.

Waiting for it to come, I worked up the nerve to raise something that had been a sore point between us for years. "Kim, we never really talk about it—"

"What's there to talk about? What happened, happened. Comes under the heading of spilt milk."

"We were both quite tanked up . . ."

"I never b-blamed you, Guy. If I b-blamed anyone, it was myself. You were being true to your nature."

"I do want to apologize for having pushed you past where you were comfortable going."

"I accepted your apology long b-before it was offered."

"Does your Magyar know about it?"

"She knows *something* happened. She knows what *buggered* means. She doesn't know it was you."

"Just as well." I smiled at a memory. "Yes, well, actually, there *was* a boy at the Metropole."

"I guessed as much. All this sudden devotion to Soviet Russia. All this talk of b-becoming NKVD spies."

"His name was Igor. At least that was the name he gave me. Jolly good chap. We fucked, of course."

"Was that wise? They might try to b-blackmail you—"

"Who could they tell that doesn't already know?"

"I take your p-point."

"Afterwards I invited him to a hole in the wall down an alleyway across the river from the Kremlin serving something that was passed off as food. Igor produced a paper bag his mother had given him. It was filled with spring onions. He shared them with me when they brought around the alleged borscht. He talked about Stalin and the metro being built by some Ukrainian named Khrushchev, he talked about the great dams that are supplying electrical energy to giant factories. It wasn't propaganda, Kim. It was the genuine article. He was patriotic. Proud to be Russian, proud to be contributing to the construction of Communism. When we parted company, he called me *comrade. Tovarish* in Russian. *Tovarish Guy*, he whispered as we strolled past Lenin's mausoleum, *just so you will know, I pick up foreigners at the Metropole and report on what they say to the secret police.*"

"That's how Igor contributes to the construction of Communism?"

"You will laugh but the answer is yes. Igor does what he can. *From each according to his ability.* And I realized—how to begin to explain this?—that our all-night exegesis of *Das Kapital* in Matthew's Café, that the weekends we spent canvassing for Socialist candidates across the railway bridge in Romsey Town—all of it was castles in the air. You were the only one of us to take himself off to where these Socialist ideals of ours were put to the test. I admire you for that, Kim. Truly. I have done nothing to compare."

"You haven't said your last word." He looked around to be sure he couldn't be overheard. "Between you, me, and the microphone that's supposed to be in every wall, Guy, I am trying to join the British Communist Party."

"Did you mail them an application?"

"I saved the p-postage. Showed up at the party's central committee H.Q. on King Street."

I was intrigued. "You just waltzed in off the street? No letter of introduction, no password, whatever? What in the world did they say?"

"A very stodgy switchboard operator turned out to be the only human in sight. He copied down my name, rank, and serial number. Cambridge Socialist Society. Vienna. Mumbling something about their having to suss me out, he asked for the names of three p-people who could vouch for me. I hope you don't take it amiss, Guy, but I gave your name, along with Don Maclean's and Anthony Blunt's."

"Then what happened?"

The pot pie seemed to have given Kim indigestion. He produced a tin of Arm & Hammer tablets from his pocket, offered me one and when I declined, took one himself. "He didn't seem particularly b-bowled over by my candidacy," he said, his words a bit slurred from sucking on the tablet in his mouth. "Said they would get back to me in six weeks time."

I think I whistled. "Six weeks! I'm not sure your best interests were served by using me as a reference. Well, what's done is done." A small straw basket with the bill in it was deposited on the table. I picked up the reckoning and divided the number in two. "What do you say we pay the piper, mate?"

I remember his answer. "Trick is to avoid p-paying the bloody p-piper, isn't it?"

3: LONDON, JUNE 1934

Where an Englishman Accepts a Proposition He Doesn't Quite Understand

I am the Teodor Stepanovich Maly, cryptonym Mann, about whom you have no doubt heard a great deal. Much of what you heard is malicious fabrication. Permit me to set the record straight. I was posted to the London *Rezidentura* in 1933, first as the principal deputy to the *Rezident* (cryptonym Marr), then, after his sudden recall to Moscow and execution, as *Rezident*. In both capacities I attempted to convince Moscow Centre to abandon, or at least scale back, efforts to recruit high-ranking British diplomats or political figures—what we professionals call *recruiting into access*—and concentrate instead on long-term penetrations: There existed an entire generation of British intellectuals who became disenchanted with the ruling classes after the Great War, who started to doubt the capitalist fairy tale of the ever expanding pie when unemployment soared in the wake of the crash of '29, who gravitated towards Marx's analysis of the inevitable decline of industrial capitalism, who with the rise of Hitler in Germany came to see the Soviet Union as the bulwark against Fascism. I had even located the epicentre of this political seism: It was in the sacrosanct halls of Cambridge University in the medieval town of Cambridge, more precisely in one of Cambridge's several colleges, Trinity. In the early years of this decade, the nascent Socialist movement on campus limited itself to reading the *Daily Worker* aloud at meetings, pamphlet writing, and late-night discussion groups where, with any luck, the members of the Socialist Society could discuss the Socialist girls straight into bed. With the arrival of a handful of genuine proletarians, namely half a dozen miners from the coal face who ate the cores when they ate apples, a local Communist cell came into existence; the miners, who roped drums of coal to their waists and dragged them out of airless tunnels, had taken part in the bitter thirty-week general strike of 1926 only to be bought off with scholarships to Cambridge. I wasn't really interested in the miners. My idea was to recruit young and eager upper-class leftist intellectuals from the Socialist and Communist ranks willing to transfer their loyalties to the internationalist anti-Fascist movement. We would then channel their professional careers in the hope they might wind up working as Fleet Street journalists or junior Foreign Office clerks. If we were diligent in selecting talented recruits, they would, with the passage of time, rise through the ranks to positions of consequence, giving us access to the state's thinking, perhaps even to the state's secrets.

Such was the proposition that Moscow Centre was

mulling with its usual lack of enthusiasm for original ideas when Harold Adrian Philby literally fell into my lap.

I should say immediately that Philby's name was not unknown to me. His potential for recruitment had been put forward in Vienna by a young Hungarian-Jewish comrade who worked for the Centre. Her name was Litzi Friedman. One of the semi-monthly reports from her controller, cryptonym Arnold, mentioned a young upper-crust British Socialist fresh from Trinity College, Cambridge; the Friedman woman described him as an ardent anti-Fascist who had motorcycled from Britain to Austria to join in the struggle against the dictator Dollfuss. Moscow Centre was intrigued enough to assign the Englishman the German cryptonym *Söhnchen* (Sonny in English) and dispatch me to Vienna to sit in on one of Arnold's meetings with the Friedman woman. I was careful to position myself in a corner of the room filled with shadow. I remember Litzi Friedman commending the young Englishman as a committed Marxist and a fast learner, someone capable of keeping secret things secret should Moscow Centre decide to recruit him as an agent. In Vienna Sonny wound up sharing a bed with Litzi Friedman where, one supposes—for her sake one *hopes*—he was as ardent a lover as he was an anti-Fascist. After Dollfuss crushed the Austrian Socialist opposition, Sonny married the Friedman woman at the Vienna town hall so she would qualify for a British passport and then fled with her to the safety of London. The centre, in its infinite wisdom, instructed me to resume contact with Litzi Friedman and sound her out again about the possibility of recruiting as an active agent the British gentleman who was now her lawful wedded husband.

This I did. I met with her in London on three occasions. At the first meeting she looked at me with undisguised curiosity. "Have we met before?" she asked.

"What makes you think so?"

"It's the triangular moustache. The man who sat in on one of my sessions with Arnold in Vienna was tall and thin like you and had a triangular moustache on his upper lip. It was you, wasn't it?"

"I have never been to Vienna," I replied.

She laughed. "It *was* you," she said. She waved a hand. "No matter."

The only thing that had changed about the Friedman woman since our paths had crossed in Vienna was her hair—I remember it being the colour of rust then, now it was pearl-grey. I found Litzi Friedman to be a moody young woman who arrived at each meeting with her hair dyed a different colour. She confessed to being bored to tears by the British and their class distinctions. I concluded that she was eager to be of service to the *internationale* but erratic in her behaviour (she was quite capable of squandering the little money her husband earned on footwear) and, if I am any judge, immature in her Marxist indoctrination. Oh, she was familiar enough with the general argument: dialectical materialism, the class struggle as the motor of social change, history as a science based on thesis, antithesis, synthesis. But she was inept at analysis that required excavating under the surface of political events. Convincing me how passionately she supported the Soviet Union seemed to be her top priority. As I wrote in the report I filed with Moscow Centre after each of our meetings, I did not consider her to be a potentially important contributor to our cause. This husband of hers, this Harold Adrian Philby, was (to employ the British idiom) a different kettle of fish entirely.

Friedman's praise of Philby was ringing in my ears when the note from the Central Committee of the British Communist Party crossed my desk. This same Philby had applied to join the party. With respect to long-term penetration agents, he was made to measure: young, ardent, idealistic, iconoclastic, disgusted with the muck the Great Powers had made of Europe after the Great War, Cambridge educated, socialist orientated, upper-class with (as I came to appreciate) an appropriate amount of guilt at not having honest working-class dirt under his fingernails. He was one of those pampered aristocrats who threw away the cores when they ate apples. In addition he was the son of an eccentric Englishman, Harry St John Philby, who had converted to Islam and gone off to live in Arabia, where he was known to be a confidant of the Saudi monarch, ibn Saud. St John was thought to have the usual *old school* connections on Fleet Street and perhaps even in Caxton House, the nerve centre of His Majesty's Secret Intelligence Service, known also as MI6. As far as the younger Philby was concerned, there was a bonus to be had: Like a great many undergraduates of his day, Philby had belonged to the Cambridge University Socialist Society, attending meetings in the beer vapours of Matthew's Café, arguing into the early hours whether there was any point in handing out the *Daily Worker* to dog-tired workers living on the wrong side of the railway bridge in Romsey Town; Philby, who according to Litzi Friedman considered himself a Marxist by the time he left university, had nibbled at the edges of the Cambridge Communist cell when it came into existence, but had by a fortunate twist of fate never actually joined, which meant that his name would be spotless as a newly minted halfpenny for the inevitable background checks his candidacy for a government or Fleet Street job would provoke.

I asked for, and received by return telegram, permission from Moscow Centre to attempt to recruit Harold Adrian Philby to work for Soviet intelligence. It goes without saying, I gave Litzi Friedman detailed instructions to be sure she and the young Philby were not being followed when she brought him to that first meeting in Regent's Park. She was to tell him only that he would be seeing someone important. Nothing more. She was to take three different taxis, getting out each time before the hack reached the destination she had given the driver. She was to use one-way streets, walking against traffic, to disrupt any automobile-based surveillance. She was to use Harrods emporium, entering through one door, going up in the lifts, descending by a staircase, exiting into the always teeming Brompton Road by another door. The entire process was not to take less than three hours.

As for me, I employed my usual technique for avoiding surveillance. The Soviet embassy was under observation day and night. I had even spotted men with binoculars and motion picture cameras on tripods behind a venetian blind in a window diagonally across the street from our principal entrance. Along with my driver and my male secretary (who concealed himself in the boot), I got into one of our limousines in the courtyard and we set off through the gates into traffic. My driver, who was quite experienced in evasion techniques, immediately identified two automobiles following at a discreet distance. Obeying my instructions to the letter, he made no effort to lose them in the congested streets. Instead we meandered through the midmorning traffic in the general direction of Hampstead and its heath. With the heath in sight, my driver turned into a narrow one-way street going the wrong way. A British bobby along the street started to wave us down until he noticed the diplomatic number plate, at which point he contented himself with ordering us to turn off, which we did. My driver pulled into an alleyway and parked in an area behind a Chinese restaurant long enough for my secretary to take my place in the back seat and me to retrieve from the boot an umbrella and a bowler hat. My limousine set off in one direction. With the bowler set squarely on my head, I set off on foot in the other direction. I had no difficulty blending into the late-morning crowds on the street. I went into an underground station and took the tube, getting off and doubling back on my tracks several times until I was persuaded I was not being tailed. It was then and only then that I made my way to the Regent's Park tube station. Emerging from the underground, I began walking at a leisurely pace through the park in the direction of the zoo to the north. I settled onto a park bench on a little-used path and regarded my wristwatch. It was precisely eleven thirty-three. I could see the Friedman woman walking towards me from the direction of the Round House, which had been opened the previous year to accommodate a pair of gorillas. Oh, these English—if they treated their workers as well as their gorillas one could almost like them. A lean young man a head taller than Litzi Friedman walked a pace or two behind her and off to one side. When they were twenty or so paces away, I raised a forefinger—a prearranged signal asking if she was sure they had not been followed. She removed her straw hat (I noticed her hair was dyed platinum blonde) and fanned her face with its brim—a prearranged signal assuring me that she had taken appropriate precautions and spotted no one behind her. She stopped to exchange a word with the young man. Smiling at him, she nodded in my direction, then started back towards the zoo. The young man approached. I stood up and offered my hand. "Hello," I said.

He shook it. "Hello."

"You will be the Harold Philby of whom Litzi Friedman has spoken in glowing terms."

"Whatever she told you was surely an exaggeration. She failed to mention *your* name."

"It's Otto," I said. I motioned towards the bench and we both sat down. "Do you mind if I call you Harold?"

"I prefer my nickname, Kim."

"Kim it shall be." I produced a pack of English cigarettes. "Smoke?"

He selected one from the cardboard package. I held the

flame of my lighter to the end of his cigarette, and then to mine. The smoke from our two cigarettes intermingled as we regarded each other. Philby said, "May I assume this has to do with my app-pplication to join the Communist P-party?"

The Friedman woman had not mentioned the stammer. "You are free to assume anything you want," I said with a cheerful laugh, "though in this particular case you would be dead wrong."

"Ahhh, yes. I see."

"What do you see?"

"I see there may b-be more to this rendezvous than meets the eye."

The night before my meeting with Philby I had gone to the trouble of writing out what I would say as if it were a script for a radio drama. I had taken to heart the advice my late predecessor had once given me with respect to recruiting agents: Tone was every bit as important as the actual words. All that remained for me to do, sitting on a bench in Regent's Park, squinting at my interlocutor because of the dazzling sunlight, was play the role I had assigned myself: I had to make him feel as if he had found a kindred spirit and a lifelong friend. "If you want to join the party," I began, "of course they will accept you into its ranks with open arms."

"I do want to join the party. I want to p-participate in the struggle against Fascism and corporate capitalism."

"The struggle takes place on many levels. You can, if you choose, spend your days selling the *Daily Worker* in working-class neighbourhoods. But from what I've heard from Miss Friedman, it would be a waste of your time and talents."

Söhnchen—as the scene I am describing was set in Britain, I should probably stick with the English translation of his *nom de code*, Sonny—Sonny appeared to be startled by what I said. "What are my talents?" he demanded.

A well-dressed woman wearing an ankle-length skirt came down the path, walking her dog on a silver-link leash. I waited until she was out of earshot. "You are, by background, by education, by appearance and manners, an intellectual. You are able to blend in with the bourgeoisie and pass yourself off as one. If you really want to make a significant contribution to the anti-Fascist movement, simple membership in the British Communist Party is not the ticket. The clandestine alternative I am proposing will not be without difficulty, without danger even. But the rewards in terms of personal achievement, in terms of actually bettering the lot of the world's working classes, will be immense."

I remember he was staring at his shoes as I went through my routine. Suddenly he looked up at me with his ice-blue eyes. "Who are you?"

"I told you, my name is Otto."

"I was not b-born yesterday. If it p-pleases you to be known as Otto, I shall call you Otto. *But who are you? Whom do you represent?*"

"Does it matter?"

He let this sink in. The moment was awkward, with his question hanging unanswered—and unanswerable—between us.

I can honestly identify the precise instant I came to like

Sonny as a person, as a comrade. He could have repeated his question. He could have allowed the silence to drag on, which would have been another way of insisting on a response. To his everlasting credit he shrugged. "I suppose I shall have to make do with an educated guess," is what he said.

I continued my pitch. "You came down from Cambridge—this alone will open doors for you in journalism, in the foreign service, even in His Majesty's Secret Intelligence Service. I am proposing that you hitch your star to the Bolshevik project of imposing proletarian order on capitalist chaos. Will you join us in the struggle against Hitlerism and international Fascism?"

"You should know that I am terrified of violence. I get sick to my stomach at the sight of b-blood."

"Who amongst us isn't terrified of violence?"

"You don't understand. I tell you frankly, I am not courageous. If I were to be threatened with torture I would admit everything. I would name names. Yours first. I would die of fright if I were to be arrested."

"Being arrested can be a marvellously liberating experience. It liberates you from the fear of being arrested."

Sonny looked at me intently. "You are speaking from experience, aren't you?"

I was speaking about the marvellously liberating experience of my predecessor, of course, but I couldn't tell Sonny that. Ignaty Reif, cryptonym *Marr*, had lived in dread of being arrested by the NKVD. His hand had been shaking when he showed me the telegram from Moscow Centre summoning him home for consultations. "Don't go, for God's sake," I had whispered. We were in the men's room of a public house at the time, urinating into adjacent urinals. "I am a loyal Stalinist," he had whispered back. "Not going would only confirm their suspicions, assuming they have any." A month after his return to Russia, Ignaty managed to send a note to me through the wife of a cipher clerk who happened to be his wife's sister's niece. *Being arrested is a marvellously liberating experience,* it said. *It liberates you from the fear of being arrested.* The note was unsigned but I recognized my friend's handwriting. The telegram from Moscow Centre that announced my promotion to *Rezident* also informed us that Ignaty Reif had been sentenced to the highest measure of punishment and shot as a German spy.

Ignaty, with his round Polish face and his Polish accent and his shiny Russian suits that were one size too large for his squat Polish body, loathed everything German, starting with the language and finishing with Adolf Hitler and his thousand-year Reich.

What I told Sonny, in response to his question, was: "I am speaking from the long and painful Russian experience under the Tsars."

"Stalin is said to arrest people in great numbers," he remarked.

"Don't believe everything you read in the capitalist press," I cautioned. "Comrade Stalin only causes guilty people to be arrested." I tried to steer the conversation onto safer ground. "Listen, Kim, if you were to be in any danger, we would exfiltrate you well before you could be arrested."

"To where?"

"Why, to the Soviet Union, of course."

"I have never been to the Soviet Union."

"You would like it." I smiled. "It would like you."

I saw him nodding with what can only be described as eagerness. He never hesitated. "Yes," he said.

I was taken aback. I had expected him to put additional questions, to seek clarifications that I was under strict instructions not to provide. "Yes?" I asked a bit incredulously. "You agree to my proposition?"

He laughed. "To be honest I am not quite sure what you are p-proposing, but I am not your belt-and-braces type. I agree."

I took his hand and we shook on an understanding that would change his life.

And mine.

4: LONDON, JULY 1934

Where the Hajj Admits to Having Something Up His Sleeve

You won't recognize my name. Good Lord, why would you know who Miss Evelyn Sinclair is? I'm nobody. I'm here because I am the daughter of somebody, which is to say somebody important. My father, Hugh Sinclair, Admiral of His Majesty's Fleet (retired), is the chief of the British Secret Intelligence Service. Father, bless his heart, is old school down to his Savile gaiters. He has a mania for secrecy. He communicates with the handful of agents he has by means of what intelligence professionals curiously refer to as *dead letterboxes*. (How in heaven's name does one *kill* a letter?) If father is under the weather or otherwise indisposed, he has me service these postal boxes. Mind you, I am not actually a paid staff member of SIS but as we are starved for funds by our masters in the Foreign Office, this saves a salary. Father, universally known as *Quex* because of the speed with which he was thought to carry out orders when he was in the navy, takes his mania for secrecy to extremes. He keeps the service records of agents and staff in his breast pocket, one index card per person. He has been known to sit with his back to the individual he is interviewing in order to conceal his features. It was only because he and the Hajj (which is what father has called St John Philby since this bedraggled, bearded Arabist converted to Islam) had been school chums at Westminister and Trinity that he consented to be seated facing him. The particular meeting I am recounting took place in an upper-floor parlour of Caxton House, the dilapidated building within walking distance of Victoria Rail Station that reeked of midnight oil and served SIS as an H.Q. Thick curtains had been drawn across the windows, blotting up any suggestion of daylight. Portraits of Wellington's pink-jowled generals, each illuminated by a small brass lighting fixture, leaned off the walls as if to eavesdrop on the conversation. A carafe filled with a decent claret and four glasses had been set out on a silver tray. Besides the Hajj and father, there were two others (I don't include myself) present: father's deputies, Colonel Valentine Vivian, who had known Philby back in India before the Great War, and Colonel Stewart Menzies, a Horse Guard thought by the very few not put off by an absence of evidence to be the bastard of Edward VII. (Dear Colonel Menzies has been known to get in a huff if one didn't employ the Scottish pronunciation of his name, which was *Miniz.)* What set father's two deputies apart was that they loathed each other. None of the Caxton House regulars could recall having seen them speaking to one another; they communicated through memorandums that were routinely burned in ashtrays, some, so it was rumoured about, before being read. Father liked the atmosphere this created. Kept the troops on the qui vive, he would say. I was, as usual, present to create a stenographic minute of the conversation—it has been said of me, with some justice, that I am the Secret Intelligence Service's institutional memory. No glass had been set for me. Just as well. I am a lifelong teetotaller, not to mention co-chairlady of the Camden Temperance Society. Three minutes before the hour St John (pronounced Sin-Jin) Philby materialized at the door. He was wearing a wrinkled white suit with food stains visible on the lapels and white tennis plimsolls. Immediately after he sat down he undid the laces. "Able to trek desert dunes weeks on end," he muttered. "Damned feet swell up after five minutes in this tarmac jungle of yours."

Perhaps a word about the Hajj would be in order: To his everlasting vexation he lived in the shadow of T. E. Lawrence—our Lawrence of Arabia, as the yellow journalists would have it. Both Philby and Lawrence had contributed to the routing of the Ottoman horde from Arabia and Palestine. Lawrence in particular had captured the popular imagination when he sweet-talked Sharif Hussain of Mecca into rebelling against the Turks, eventually driving them north through Sinai and Syria. In part because of arguments advanced by Lawrence (in some cases quite shamelessly in newspaper interviews), the Sharif's son, Faisal, was crowned king in Damascus in 1920. Lawrence wanted to go the whole hog and install princes of the House of Hashim on thrones in Iraq and Transjordan, and the F.O. came to see things his way. Philby thought Lawrence had got it bass-ackward (to use the polite version of one of father's saltier expressions). The Hajj argued that the British were betting on the wrong horse; that they should be putting their money on ibn Saud and his Wahabi nomads in the Arabian desert, who were living in tents atop an ocean of petroleum. "Factories that run on coal are switching to petroleum," the Hajj would tell father, his only-just-kempt beard quivering with aggravation. "Am I wrong in thinking the keels being laid down now are going to be propelled by bunker oil."

"I am afraid that is a state secret," father would reply evenly. "If I were to tell you, old boy, I should have to kill you."

At the time St John Philby had rewarded father's rare stab at humour with a weak smile. As I recall the scene, I seem to remember father shrugging amiably. In the quarrel between the two rats of the desert, Philby and Lawrence, *Quex* was never quite sure his Trinity chum hadn't gotten it right.

As concerns the meeting at hand: Once the social amenities were out of the way, Colonel Vivian, who tended the counter-intelligence portfolio in father's shop, tapped Philby on a kneecap. "You will probably have heard," he said.

"I caught a glimpse of the headlines coming through Victoria," Philby replied. "Do you know more than what's in the newspapers?"

Father said, "It is Valentine's brief to know more than they print in the papers."

"He makes half of it up," Colonel Menzies interjected under his breath.

It was never difficult to get Colonel Vivian's goat. "I shall carry on as if I hadn't heard that," he said, but he had heard it and the register of his voice was not quite the same. "Ten Austrian Nazis from SS Regiment 89 were behind yesterday's assassination of Dollfuss. They talked their way into the Chancellery building and shot him dead when he rose to his feet to greet them. It was, of course, an attempt at a putsch. Herr Hitler will certainly have been behind it. The assassins were apprehended by the Austrian gendarmerie. I have it on good authority the scoundrels are to be shot. It was thanks to the Heïmwehr militia units, which remained loyal to the government and attacked the Nazi formations before they could launch the coup d'état, that the plot failed."

"Wasn't that boy of yours prowling Vienna?" father asked Philby.

"Dashed off to Austria to polish his German after he came down from Cambridge. Made a beeline for Britannia immediately after Dollfuss crushed those Communist riots last February."

"What's his name again?"

"Kim."

"That's it. Kim. After Kipling's Kim, if memory serves."

"Yes."

"Expect him to become a spy like Kipling's Kim, do you?"

"I can think of worse fates."

Father opined, "I can't." Colonels Vivian and Menzies

laughed appreciatively. Father continued, "Your boy was smart to return to England. In my view, a failed putsch or two won't stop Hitler from seizing Austria."

Philby said, "Great Britain is making the colossal mistake of seeing Hitler as the principal adversary."

"Have you had occasion to read *Mein Kampf*?" Colonel Vivian inquired of Philby.

"Have you had occasion to read the terms of the Versailles treaty?" Philby retorted. "What could be more normal than the Germans wanting to re-arm, to take their rightful place in Europe? Austria is their back garden, their *elbow room,* as they put it."

"The Versailles treaty was the price the Germans had to pay for waging the war," Colonel Vivian asserted.

"It was the price they had to pay for *losing* the war," Philby insisted.

"More claret?" father inquired.

"I was under the impression Muslims didn't drink," Colonel Vivian remarked when the Hajj accepted a refill.

"There is no prohibition in the holy Koran against consuming alcoholic beverages," Philby said. He was not to be easily sidetracked. "I make no secret of my exasperation with British foreign policy, Hugh," he told father. "I consider it wrongheaded, especially insofar as we flaunt the dreadful Balfour Declaration encouraging the Zionist delusion of returning to Palestine."

"You would have us accept this clown Hitler as an equal in Europe?" Colonel Vivian asked. He looked at father and raised his hands, palms upward, as if he had made the point that clinches an argument.

"Like it or not, Herr Hitler *is* an equal," Philby said. "If the British establishment views him as a clown, it's because the British press keelhauled the German chancellor with personal ridicule. The British government is every bit as responsible as Herr Hitler for the tension in Europe."

"You see no solution?" father asked. He seemed genuinely bemused by the Hajj's orneriness. Knowing father, I suspect he appreciated opinions that had their origins in an eccentric temperament.

"There would be a solution if the F.O. weren't too dimwitted to explore it. What is needed is a Christian settlement to the quarrel."

"As Christians, oughtn't we to be concerned about Hitler's attitude towards Jews?" Colonel Menzies inquired.

"As a militant anti-Zionist," the Hajj replied, "I don't give a hang how Herr Hitler treats his Jews so long as he doesn't pack them off to Palestine. They are, after all, *his* Jews, Stewart." Philby looked directly at father. "The great enemy of Western civilization is not Herr Hitler and Germany, it is Generalissimo Stalin and Soviet Russia."

Father said, "I don't quite see things the way you do, old boy. You are obsessed with Soviet Russia. Have been as far back as Trinity, where I remember your spouting off about that chap Trotsky and his Petrograd Soviet. What year would that have been, Evelyn?"

"Nineteen oh five, father."

"Oh five, of course. My predecessor at SIS, Smith-Cumming, was obsessed with Communism, too. Tried to overthrow the Bolsheviks after their little palace revolution—damn near succeeded. I'm talking about Bruce Lockhart's caper, which got us nothing but bad headlines for our troubles. Smith-Cumming devoted a good part of SIS's extremely limited resources to what he perceived to be the plausible Soviet threat of world revolution. When I took over here after Smith-Cumming met his Maker—damnation, what year would that have been, Evelyn?"

"Nineteen twenty-three, father."

"That's it, twenty-three. The inability to recall dates is a symptom of premature dotage, what? I was saying—what was I saying? Ah, yes, that we kept our more or less orthodox espionage efforts directed against the Soviets until Herr Hitler appeared centre stage. Given F.O. restrictions on our purse strings, not to mention F.O.'s unshakeable conviction that Herr Hitler had become our principal adversary, we were obliged to shift gears."

"Quite right," Colonel Vivian said.

Father didn't appreciate interruptions. "As I was saying, we were obliged to shift gears, which is to say redirect our resources from Soviet Russia in order to target Fascist Germany."

"Quite wrong," the Hajj said.

Philby was one of the very few who could cross father so directly. "How so?" Quex asked pleasantly enough.

"The future is perceptible to those who are not fearful of gazing into the crystal ball," the Hajj said. "Europe is heading for another Great War. Soviet Russia, with its limitless manpower, with Stalin's ruthless thirst for conquest, will emerge from it to dominate Europe. The Soviets, keen to recover lost territories, will dress up old Tsarist appetites in Communist ideology. Revolutionary movements financed and encouraged by the Soviets, and ultimately loyal to the Soviets, will spring up in the most unlikely places. The empire will be at risk. India will be the first to go."

Colonel Menzies had been following the exchange attentively. "What would you have us do, St John, that we are not already doing?" he asked.

"Can we suppose you have something up your sleeve?" Colonel Vivian inquired.

The Hajj: "Be a damn fool turning up here if I didn't."

Father: "Could you tell us about it?"

The Hajj: "I shall have to kill you all immediately if I do."

I have a marginalia here that reads: *General laughter*.

Father: "You haven't interrupted your exploration of Arabia's Empty Quarter to hold back on us, old boy. Do spit it out."

What follows in my minutes of the meeting is a half page of shorthand notes that were blacked out by father.

My minutes resume with my observation that father was tapping the fingertips of his right hand on the knuckles of his left hand, a secret signal to me that the interview had run its course. "Excuse the interruption, father—"

Quex turned on me in mock irritation. "What is it now, Evelyn?"

"It is almost four. You are supposed to be on the carpet of the F.O. at four forty-five sharp to discuss the proposed cutbacks in SIS funding." I seem to recall father's nautical chronometer on the wall behind his desk delicately sounding eight bells as I said this.

Father turned back to the Hajj. "Can we agree that this meeting never took place?"

"What meeting?" the Hajj said with what can only be described as a conspiratorial smirk, which, come to think of it, made him look nearly human. One caught a glimpse of what a woman might see in this unconventional figure of a man.

Father rose stiffly to his feet. "Jolly decent of you to drop by and share your views with us, St John. Always fascinating to hear what the world might look to be from Jiddah."

"Hear, hear," Colonel Menzies said.

"My sentiments precisely," Colonel Vivian agreed.

St John Philby reached down to tie up the laces of his plimsolls. "Yes, so you're turning me out to the mercies of your tarmac jungle, are you?"

Father said, "Quite."

At this point my minutes replicate the words that appear on the silver screen moments before the last reel of a film runs free: *The End*.

5: LONDON, AUTUMN 1936

Where Three Birds are Killed with One Stone

If the recruitment phase can be said to come under the heading of art—seduction, whether of a prospective lover or a prospective espionage agent, is certainly an art—what followed can best be described as craft. Or more precisely, tradecraft, to use the term we professionals employ. Setting up meetings was the first order of business. The tradecraft involved was fairly straightforward. Harold Adrian Philby, nickname Kim, cryptonym Sonny, and yours truly, Teodor Stepanovich Maly, the London *Rezident* Sonny knew only as Otto, would meet at nine- and eleven-day intervals (the irregularity was a precaution) at alternating locations, with fallback locations if for any reason one of us failed to turn up; with telephone numbers where seemingly innocuous messages could be left on new Swiss magnetic-tape answering machines, which I had to justify before Moscow Centre would permit them to be included in the *Rezidentura*'s budget. As I recall, the first several meetings were devoted to the creation of a *persona*, which is defined by the august Oxford English Dictionary, second edition, 1934 (a copy of which was, thanks to me, in the Soviet Embassy library), as the role one assumes in public, as distinguished from the inner self. The role Sonny would henceforth assume in public was that of an upper-class educated English gentleman who, like many of his schoolmates, had flirted with Socialism during his Cambridge years; had gone so far as to motorcycle to Vienna to help refugees fleeing from Nazi Germany; had married a Jewish girl in order to qualify her for a British passport and bring her to safety in England. With the passage of time, this same young man had come to his senses with respect to politics, which is to say he had matured into a right-of-centre conservative who wanted nothing more than to settle down to career and family and get on with life. We worked out the general lines in our first sessions and the details in subsequent sessions. I found Sonny to be a quick learner—it often happened that I started a sentence and he saw where it was going and finished it for me.

He kept me up to date on the progress he was making in the construction of his *persona*. He sorted through his books and got rid of the ones that would identify its owner as someone with leftist sympathies. He cancelled his subscription to the *Daily Worker* and subscribed instead to *The Times*, with its vaguely pro-German orientation. To give credibility to his new conservative *persona*, Sonny joined the Anglo-German Fellowship, a group organized to improve relations between England and Germany, going so far (with my encouragement) as to frequent the German embassy in London; making use of his press credentials as a subeditor of the *Review of Reviews,* he had several conversations with the German ambassador, Herr Ribbentrop, during which Sonny was careful to repeat his father's mantra about the need for a Christian settlement to British-German differences. Most importantly, Sonny began cutting his links with his leftist Cambridge friends.

I instructed Sonny to make the effort to get on better terms with the man he invariably referred to as his *sainted father*, St John Philby, who was less than pleased when his son turned up in London married to a Hungarian Jewess-cum-Communist. Kim wrote his father a rambling letter in which he explained away his leftist sympathies as misplaced youthful idealism and described his conversations with Ribbentrop. This worked out so well that Kim and his wife were invited to lodge in his father's London flat. It was at this point that I gave Sonny his first espionage assignment: I instructed him to go through his father's papers to see if there was any connection between St John and the chief of the British Secret Intelligence Service, the mysterious Admiral Sinclair. Sonny passed this initial test with what the English refer to as *airborne colours*: He brought me duplicates of three letters, copied off by Sonny in miniscule handwriting, each signed by someone named *Hugh*, which I knew to be the Christian name of Admiral Sinclair. Apparently he and St John were acquainted with each other from Westminster and Trinity College, Cambridge. In one of the letters, Hugh brought St John up to date on mutual friends from those days. Regrettably, the letters revealed no state secrets. In the last of the three, bearing a quite recent date, Admiral Sinclair invited St John to come by Caxton House for a drink the next time he found himself in London. From the way the invitation was worded, I gathered that St John Philby was not an actual member of the British Secret Intelligence Service but, given his close relationship with the Saudi ruler ibn Saud, more like an occasional consultant.

Sonny's second assignment—one of the most important missions in the business of espionage—was to suggest which of his old Trinity College friends might be recruited to work for the Communist *internationale* and, eventually, Moscow Centre itself. Kim turned up at our next meeting with a list, written out on the back of an envelope in the simple book code (page number, line number, letter number) I had taught him. It was impossible to decipher unless you knew which book he was working from. In this particular case it was the copy of the Hilton novel *Lost Horizon* that his father had given him when Sonny came down from Cambridge. Both Sonny and I had been fascinated by the book's tale of a mythical Himalayan utopia called *Shangri-La*. (I remember him joking that if he were ever to be unmasked as a Soviet spy, he wanted to be exfiltrated to *Shangri-La*. Being a staunch Communist, I assured him Stalin's Soviet Russia was the nearest thing to a *Shangri-La* on earth.) I still have Kim's envelope which, deciphered, reads:

Donald Maclean
Guy Burgess

Anthony Blunt
John Cairncross

Sonny knew them all from the Socialist circle at Cambridge. When we went over the list at one of our sessions, he described Maclean (who was immediately assigned the cryptonym *Orphan*) as a fervent Marxist and one of the original organizers of the Cambridge Communist cell. Sonny seemed to think that Maclean was our best bet: twenty-two years old, raised on the Island of Tiree off the Scottish coast, he had earned a first at Cambridge in foreign languages and seemed destined for a brilliant career in the Foreign Office.

I discussed Maclean with my deputy at the *Rezidentura,* Anatoly Gorsky, cryptonym *Kapp*, then sent a memorandum to Moscow Centre with Maclean's pedigree and our estimation that, in accordance with my strategy of long-term penetrations, we ought to attempt to recruit him. When Moscow Centre failed to respond I began to wonder if my telegram had gone astray. I sent it a second time. The response, which came back that evening, was terse to the point of rudeness.

From: Moscow Centre.
To: Teodor Stepanovich Maly.
Subject: Recruitment of Orphan by London Rezident.
Reference: Your telegram of 12 November 1936.
Authorization granted. Try but if the milk curdles, you must drink it.

No one to my knowledge has suggested that working for Moscow Centre had anything in common with a pleasure cruise.

I assigned Sonny the task of recruiting Maclean. He was reluctant at first. "How the hell do I raise the matter in a way that doesn't compromise me if he says no?"

"From what you've told me, I think he is enough of a Marxist to forget the conversation took place if he should decide to decline," I said.

"I've never done anything like this before. What do I say?"

"Say what I said to you: You can sell the *Daily Worker* on street corners or you can join in the common fight against Fascism."

"By golly, I'll try," Sonny said. And he did. He went up to Cambridge and took Maclean to supper at a local watering hole. Making the pitch turned out to be easier than Sonny had imagined. Maclean suspected that Philby himself had been recruited by the Soviets and said so. How else to explain his recent cutting off contact with the Cambridge crowd? Sonny played his cards close to his spencer, as the English say. He didn't admit anything, but he didn't deny it either. And when he came to the point—when he asked Maclean if he wanted to join in the struggle against Fascism—*Orphan* (as I now called him in my reports to Moscow Centre) simply smiled. "Who are you working for?" he asked. "The Kominturn? The Third *Internationale*? The NKVD? What the cheap Fleet Street sheets call Moscow Centre?"

Sonny told me he smiled back and said, "All of the

above" as if he were responding to a multiple-choice question on a Cambridge quiz.

The two apparently burst out laughing.

Which is how Maclean came to be recruited.

Guy Burgess, the second name on Sonny's original list, was another matter altogether. Sonny himself expressed serious reservations about the recruitment of Guy Burgess. As an undergraduate, Burgess (who was assigned the cryptonym *Maiden*) had dazzled his contemporaries and his professors alike with the reach of his intellect, so much so that he had been elected to the elite Cambridge Society of Apostles. Curiously, at a recent lunch with Kim, Burgess had gone so far as to suggest that he and Sonny should become Soviet spies.

"What did you say?"

"I told him he was mad."

"Was he?"

"Knowing Guy, it's quite possible he was passing off a serious idea as if it were a joke."

"Assuming he is willing to work for Moscow Centre, would he submit to discipline?"

"I am b-bound to tell you that Guy is an *enfant terrible,*" Sonny replied. "He used to go to leftist demonstrations in his roadster, driving up onto the pavement and revving the engine to scatter counterdemonstrators. It's a miracle he wasn't arrested. The heart of the p-problem is that Guy flaunts his homosexuality every occasion he gets. It would take a skilled Soviet controller to restrain him."

"There might be advantages to being homosexual."

"I'm not sure I follow you."

"A great many upper-class Englishmen—in government, in parliament, in banking, in the press—are said to be homosexual, or at least bisexual. A homosexual intelligence agent could have the same success seducing targets as, say, a beautiful female agent. Professional intelligence operatives call that a honey trap. I shall discuss Burgess with my associates in the *Rezidentura*."

Before we could reach a decision, this Burgess fellow forced our hand. He obviously had a sixth sense for the subtleties of undercover work because he quickly grasped that both Sonny and Orphan were cutting their ties to their Cambridge Socialist comrades. He raised the subject with Orphan directly, telling Maclean that he suspected something was afoot. "You fellows don't fool me—posing as repentant Socialists turned conservative. You and Philby are up to something." Maclean, exasperated, told him: "Shut your trap, will you. I am still who I was. I can't say more." Burgess said, "No need to say more. You and Kim work for Moscow." I can tell you that he wormed enough out of Maclean to come round to see my man Philby in London. "I have put two and two together," Burgess exclaimed, according to the detailed report of the conversation Sonny provided.

"Did you arrive at four?"

"I most certainly did," Burgess said. "One would have to be deaf and dumb not to have seen it. You and Don Maclean have been recruited by the Soviets. Own up, Kim. You do remember it was me who first suggested we spy for the Russians? How in the name of our long friendship can you cross this Rubicon without taking me with you? I feel obliged to tell you I consider it extremely disloyal of you to leave me behind."

Which is how Guy Burgess came to be recruited.

The months following Philby's coming on board—I may say the two years—were devoted to his education as a spy. In our Soviet Union, prospective agents are given four years of round-the-clock schooling at a secret training camp before they are sent into the field. Breaking in an agent in a hostile environment, which is what England represented for us, is an enormous challenge for both the teacher (in this case me) and the student; I had to cover a four-year curriculum in semi-monthly meetings, each of which lasted forty-five minutes. In addition to learning various simple cipher and secret writing techniques (Moscow Centre favoured using urine as ink, unlike the British, who preferred lemon juice), he had to master the art of getting lost in a crowd even in the absence of one: of becoming inconspicuous. For this he had a natural talent; in any given group of people, Sonny was the last one you'd take for an espionage agent. He had to perfect the art of making sure he was not being followed without alerting the person who might be following him that he was making sure he was not being followed. All tricks of the trade, so to speak. Tedious stuff, but essential to a Soviet espionage agent operating in a capitalist environment, meeting regularly with his control, in Philby's particular case trying to explain away a distinct left-wing footprint as youthful exuberance and establish himself as a solid conservative citizen of Great Britain.

During this incubation period, Philby applied for various

low-level posts in government, at the Foreign Office in particular, and later on Fleet Street in the hope of being offered a position that would lead to a career in journalism. None of these applications even reached the interview stage. When I analysed the situation with the comrades in the *Rezidentura*, we concluded that Philby must be on some sort of black list. We excluded the possibility that British intelligence was aware he'd been recruited by us; he would have been arrested if that were the case. We also excluded the possibility that it was his left-wing Cambridge past that was impeding his career; both Maclean and Burgess, despite having similar *curricula vitae* as Philby, seemed to have a foot in the door of the Foreign Office. Which narrowed the problem down to Philby's involvement with the Socialist-Communist movement in Vienna during the Dollfuss affair, and most particularly his marriage to a Hungarian-Jewish woman known to be a Communist activist (and perhaps suspected of being an agent for the Narodnyi Komissariat Vnutrennikh Del—the Peoples' Commissariat for Internal Affairs).

It was towards the end of 1936 that I devised a course of action that would neutralize both these obstacles with one stroke.

"Crikey Moses! Did I hear right? You want me to go where?"

"Spain."

"My sainted father took me on a tour of Moorish Spain when I was in my teens. Might be a b-bit dodgy going back now, what with a civil war raging?"

"But that's the point of your going, Kim. What could be

more natural than a young Cambridge graduate, stuck in a career rut as a subeditor for a weekly review, striking out on his own as a freelance journalist? Sell off your books and records to explain away how you finance the trip. Perhaps you could ask your father for a small loan—he funded your trip to Vienna, didn't he? You could write articles from the battlefront. Get your byline into London newspapers. If you do decently, one of the broadsheets—perhaps even *The Times*—will hire you as a permanent correspondent. Your career will be up and running. No telling where you could wind up. There are more than a few in the Foreign Office, even the British Secret Intelligence Service, who started out as journalists."

Philby began to see the merits of my idea. "Covering a war could be exciting. I will admit that my heart is with the Republicans—not a few of my Cambridge comrades have enlisted in the International B-brigade and are fighting against the Fascist *Falange* in Spain. It would be b-bloody marvellous to get their stories into the newspapers."

"You wouldn't be reporting from the Republican side, Kim. You would report from Franco's side."

"You want me to write about Fascists!"

"Absolutely. There are dozens of famous journalists covering the Republicans—that American Hemingway, the Hungarian Capa, the Englishman Orwell. You would be hard put to compete with them. But as there are so few journalists reporting from the Nationalist side, your dispatches would likely be front page news. They would be dispassionate, unbiased, balanced, even slightly pro-Franco, which would dispel any suspicion you were at heart a Communist and pro-Soviet. Your loyalty to the British government would be visible in print. Mark my words, Kim: Doors will open for you."

Philby thought about this. "What about Litzi?" he asked.

"What about Litzi?"

"Would she accompany me to Spain?"

"It would be best if she remained in London."

"But that would involve a separation."

When I didn't immediately reply, Philby said, "Ahhh. I am quite thick not to see what you're p-plotting."

"What am I plotting?"

"One way or another, you want me to leave Litzi. Covering the Spanish war would kill two b-birds with one stone. Paint over my Socialist background with a right-of-centre veneer, mark p-paid to my marriage to a known Communist."

"Three birds with one stone, Kim. We have informants on the Republican side but next to nothing on Franco's side. As an Englishman with a reputation for being a friend of Franco's principal sponsor, Germany, you would be ideally positioned to obtain information on Franco's order of battle, on troop movements, on the matériel and pilots that Hitler and Mussolini are providing to the fascists."

I remember we were sitting on the bench across from the new Battersea Power Station on Kirtling Street at the time of this conversation. It was lunch hour. Men with identical bowler hats planted on their heads strolled the sidewalk. A boy in knickerbockers hawked newspapers on the corner, calling out the headlines in a shrill singsong voice. *Edward planning to abdicate throne to marry American divorcée Simpson. Defying League of Nations Hitler tightens grip on Rhineland.* I was wearing my bowler and balancing my umbrella across my knees. I retain an indelible image of Kim shelling peanuts to feed the pigeons prowling the gutter. He concentrated on the pigeons for a long while. Finally he said, "How do you think they learn to eat the nuts and not the shells?"

"Painful experience."

"That's a coincidence—it's my alma mater. The school of p-p-painful experience." He nodded as if he had come to a decision. "Of course I shall have to speak with Litzi."

"I have already spoken with Litzi."

He turned to me in surprise. "When? She didn't say a word about it to me."

"She is still under Centre discipline. I instructed her not to. We met last week at the tearoom in the Brook Street hotel. I explained to her what I had in mind for you. Litzi is a good soldier, a good Communist. There is a line in English poetry that describes her perfectly: *They also serve who only stand and wait.* When we spoke, she said she'd seen the writing on the wall when you told her you'd agreed to be recruited—she understood that you and she would eventually have to separate. She realizes she is a liability to you, a drag on your career. She realizes this has to end if you are to be of service to the anti-Fascist *internationale*. People would understand your marrying a Jewess to save her from persecution. People will understand your decision to leave her once she was safely in England."

"I shall need to think this through," he said.

"By all means, think it through."

"I do have a choice?"

I gripped his arm. "You have a choice—you can take the leap and become an important contributor to the cause, or you can join the British Communist Party and"—here I pointed to the boy hawking newspapers on the corner—"call out *Daily Worker* headlines to illiterate coal miners."

When Sonny showed up for our meeting eleven days later, he was carrying an English-Spanish dictionary. He riffled through to a page he had dog-eared and read off what he had written in the margin: "*Voy a España para informar sobre una guerra.*"

"*Muchas gracias*," I replied.

By early 1937 I considered Sonny sufficiently proficient in tradecraft for him to depart for Spain. At our last meeting, on the Regent's Park bench where we'd first met, I gave him a sheet of very thin rice paper. In a column down the left-hand side I had listed the things we were interested in: *tanks, trucks, repair facilities, airports, bombers, fighters, artillery, mortars, machine guns, battalions, regiments, divisions, German or Italian advisors, German or Italian pilots.* Down the right-hand side I had listed innocuous words: *because, eventually, weather, incredible, tasty, sunset, lunch,* that sort of thing. I instructed him to post a love letter once every week to Mlle Dupont at 79 Rue de Grenelle in Paris. Every fifth word in the letter would be a code word. If he wanted to report seeing eighteen tanks at a repair facility, the fifth word in the letter would be *18,* the tenth would be *because,* the fifteenth, *weather*. From time to time he would be summoned to one of the French towns just across the frontier where foreign correspondents went to avoid censorship when they filed stories. There he would meet with his field controller, Alexander Orlov, cryptonym the *Swede*. Orlov would be sitting at the local train station café when the church bells sounded noon. He would be wearing a Panama hat with the brim turned down to shade his eyes and reading a copy of the new American magazine called *News-Week*. The Swede would debrief Philby and supply him with fresh code sheets, cash, and instructions. "I can promise you that Moscow Centre considers this a high-priority assignment," I said. "Important comrades in the Soviet capital will be watching to see how you perform."

"They said that?"

"They didn't have to. Sending Orlov, who is one of our most experienced field agents, to be your controller tells the whole story. I know Orlov personally. He was a war hero—he distinguished himself fighting with the twelfth Red Army on the Polish front after the Bolshevik Revolution. Don't be put off by his manner. He is a gruff, no-nonsense fellow but a loyal party member and a steadfast comrade. You can trust him with your life."

I remember Sonny running his thumb down the list on the left-hand side of the thin sheet of rice paper. "It appears as if I shall have to."

6: SALAMANCA, SPAIN, DECEMBER 1937

English Discovers There is No Way Out Except Up

There is a downside to being a celebrated film and theatre actress, which is my professional description—gentlemen simply assume you're playing a role offstage as well as on. English, as I christened him the moment I heard his posh British stammer, must have thought this to be the case. I become aware of him across the luncheon table at the Grand Hotel in Salamanca, Franco's military H.Q., saying little, eating less, sucking on tablets he retrieved from a small tin, all the while smoking one of those vile French cigarettes favoured by the working classes. He appeared to be mesmerized by the German military advisors decked out in a mixed bag of Gilbert and Sullivan frippery, eating at the long table reserved for them in the middle of the dining room. The Colonel Wolfram von Richthofen, a cousin of the legendary German ace from the Great War Manfred von Richthofen, was entertaining a cluster of young Condor Legion Messerschmitt pilots, using his hands to conjure up two planes locked in a deadly dogfight. Every now and then one of the Italian Fiat pilots at a nearby table would leap to his feet to toast his German comrades. Shrugging off the greatcoat draped over his shoulders, Richthofen, the Condor Legion's chief of staff, would half rise out of his chair to acknowledge the salutation. It was only when we came to coffee and brandy that English seemed to notice my presence at all. He raised his marvellously robin's egg-blue eyes and fixed them on me, as if there were already a connivance between us; as if it was written that we would become intimate. When we finally found ourselves alone after the meal—our host, Randy Churchill, counting on the pound sterling to trump the Spanish peseta, had gone off to renegotiate the bill—English called to me over the clamour of the restaurant, "So what role were you p-playing today?"

"Sorry?"

"What role? Whom were you trying to b-b-be?"

"That's a goddamn arrogant question to put to someone you don't know."

Detecting the mischievous glint in his eyes, I tossed a shoulder in vexation. "I was *trying* to be the Canadian actress who keeps men at arm's distance by a wisp of wintriness in her voice, an ironic curl to her lips when she smiles."

"Have you actually rehearsed in front of a m-mirror?"

"Who the hell are you?"

"You do it very well, the wintry voice, the ironic curl deforming an otherwise delicious smile. I got the uncomfortable feeling even arm's d-distance might be too close to the flame for comfort. Well, ta ta. I must be off."

"Who was he?" I asked my luncheon host when he came back. "The Englishman diagonally across from me?"

"Dear girl, that's Philby. He's *The Times* correspondent in Spain. Has he gone and put his foot in his mouth again? The Orientals are said to say *a closed mouth gathers no feet*, but our man Philby lives by another creed. He is afflicted with the absolutely revolting habit of saying what he thinks."

Several days afterwards I ran into English again. I remember I was wearing a form-hugging ribbed turtleneck sweater and a pair of high-waisted hopsack trousers of the kind Marlene Dietrich had modelled in Edna Chase's *Vogue*. He was dressed in a casual corduroy suit and tie and was banging out Cole Porter's "Let's Do It, Let's Fall in Love" on the upright piano in the Grand Hotel basement bar. A gaggle of foreign correspondents and their lady friends had gathered round him. Those who knew the song were singing snatches. "Moths in your rugs do it, What's the use of moth balls?" Somehow the seawall of bodies parted and he caught sight of me. The playing stopped abruptly. English threaded his way through the crowd until he was standing before me. "I have been known to give a p-passable imp-personation of our lord and monarch, George Six. We b-both of us stammer. Would you care to hear it?"

"No."

"Ahhh, beware of actresses bearing grudges. You didn't appreciate *arm's d-distance might be too close to the flame for comfort*."

"Didn't."

"Can I make it up to you? Stand you a snakeb-bite?"

"Snakebite?"

"A drink. From a glass. With a straw if you p-prefer." He offered a paw. "Philby. Kim Philby."

I looked down at his hand thinking it might be the snake that could bite, then, laughingly, gave in and accepted it. "Randy Churchill told me who you were. You cover Spain for Geoffrey Dawson's rag. Remember reading your notice in *The Times* when Franco took Gijón—I supposed *from our special correspondent in Spain* meant you. Something about towels draped from windows as tokens of surrender, something about empty shops, a silent population. Sounded almost as if you'd been there."

"I was there. I was describing what I saw." He realized he was still clinging to my hand and abruptly let it go. "I know who you are, too," he announced somewhat awkwardly. "Frances Doble, Bunny to her mates, pushing thirty-five but nobody is quite sure from which side, spoilt daughter of a Canadian banker, spoilt ex-wife of a minor b-baronet, spoilt film and theatre actress who played the lead opposite the matinee idol Ivor Novello in Nöel Coward's *Sirocco*. According to *Picture Show* you are said to have an exquisite figure." He treated himself to a long cheeky inspection of my body. "I'd say *P-picture Show* was spot on."

"You *have* done your homework."

He produced a smile. Of the two of us, it was English who possessed the more delicious smile—it could thaw out the iciest grudge. "Homework is what I do for a living," is what he said.

Eager to hold up my end of the conversation, I'm afraid I began to babble. "In *Sirocco,* Ivor Novello chased me round a table till he tackled me to the floor and stretched out on top of me, his hips moving in passion. Dear God in heaven, they told me Ivor preferred boys but onstage he could have fooled me. I could feel his panhandle in my groin."

"You must tell me more about Ivor Novello's p-panhandle," English said, taking a grip on my elbow and steering me towards an empty table at the rear of the bar.

A man I'd never seen before accosted English, blocking his path, putting a trembling palm on his shirt front. "You are a lout, Philby," he said quite loudly, his words slurred, his breath reeking of alcohol. "I have read your dispatches suggesting that Republican mines and not Fascist incendiary bombs destroyed Guernica. You have betrayed your Cambridge friends who died defending Republican trenches, you have betrayed the great Democratic cause of this century. You are on the wrong side of history."

I saw the fingers on English's right hand clench into a fist and I thought he was going to strike the man. "You are drunk," he said, dominating his emotions, shouldering past him and pulling me along behind him. He turned back for an instant. "I am exactly what I have always b-been," he said.

"And what would that be?" the man called after us.

"My sainted father's boy," English said so softly I am sure I was the only one who heard him.

"Sorry b-bout that," he said as we settled into a booth facing each other.

"Happen often?"

"P-people feel strongly about civil wars. That's why otherwise sane men wind up murdering each other for a few square yards of dirt."

"Do you feel strongly about this war?"

"I have no opinion one way or the other. I am p-paid to describe what I see. What about you?"

"I am not a Nationalist. I am a Royalist. I favour Franco winning in the expectation that he will restore the Bourbon monarchy."

"Codswallop. If *el Caudillo de la Última Cruzada*, as Franco styles himself, restores the monarchy, he will seat his own arse on the throne."

"I can only hope you are misreading his intentions."

"What brought you to Spain?"

"A random wind. I chanced to meet King Alfonso in London, it will have been shortly after he went into exile in 1931. He turned up at one of my after-theatre champagne bashes. He had the face of an animal but the heart of a Spaniard. He talked nonstop of Spanish bulls, of Spanish music, of Spanish women. My fascination with Spain dates to my friendship with Alfonso. He suggested I come see for myself. When I reminded him there was a civil war raging, he laughed and said violence was also characteristically Spanish. To make a long story shorter, I did come to see for myself. Been here since. What 'bout you? How did you wash up on this shore?"

"Same way I washed up in Vienna few years b-back—several of my Cambridge mates dared me to go. Sold my books and records to p-pay my way, came as a freelance for a few months, wrote one piece that caught the eye of my masters at *The Times.* They offered me the situation. Which is how I came to be hanging about Franco's military headquarters in Salamanca." English looked at me in a way I'd seldom been looked at before. "Which is how I came to share a table with the most beautiful woman in Spain."

I heard myself murmur, "I'll wager you say that to all the girls."

He smiled innocently. "I say it to some of them. In your case it happens to be true."

Daiquiris appeared as if by magic on the table. It dawned on me that English had ordered them before I'd actually agreed to join him for his snakebite. Behind the shy smile he was a smug piece of work. I remember asking, "Can I presume you no longer fear singeing yourself on my flame?"

"I still fear your flame, but I like to live d-dangerously."

"Randy told me about your living dangerously," I remarked. "He said you were nearly stood against a wall and shot in Córdoba."

"Randolph was embroidering, as always."

"What did happen in Córdoba?"

"I went there on a whim when I saw a p-poster advertising a bullfight. I made the mistake of not bothering to get a pass to a restricted area. Late that night two *Guardia Civil* types armed with rifles and bayonets b-busted into my room. They searched my valise and the room whilst I dressed. Then they marched me off to the local lockup. An officer, who clearly had it in for the English because we have declined the honour of establishing diplomatic relations with Franco's Nationalists, ordered me to empty my p-pockets. That's when I remembered the sheet of rice paper filled with codes folded into a tin of Arm and Hammer indigestion tablets in my pocket. If they had found that I would have been in a real jam."

"What on earth did you do?"

"I pulled my wallet from my hip p-pocket and tossed it onto the table. The two soldiers and their officer pounced on it. Whilst they were going through my press credentials I managed to roll the folded rice paper into a ball with my finger tips. Then I popped it into my mouth as if it were an indigestion tablet and sucked on it until it dissolved."

I sipped my daiquiri. "Of course I don't believe a word about your sucking on the code."

English smiled. "I was trying to impress the p-pants off you."

"Why would you want to do that?"

The smile vanished. "In the hope of impressing the p-pants off you."

I will admit to a weakness for men who don't beat about the bush. "Let's do it," I said, pilfering a bit of Cole Porter's lyrics.

"Lovely. Let's."

"My room or yours?"

"Mine is right under the German contingent. Lifts don't run at night. The ones who pilot the Heinkel 45s tramp off at four in the morning to bomb the Republican lines."

"Mine is next to the Italian pilots, but they don't leave until six."

English said, "By six we ought to be just drifting off to sleep."

He was not far from the mark. By six I had lost count of how many times we'd made love. We were sitting up in bed smoking (my Old Golds; I couldn't support the odour of his Gauloises Bleues) when we heard the Italian pilots padding along the corridor towards the staircase on their stockinged feet. The sound of them whispering in Italian made us both giggle. "You're a good storyteller," I said. "The business about the code in Córdoba—the more I think about it, the more it rings true."

"I can be convincing when I try."

"It wasn't your being convincing so much as everyone assumes *Times* correspondents work for the British Secret Intelligence Service. Randy Churchill is persuaded you're SIS. Are you a spy, English?"

"No."

"If you were, would you tell me?"

"No."

"That puts us right back where we started."

"We can never go b-back to where we started, Frances."

It was as close as he would ever come to a declaration of love.

His story of sucking on the code as if it were an indigestion tablet haunted me. As our life lines intertwined with the passage of time—we each kept our rooms in the Grand Hotel but he spent most nights in mine when he wasn't on the road—I began to understand that English did have a secret life. It's the sort of thing a woman knows intuitively about a man. Oh, he was drinking heavily, although he held his liquor with the best of them—you had to be sharing a bed with English to know he was inebriated. No, no, it was much more than his reliance on alcohol. Instead of my keeping him at arm's distance, he was keeping me at arm's distance. I could get only so close to him before I hit what I came to think of as his invisible wall.

I tried to penetrate it, to climb over or round it, all without success. Weeks into our love affair, I tried another tack. "Whom do you admire?" I asked.

"What makes you ask?"

"You can tell a lot about a man from whom he admires. Statesmen? Sportsmen? Seamen? Businessmen? Gamblers? Writers? Gigolos?"

He gave the question some thought, nursing his umpteenth gin, rubbing the rim of the glass with a forefinger until it produced a soft moan. "I admire rock climbers," he finally said.

"That's certainly creative. And why rock climbers?"

"Once they start scaling the face of a cliff, I'm t-told there is no turning back, no way out except up. If you get weak-kneed, if your arms or your n-nerve give out, you have no choice, you must keep on climbing."

"Is that how you see life in general?"

He appeared startled by my question, almost as if he had caught a glimpse of a side of himself he hadn't remarked before. "Now that you mention it, I suppose it is."

By December of 1937, the war that was said to be laying waste to the Iberian peninsula had become rather abstract to me. I had never heard a rifle fired in the hope of killing or maiming a fellow human being, so I was incapable of summoning an image of trenches filled with soldiers shooting down ranks of attacking soldiers. Try as I might, I was unable to see the war through English's eyes. To give him his due, he attempted to educate me. He recounted dreadful episodes of mayhem committed on both the Nationalist and the Republican sides. I remember one tale about the wife of a Communist leader who was raped by every member of the firing squad before being executed. We actually got into a quarrel over it—I argued that English had no way of knowing if the story was a true account of an atrocity or propaganda. He retorted that his source was unimpeachable, but of course he refused to identify him.

English had the habit of fortifying himself with gin before attending the daily briefing given by the general staff's press attaché on the hotel's fourth floor, and he took everything that was said there with a grain of salt. He played *pelota* twice a week with the chief of military censorship, Pablo del Val, in the hope of getting a scoop. The only thing he got for his trouble was muscle cramps. He managed occasional field trips when the Nationalists removed the leash on which journalists were kept, but he and his colleagues were escorted everywhere by a team of Franco's press officers and were only permitted to interview pre-selected Nationalist soldiers or officers. English traded war stories with various of his Fourth Estate friends at the table reserved for foreign correspondents in the hotel's basement bar. I was often present but I had difficulty following the conversation, laced as it was with military jargon and references to unfamiliar geography. I did gather, as Ernie Sheepshanks of *Reuters* put it, that the handwriting was on the wall: Nobody covering Franco's H.Q. thought the Republicans could triumph, let alone cling to the territory they held. One of Mussolini's own sons, Bruno, commanded an Italian bomber squadron—I'd been introduced to him at a cocktail party marking the first anniversary of the arrival of Franco's Moorish army in Spain. I remember his saying much the same thing, although his gloating tone of voice was repugnant.

Days before what turned out to be one of the coldest Christmases in memory, the Grand Hotel was abuzz with excitement. To everyone's astonishment, the Republicans—goaded on by their Soviet advisors, so it was presumed—had captured the provincial capital of Teruel. English pointed it out to me on the map. It was inland on the Mediterranean side of the peninsula, circled in red by one of the German or Italian aviators who had bombed it. There was a heated debate at the correspondents' table about the merits of the Republican campaign. The consensus was that a quick propaganda victory might boost flagging morale but would not translate into a strategic advantage. Robson of *The Daily Telegraph* had actually been to Teruel when the Nationalists first took it. As foreign journalists were refused permission to visit the Teruel front, a good deal of the local colour in English's notices came from Robson: Teruel was a bleak, walled town with Siberian winters; soldiers fed broken furniture into fires to melt snow for drinking water; both sides could expect more casualties from frostbite than bullets; whoever held La Muela, the hill dominating the town, could expect to win the battle. English's dispatches were so detailed, he actually received a telegram from *The Times*'s foreign editor, Ralph Deakin, complimenting him. Another regular at the correspondents' table, the Associated Press's Ed Neil, claimed to have a source on the Nationalist's general staff who reported that Franco, unwilling to allow the Republicans even an insignificant triumph, had massed an enormous army on the Teruel front. It was Neil who kept us informed of the Nationalist counterattack. After *softening up* (what a revolting expression) the Republicans with the heaviest artillery barrage of the war, the Nationalist soldiers stormed the Republican positions. Fighting raged in the centre of the town around the churches of Santiago and Santa Teresa. *Dinamiteros* braved heavy fire to blow up Republican T-26 tanks dug in around the bullring in a suburb. With Teruel safely back in Nationalist hands, Franco's press people finally laid on a junket to the front.

Teruel. Even now, long after the fact, the word makes my blood run cold, not because of the battle, of which I know little more than what was reported in the headlines. No, my blood runs cold because I was personally acquainted with five casualties of the Teruel campaign. The abstract civil war became sickeningly real.

Here is English's account of the junket to Teruel at the very end of December, which I heard a dozen times if I heard it once. I can honestly say that until we went our separate ways, some two years after we'd met, talking about the trip—to me, to other correspondents, to visiting members of a Parliamentary commission, once to a German embassy officer who had been playing *die Wacht am Rhein* on the bar's upright piano—seemed to be the only way English could make it through the day. Or the night that followed.

English shared an automobile with four regulars from the Grand Hotel's basement bar: *The Daily Telegraph*'s Robson, *Reuters*' Sheepshanks, the AP's overweight and forever dieting Ed Neil, and the very young and very amusing *News-Week* photographer Bradish Johnson. The five of them set off in a snow blizzard so blinding they only managed to stay on the road by following the tail lights of the press officer's car, which in turn followed the tail lights of an army supply truck. English was wearing the coat of an Arab prince his father had given him, it was bright green on the outside with a red fox fur lining. Icy winds swept the wastelands of Aragon around Teruel as the journalists passed through villages acrawl with soldiers heading for the front and civilians fleeing the battle. The group stopped for lunch at the canteen of a makeshift landing field that used a stretch of roadway as runway. From the toilet window English could make out soldiers chipping ice off the wings of Fiat fighter planes. In the village of Caudé, north and west of Teruel, English persuaded Franco's press chaperone to let him interview a wounded officer limping towards the rear. Passing a water well, English chanced to look into it and saw that it was filled with dead bodies—whether civilians or military he could not make out as they were covered with snow. The brief conversation he was able to have with the wounded officer was drowned out by an artillery battery a hundred yards away shelling Republican lines.

Once past Caudé, English—who was driving—pulled

up next to a snow bank and went off to relieve himself near a dead horse with its frozen legs thrust into the sky. His description of trying to open the buttons on the fly front of his trousers while wearing mittens still brings tears to my eyes. In the end he took off one mitten and undid the buttons and quickly pulled the mitten back on for fear his fingers would become frostbitten in the subzero temperature. Returning to the two-door automobile, English found he had lost his place in front. Bradish was pouring rum into tin cups. "Come on in out of the cold," he called. English walked around to the passenger side. Sheepshanks pulled his seat forwards and English squeezed onto the rear seat next to Ed Neil. There apparently was a spirited discussion underway about whether the winters in Aragon were colder than a witch's tit, but as nobody could claim firsthand experience with witches' tits, the question was left hanging. Bradish revved the motor to activate the small heating unit. Before he could shift the automobile into gear a giant hand lifted the vehicle into the air and then dropped it back onto the ground. English never heard the explosion of the Republican shell that landed (so he was later told) next to the bonnet. He remembered only an ear-piercing silence, then soft groans. Soldiers pried open the car doors, which were shredded with shrapnel holes. Bradish Johnson, his face blackened, fell out headfirst onto the road, lifeless. Poor Sheepshanks, sitting next to Johnson, was gasping for oxygen and suffocating because he couldn't get enough. His head was torn open, what English took for brain matter was seeping out. The soldiers pulled

Robson and English onto the road and then wrestled Ed Neil out from the rear seat. His left leg was torn to the bone with metal splinters. English, who was bleeding from a gash in his scalp, pressed a mitten to his own wound to stop the flow of blood. He bent over Neil, whose lips formed words. He finally managed to whisper "Do me a favour, keep an eye on my typewriter, will you?"

A military ambulance took the five journalists to a dressing station at Santa Eulalia. Robson and Bradish Johnson were pronounced DOA. Sheepshanks never regained consciousness. The surgeons did their level best to save Neil's leg, after which they did their level best to save Neil when gangrene set in. He died late in the evening of the following day. As for English, once the doctors stitched up the wound and bandaged his head, he was, medically speaking, fit as the proverbial fiddle. I, of course, knew nothing of all this until, on the first day of 1938, which chanced to be English's twenty-sixth birthday, he turned up in the hotel dining room, a bandage around his head, dried blood on his jacket. "I b-b-badly need a b-b-bloody drink," he said.

His hands trembled so violently he had to use both of them to manoeuvre the brandy glass to his lips.

It must have been close to midnight before he ceased trembling entirely. Lying next to him in bed, our hips touching, I could sense him asserting control over his body. When he was still, I whispered in his ear. "Your strengths are evident. Your weaknesses aren't."

"I don't p-permit myself weaknesses."

I thought about that for the time it took to smoke half a cigarette. Finally I said, "Surely that *is* your weakness."

"Ahhh. I see your p-point, Frances."

English, of course, was an overnight sensation. Photographs of him appeared first in the local Spanish papers, then the story of *The Times* correspondent who had cheated death while those around him were killed spread to England and Continental Europe. In the hotel bar, utter strangers would come over and shake his hand. Looking back, I can see that this newfound fame may have contributed to our drift apart. Up to the Teruel business, I was the celebrity in the couple. Brits or Canadians would occasionally recognize me from one of my films—usually *The Water Gipsies* or *Dark Red Roses*—and ask for an autograph. Now when Brits or Canadians—or Frenchies or Italians or Germans or Dutch, for that matter—accosted English, he would quickly introduce me: "You will surely recognize Frances Doble," he would say and more often than not I was favoured with a polite smile or a perfunctory nod before the individual turned back to English, who clearly occupied centre stage. Oh, please don't jump to the conclusion that I was jealous. I honestly don't believe I am capable of jealousy. I suppose it's simply that my ego required a certain amount of nourishment and, like most actresses flirting with middle age, it made me uncomfortable when I didn't get it.

English and I got into more spats than usual over ridiculously minor matters such as who had first suggested this or that restaurant, why he always came to my room (after Teruel, the German pilots were getting up at the same hour as the Italian pilots, and in any case we were so tired we never heard them stirring in the corridor) and why I was never invited down to his. All of these small increments of a disintegrating relationship came to a head when English's *pelota* partner, the chief of military censorship Pablo del Val, telephoned one Saturday morning not long after English's return from Teruel. (Talk about being taken for granted, he rang *my* room and without so much as a *buenos dias* demanded to speak to English.) As English held the telephone away from his ear, I caught the conversation.

"Philby, I'm coming round to get you at six tonight."

"But we aren't supposed to be playing *pelota* until Tuesday," English remarked sleepily.

del Val's hysterical laughter crackled over the telephone line. "It has nothing to do with *pelota*, which in any case you are miserable at. Generalissimo Franco is going to decorate you for your heroic actions on the battlefield in the struggle against Godless Communism."

English and I had a spat over whether I should accompany him, he insisting, me desisting, but I gave in if only to shake the hand of the great leader whom I expected would restore the monarchy to Spain. That evening we found del Val waiting impatiently in the hotel's elliptical driveway, his black Mercedes-Benz motorcar at the head of an imposing convoy of vehicles filled with journalists. He was a bit flustered to see me on English's arm, but I ducked into the backseat before he could utter a word. Shaking his head grumpily, del Val took his place next to the driver. We had a police escort all the way to the palace in Burgos that

Franco used as a home and a headquarters. We wound up practically running through a series of enormous rooms filled with army and air force officers sitting like schoolchildren at small desks, and a grand ballroom with artists on a scaffolding restoring frescos on the ceiling, until we arrived at an antechamber where rough-looking men in identical shiny black suits searched English, and a female wearing a badge that identified her as a sanitary officer searched me. (She didn't shilly-shally, in full view of all the men, about patting down my breasts.) We were ushered into a windowless round room with military maps tacked to the walls. A gaggle of journalists crowded in behind us. Three men in uniform were leaning over a map spread across a large table. I realized the short one was Generalissimo Franco in the flesh. del Val coughed into his cuff. Franco looked up, unsure of what was expected of him. A young officer with the gold braid of an aide-de-camp approached and whispered in his ear. "Pensé que iba a venire mañana," Franco said in a loud voice. del Val said, "Hoy en dia, excelencia." Franco shrugged. "Vamos a harcerlo." The young officer handed Franco a small wooden box. He opened it and removed what turned out to be the Red Cross of Military Merit. The Generalissimo made his way across the room to English, stood on tiptoes and, with some difficulty, succeeded in pinning the medal onto the breast pocket of his corduroy jacket. Flashbulbs exploded. Franco mumbled his way through a short speech, which I didn't catch a word of. English thanked the Generalissimo in English. del Val translated it phrase by phrase into Spanish. Franco nodded and reached to pump English's hand.

Flashbulbs popped again. English started to introduce me—"Please meet my friend, the Canadian film actress Frances—" But Franco had already turned back to the map on the table.

There was an impromptu bash at the Grand Hotel basement bar the next night. Correspondents from a dozen or so countries clustered around English, each waving his copy of a local or regional newspaper with a photograph of English, a decidedly sheepish grin on his face, being decorated by *El Caudillo* splashed across the front page. Bill Carney of *The New York Times* asked English for his impressions of Franco. "Tell the truth, the whole thing was over in the b-bat of an eye," he replied. "Didn't have a chance to form an impression." Randy Churchill clapped English on the back. "Well done, old boy. You're bound to get a raise from your masters at the British Secret Intelligence Service—they will be elated to have one of their operatives seen shaking Franco's hand. Doors will open that have heretofore remained shut. Nationalist generals will usher you into their map rooms and point out the disposition of their troops. By Jove, any intelligence service in the world would consider this a major coup."

English laughed off the suggestion that he was employed by the SIS. "I don't work for any intelligence service, much less the B-brits. So none of them can claim a coup."

"If you swallow that," Randy told Carney with a knowing wink, "I have some prime fen for sale in County Galway that will be of interest to you."

Around about midnight I tugged at English's elbow.

"Don't be too awfully long," I told him. "I'm fagged out."

"Shouldn't think I shall be coming by tonight," he said. "Bit b-bushed myself."

"You could always come round simply to sleep."

He managed one of his delicious smiles, the kind that can thaw out the iciest grudge when you first experience it. "I'll take a rain check," he said.

I am afraid irritation got the better of me. I snapped, "Tough luck, English—I haven't been reduced to giving rain checks to my bed."

7: BIARRITZ, APRIL 1938

Where Alexander Orlov, Cryptonym the Swede, Discovers That the Englishman is Armed

I have heard it bandied about that, as a matter of tradecraft, the reasonably professional British Secret Intelligence Service, along with their American cousins, the embarrassingly amateurish Office of Strategic Service, use safe-houses or safe-apartments or safe hotel rooms for clandestine meetings, while we Russians are thought to favour public places on the theory that the more public the place, the easier it is to go unnoticed in the crowd. You will be amused to learn that tradecraft has nothing to do with these preferences. In my experience, which consists of two decades of clandestine activities, the British and the Americans rent safe houses because money is burning a hole in their trouser pockets. Our NKVD, hostage to its proletarian roots, counts kopeks. A Russian controller, which happens to be my current job description, would leap at the chance to debrief his agents under a roof, if only to keep out of the rain. For shit's sake don't quote me, but the problem is Moscow Centre. The problem is the fuckers on the fifth floor of the Lubyanka who pore over our expense notes like chimpanzees hunting for lice in the hair of their offspring—these budget commissars refuse to authorize the rental of safe houses or safe apartments or safe hotel rooms when, without spending a ruble, we are, so they argue, perfectly able to meet agents outdoors. In parks, in cafés, at motorbus or train stations and the like. The one time I rented a room in Paris to debrief a secretary to the *chef de cabinet* in the office of French Prime Minister Daladier (she had flatly refused to meet me at the Gare de Lyon), the Soviet embassy's code clerk wound up being rousted from his bed at two in the morning to deal with a blistering telegram (tagged *Priority Immediate,* which meant it had to be deciphered the moment it came in) addressed to me. The son of a bitch of a code clerk passed it on, pasted in strips across a blank page in his steel-covered message book, with a graceless smirk. "To the attention of Alexander Orlov," the plain text memorandum began. "The 5,000 French francs you squandered on a room at the Hotel Meurice last month, along with the 100 franc gratuity to the concierge, have been deducted from your wages. Be so kind as to follow Centre guidelines to the letter. We direct your attention to Standard Agent Operating Procedure Rule 7 subparagraph Kh: Meetings with undercover agents are to be conducted in public areas."

Kopek pinching pricks!

All of which explains what I was doing on the terrace of a seedy workers' café outside the train station in the French resort town of Biarritz, my Panama hat with the turned-down brim shading my eyes from the midday sun, drinking cheap anisette while pretending to read a copy of the American magazine *News-Week* (purchased at a *papeterie* in Bordeaux with my own money) in which I'd concealed new codes and cash. The Englishman was as usual maddeningly punctual. The bell in the church tower across the square was announcing the noon hour as he settled onto the chair across the table from me. He was wearing worn corduroys, a khaki desert jacket and a threadbare silk scarf knotted loosely around his neck. A gauze field dressing protected the gash in his scalp from the fine sand dust rising off the pavement with each gust of air. His face appeared thinner, his eyes more heavy-lidded than I remembered. He looked as if he was coming off an all-night binge. He looked as if he could use a holiday, which is something spies never get to take. I made a mental note to pass on to my superiors: The agent Moscow Centre knew as Sonny was paying the piper for leading a double life.

"Good morning to you, Alexander," he said. He waved a palm to catch the eye of the waitress and ordered American coffee. "Or should one say g-good afternoon now that it is *after* noon?"

I wasn't comfortable with small talk. "Either, or," I remarked.

The Englishman pulled a small metal tin filled with tablets from a jacket pocket. He offered me one and when I wagged a finger, he carefully selected a tablet and popped it into his mouth. "Chronic indigestion," he said. "Spanish use too much olive oil when they cook. In B-basque country you can smell a kitchen for kilometres. Imagine the havoc that p-produces in your average British digestive tract."

"Imagine," I agreed. "How is your head wound?"

"The gash became infected. Spanish surgeons had to open it up and clean it out before drowning it in tincture of iodine and stitching it back up. The red on the gauze is iodine, not blood. I get the occasional migraine which I treat with aspirin and alcohol."

A thin teenage girl almost lost in an ankle-length white apron set a glass of coffee and a second glass of water on the table in front of Philby. He helped himself to two cubes of sugar, then glanced around as he absently stirred the coffee. A double line of schoolchildren, each of them dressed in identical blue smocks and clutching the shoulder of the child in front, was being led diagonally across the square by a very short priest holding a wooden crucifix high over his head. Philby regarded them so intently I wondered if it reminded him of a scene from his own childhood.

Inspired by the sight of the crucifix, I asked, "How is Catholic Spain treating you?"

"Like the heretic I am. The awful truth, which doesn't endear me to my Spanish friends, is I miss the Moors—I am sorry they were hounded back to North Africa. Their poets, their architects, their scholars enlightened Catholic Spain." He leaned towards me and, lowering his voice to a thick whisper, said, "Alexander, Franco's newspapers are filled with stories of p-purge trials, of executions, in Moscow. They gloat that the revolution is devouring its children—Zinoviev, Kamenev, Rykov, even B-bukharin, the man Lenin himself called the darling of the p-party. What's going on? How do you explain this? Can there be a grain of truth to the charges that these giants of the revolution were foreign agents?"

I had, over time, given this matter of life or death not a little thought. The purge of the party that began in the early part of the decade had in due course reached into the ranks of our NKVD. Quite a few of my colleagues in the field had been recalled to Moscow; some had been found guilty of being foreign agents and suffered the consequences—a bullet in the nape of the neck. Others had simply disappeared. What would I do if I were to suddenly receive a telegram summoning me home for *consultations*? I would shit in my pants—it would be every bit as dangerous not to go as to go. The NKVD has a long arm—on more than one occasion I had been that long arm. I suppose I could always solve the dilemma by defecting to the West, but that would leave my family—my wife and daughter, my parents, my brothers and sisters and uncles and aunts—exposed to punishment. (In the eyes of the People's Prosecutor, a relative of an enemy of the people is also an enemy of the people.) If it ever came to that, I would have to come up with a scheme to protect my family. The Englishman was watching me intently, waiting for an answer to his question. "From an operational point of view," I told him, "everyone must be seen as a potential foreign agent."

"What about me? Do you think I could b-be a foreign agent?"

"I keep the possibility on file in one lobe of my brain."

"Why on earth do you meet with me, then?"

I could see my answers were making him uncomfortable.

This Cambridge fellow who stammered his way through a conversation was visibly pushing himself to the edge to spy for the Soviet Union. And yet . . . and yet one could perceive in him the faintest suggestion of deeper currents, of loyalties beyond the surface loyalty to us. To family perhaps? To friends? To his privileged class? To England? "I meet with you," I finally told him, "because you are our principal agent in Spain. Moscow Centre trusts you. So do I."

"You took your sweet time replying."

"I take my sweet time all the time. Like a good night's sleep, it's a habit that contributes to longevity."

"Yes, well, but you avoided my questions about the p-purge trials. Were Zinoviev, Kamenev, Rykov, Bukharin agents of a foreign p-power plotting against Stalin?"

"I am not in a position to know if they actually plotted against Comrade Stalin or simply intended to," I said. "But I believe they would have if they could have—the struggle for power in the Kremlin that began with Lenin's death in 1924 is unfortunately still going on. Comrade Stalin anticipates there will be a war with the German Fascists by 1943 at the latest. He is wisely securing his rear to avoid being stabbed in the back when war comes."

"Ahhh, I'm beginning to see why you always sit facing the café window—you're afraid of being stabbed in the back, you're keeping track of what's going on b-behind you without appearing to."

I grunted in agreement. "It's a bit of tradecraft that doesn't cost Moscow Centre a kopek," I said.

"I'm not quite sure I understand."

I decided not to explain. "What route did you take getting here?" I asked.

"Train to San Sebastián, then caught a ride in a Red Cross truck to Bayonne and took that new tramway to Biarritz. I was obliged to spend a night in Bilbao on the way—the rail line after Bilbao had been cut by a mudslide. I chatted up a German military attaché in the bar of my hotel. Nice chap. Heinrich von something." Philby rummaged in the breast pockets of his desert jacket with his fingertips but couldn't find what he was looking for. "B-bloody hell, he gave me his calling card but I seem to have mislaid it. Heinrich was so impressed to come across someone who had spoken with Ambassador Ribbentrop, he invited me to supper in the officers' mess at an aerodrome near the city. Whilst driving past an enormous hangar, I could see airmen assembling several fighter planes that seemed to have been shipped in large crates. The attaché told me they were Willy Messerschmitt's latest model—Bf 109Fs, with 1,100 horsepower engines. He boasted about their being able to fly rings around the Russian fighters the Republicans managed to put into the air."

"Did he mention the 109's armaments?"

"No. And I didn't ask. Should I have?"

I shook my head. "You were smart not to. You want to be careful not to appear overly curious." I took my sweet time sipping my anisette. "In any case, with or without the new 109s, the war against Franco is lost."

"Is that what Moscow Centre thinks?"

"That's what the world thinks. The forces Franco gathered under the Nationalist banner—monarchists, Fascists, priests, career army officers—control the Basque country and the heavy industry in Bilbao. You yourself reported that Franco could muster five armies supported by some four hundred aircraft."

"The Republicans still have Barcelona and its port," Philby said. "Comrade Stalin could send in masses of armaments . . ."

Knowing me, I would have smiled one of my knowing smiles. I said, "Comrade Stalin will need those masses of armaments to defend Soviet Russia when war breaks out with Germany. The Republicans' only hope is to stay put in their trenches and try to hang on until the European war erupts, at which point the weights on the scales might conceivably shift."

I was struck by the expression on Philby's face. He looked genuinely distressed. Clearly the moment had come to raise the delicate matter of the special assignment from Moscow Centre. "There is one other hope for our Republican friends and their Communist allies . . ."

"Yes?"

Philby ran a finger under his scarf, as if it were chafing his neck. I thought silk didn't chafe but then what did I know? I only owned itchy woollen scarves. I said, "Generalissimo Franco is the Republicans' only other hope."

"I beg your p-pardon?"

I couldn't contain a laugh. The special assignment Moscow had instructed me to pass along to Sonny was manifestly ridiculous. Still, I had little choice but to do what I was told. "If he were to die suddenly—"

"Why would Franco die suddenly?" I noticed the heavy

lids on Philby's eyes blinking open as he grasped where this was going. He leaned half across the table. "How would Franco die suddenly?" he whispered.

"Someone might assassinate him."

"You're surely not suggesting that that someone might be me?" He stared at me incredulously. "You are, aren't you? What a pisser. You're actually asking me to kill Franco!"

His lack of sophistication was getting on my nerves. "I'm not asking you anything. Special assignments don't originate with controllers in the field. I'm the fucking middle man, passing along an order from Moscow Centre. Wise up, Kim. A special assignment of this nature could only come from Comrade Stalin himself."

"Do I have this right? Joe Stalin wants Kim Philby to assassinate Francisco Franco?"

"The moment has come to educate you on how things like this work," I said. And I did. At some length. The tale usually begins with Comrade Stalin watching late-night motion pictures with his Politburo cronies in the Near Dacha outside of Moscow. Along about the second or third reel, he might make a casual remark, which then works its way down the chain of command, gaining authority and urgency with each retelling.

Nodding as if he were punctuating my sentences, the Englishman heard me out. "How can you be sure of this?" he demanded. "Have you encountered Comrade Stalin? Do you know him personally?"

"I worked for him during our civil war in the city we now call Stalingrad. He was a tough biscuit, as the Americans say."

"I believe the expression is tough *cookie*."

"Biscuit. Cookie. He is as tough as the stunted trees in the Arctic steppe. In Stalingrad several of us pooled our resources and bought him a beautiful 9 millimetre Beretta to mark a particular occasion, the details of which I won't go into. Comrade Stalin was extremely proud of his Italian pistol—he showed the bare-breasted goddess engraved on its barrel to everyone. In Stalingrad he carried the pistol wedged into the wide belt of his tunic. I remember him once saying he slept with it on the table next to his bed."

"The only thing I'm armed with," Philby told me, "is humour and trepidation. I don't even own a handgun. I wouldn't know how to use one if I did."

"You point it and pull the trigger."

"If I ever pointed a handgun at another human, even someone as god-evil as Franco, I'd shut my eyes so as not to see blood spilled. If I shut my eyes I couldn't hit the broad side of a barn, forget about the chest of a man." He shrugged the way English people shrug, which is to say he lazily raised a shoulder as if he were dispensing energy frugally. "I saw my father bleeding from a cut on his hand once when I was a child. We were exploring the souk in Damascus. Know what I did? I p-puked over a p-posh *djellabah* at a tailor's stall. The only way my sainted father could quiet the bugger was to buy it. For years he would tease me about his having wasted good Syrian *piastres* on an article of clothing that was far too big for me. I suspect my chronic indigestion, perhaps even my stammer, date back to Damascus. I took the story about the *djellabah* being too big as metaphor."

"You didn't fit the image your father had of what a son should be."

"Something along those lines."

I remember thinking, I need to soothe the Englishman's ruffled feathers. I remember saying, "You don't have to actually kill Franco, Kim. You only have to appear to go through the motions of organizing an assassination. Send me reports on his security precautions as if you are taking the special assignment seriously. By the time Moscow figures out you're not going to assassinate Franco, the Republican armies will have collapsed, putting an end to the civil war. Franco, Spain's dictator in residence, will be beyond reach in a palace in Madrid and Moscow will turn its attention to the threat closer to home: Adolf Hitler."

Philby sat there shaking his head in bewilderment. My words obviously hadn't registered. "I haven't the foggiest idea how one goes about killing someone, Alexander. Otto never educated me along these lines in London. I did simple codes, I did secret writing, I learned how to spot when someone was following you, I was quite good at getting lost in a crowd even in the absence of a crowd. Nothing about assassinations. How do they expect me to do it? With a knife? A p-pistol perhaps? Ahhh, p-poison. Surely p-poison. Spies are supposed to be skilled at p-poisoning p-people. Or perhaps they would like me to strangle him. He is quite short, you know, though come to think of it quite brawny. Don't know if I could pull it off. Assuming I was up to it, what am I supposed to do—strangle the bloke with one of my shoelaces, which is about the only p-personal item the bloody bodyguards left me when I've been in the same room with Franco?"

I reached across the table to grasp his wrist. "Get a hold of yourself, Kim."

Two particularly attractive girls, French judging by their mouthwateringly bare shoulders, were strolling past the fountain at the centre of the square, their arms linked, their laughter drifting across the cobblestones. With the sun's rays slanting in between the wind-bitten sandstone apostles atop the church cornice, their long dresses had turned transparent. Philby noticed me staring at something in the café window and followed my gaze. He snickered admiringly. I heard him say, "I suppose you've killed people in your day."

I wasn't sure if it was intended as a statement or a question. Thinking an episode that might have come from one of those twenty-franc pocket detective novels, but didn't, would distract him, I said, "I was in a cheap hotel in Nice a month ago when two French detectives burst into my room."

"What did you do?"

"I was sleeping in my underwear when the overhead bulb snapped on. I sat up, blinking hard to be sure I wasn't dreaming. I wasn't dreaming. They were both standing at the foot of the bed, their feet planted wide apart in the orthodox firing position, pointing pistols at my solar plexus. I recognized their pistols—each had his fist around a 6.35 millimetre blowback, what the fucking French call *Le Français*. I held up my hands, palms out and looked over at my own pistol—a lovely little P08 Luger Parabellum—in the holster hanging on the back of a chair out of arm's reach. They followed my eyes. That was their fatal blunder. I slept with a double-barrelled American Mossberg under the blanket. I had sawed off the barrels myself so the shot pattern would spread and it would be hard to miss at close range. I shot them dead, one barrel each." I threaded my fingers through my hair, which I kept cropped in the style popular with Red Army non-commissioned officers. "It wasn't a pretty sight, I will be the first to concede. There was a fair amount of blood spattered over the wallpaper depicting sheep grazing in a meadow. For sure, you would have thrown up. I dressed and climbed out the window and made my way to the street on one of those newfangled steel fire escapes they install on public buildings nowadays."

"How does it feel? To shoot someone to death?"

"It feels a damn sight better than *being* shot to death."

Philby polished off the last of his American coffee, which must have been cold by now, though that didn't seem to faze him. He reached for my copy of *News-Week*. "I take it this is for me?"

"You'll find a new code sheet stuck in the pages, along with what hard cash I could squeeze out of the pricks on the fifth floor. Keep addressing your picture postcards to Mademoiselle Dupont at 79 Rue de Grenelle in Paris."

Philby gestured with his jaw towards the thin cardboard box on the chair next to me. It was tied with rose-coloured ribbon. "Is that for me, too?"

"No, no. That's a robe for my wife. The British designer Captain Molyneux has a shop in Biarritz. Want to hear something funny? I recognized one of the customers when I bought this—it was Théodore Alexandrovitch, the grand duke who fled Petrograd after the Bolsheviks came to power and washed up in a palatial seaside villa not far from Biarritz. The voluptuous young beauty being fitted for the robe the grand duke eventually bought was definitely not his wife."

I didn't tell the Englishman how I knew this. I didn't want to bore him with the story of the prostitutes in my employ at a local *maison close* and my running fight with the kopek-pinching pricks in Moscow who decided the wages I paid the girls came under the heading of personal, not professional, expenses.

Philby grinned. "Perhaps you could blackmail the grand duke."

I grinned back. "You may have a future in espionage after all."

8: GIBRALTAR, JULY 1938

Where Mr. Philby of *The Times* Regrets Not Being a Vegetarian

The London *Rezident* had sent me out in the belief that nothing would be more inconspicuous than old Cambridge mates getting together for what Kim referred to as a snakebite, and the Rock Hotel, part way up the slope in Gibraltar with its amusing view of the harbour below and the Straits beyond, was a more or less convenient venue for the both of us. I'd discovered a telegram waiting for me at the reception desk. "Would you be Mr. Guy Burgess, then?" the concierge inquired.

"I would be if I could be," I shot back.

He looked confused. "Is that a *yes*?"

"Yes, it's a yes." He handed me a Western Union form with the message pasted in strips across it: Kim, it seemed, was running two days behind schedule, something to do with a village halfway between Valencia and Barcelona named Vinaroz falling into Franco's hot hands, cutting the

Republic in two. *The Times*, deciding this strategic victory merited a dispatch, ordered its special correspondent to the scene. I wasn't about to hang around the Rock Hotel with the dowager matron saints who, at any given hour, could be found on the terrace strapped into their rigid corsets staring out at Africa as if it might go away if they looked at it long enough. If I'd hung around, what with my being a Foreign Office minion on a secret mission (which I had declined to deny when the concierge supposed this to be the case), one of them might actually have engaged me in conversation. No, no, a preemptive strike was clearly called for. And Algeciras, across the bay, was the logical target. Been there before, couldn't wait to rejuvenate my memories. There was a section of town the locals called The Hill, and a cabaret nicknamed Anal Canal run by two Scottish faggots. The unpaved street was teeming with bastard urchins retrieving discarded cigarette ends and if they were still alight, smoking them down to their filthy fingernails. The waiters were all beautiful Portuguese Nancy boys dressed in tight French sailor suits—striped shirts, tight-arsed bell bottoms, a blue cap with a red pompadour—and reeking of delectably cheap perfume. You could have any one of them plus a bottle of watered champagne for the asking plus five pounds sterling. Two stark-naked lesbians, their lips and labia painted crimson red, were wrestling on a mat set out on the small proscenium. The general idea appeared to be to reduce your adversary to semi-consciousness and then bring her back to life with a revolting demonstration of mouth-to-labia resuscitation. I will be the first to concede I was worn to semi-consciousness when the taxi deposited me at the foot of the Rock Hotel two days later.

"You look as if you've been through a war," Kim said.

He still had a small gauze bandage stuck with adhesive over the gash in his head—all that remained of the turban-like dressing visible when a photograph of our English war hero appeared in the London sheets. "Clearly it's you who has been through a war, old boy," I remarked as we settled onto straw chairs round a table at the far end of the terrace, within eyeshot but out of earshot of the dowager brigade. Kim produced one of his foul-smelling French cigarettes that kept mosquitoes at bay, so he'd claimed when he chain-smoked at Cambridge. The book of matches slipped out of his fingers. He leaned over to recover it, inspecting the underside of the table in the process.

"I see you have acquired a bit of tradecraft whilst in Spain," I said.

"One lives and learns, or should that be *learns* and *lives*?"

I set my folded copy of the *Picture Post* on the table. "How's your Magyar spouse?" I asked.

Kim casually picked it up to inspect the photojournalism, in the process pocketing the envelope with the eighty pounds Sterling and the new codes typed on rice paper. "When last I saw her, which was some months back, she seemed to be muddling through," he said.

I must have cleared my throat, which is what I have been told I do before delivering unpleasant news. "I am afraid I am the bearer of rather distressing tidings," I said.

"Yes?"

"Our London *Rezident,* Otto, has been summoned back to Moscow."

"P-perhaps it was for routine consultations."

"His wife was instructed to return with him."

"Ahhh." Kim let this sink in. "What do you make of it?" he asked.

"What with all the rumours of purge trials in Moscow . . ."

"Surely these rumours are capitalist propaganda," he said.

I expect I shrugged. "Where there's smoke there's fire. The way I see it, Stalin would be a sap not to cleanse the rear of fifth columnists before the war with Germany breaks out."

"Otto is not a fifth columnist."

"I should think not, in which case no harm will come to him in Moscow. Got to know Otto fairly well when he was putting me through my paces in London. Decent chap, steadfast Communist, damn good *Rezident*, professional to his fingertips. Last time I saw him was in a Soho pub. He turned up sporting a bowler and carrying an umbrella—I gathered it was his disguise to stymie the MI5 twits trying to follow him. I told him he ought to have gone the whole hog and shaved the triangular moustache on his upper lip—as there weren't two like it in London, rather made him stand out in a crowd. He said his father had fought in the Bolshevik Revolution wearing a triangular moustache, it was a family tradition sort of thing. The old sod even told me his real name. It's Teodor. Teodor Maly."

"He has done such a splendid job recruiting us, hard to

see what Moscow Centre could p-possibly hold against him."

"I should think you are prosecution exhibit number one."

"Come again."

"That night in Soho, he polished off an entire bottle of vodka and let down his hair. He confided that what Moscow Centre held against him was you."

"You want to spell that out, Guy?"

"You met the Swede across the border in Biarritz two months ago."

"It was closer to three. No matter."

"The Swede debriefed you on Nationalist order of battle. He debriefed you on the latest model Messerschmitt to reach Franco. He passed on to you new codes and a bit of cash. Then he brought up the business of a special assignment."

"Even he had to laugh when he raised the subject, it was that ridiculous."

"An order of that nature could only have come from Stalin," I said.

"The Swede told me how these things work. Stalin, who apparently stays up until all hours and drinks like a Georgian *muzhik*, might have said something about how the war in Spain was lost, the only hope being if we could kill off Franco. A Politburo colleague would have repeated it to one of his minions the next morning, at which point the order started down the line."

"Still, if it originated with Stalin . . ."

"How would *you* assassinate Franco, Guy?"

"I didn't get the special assignment. You did. How is for you to figure out. Also the getaway."

"I can't believe two old boys from Cambridge are having this conversation. You know I go queasy at the sight of b-b-blood. B-bloody hell, it's one thing to spy for the good guys, quite another to start knocking off the chaps they don't fancy."

"Christ, don't get pissed at me. I'm only the messenger." Several of the matron saints glanced in our direction but I indicated with a wave of the back of my hand that they would do better contemplating Africa. "What did the Swede tell you?"

"He said I ought to act as if I were enthusiastic. I should come on as eager to carry out orders once I figure out how. He told me I should report on Franco's security precautions as if I had every intention of assassinating him. He said by the time they figured out I wasn't up to the assignment, the war would be over and Franco would be beyond reach in Madrid."

"Did you at least file reports on Franco's security?"

"I did, actually. Franco is surrounded by loyal Andalusian bodyguards who have been with him since he led the Spanish contingent in the Rif Wars in Morocco. I spelled out the procedure to apply for a pass to enter a government building—one needs a p-passport along with two corroborating identity documents. When Franco leaves the palace in Burgos, there are anywhere from twelve to fifteen identical automobiles in his convoy. The cars leapfrog past each other en route. Even if you knew which car Franco started out in, you'd have no way of knowing which one he was in three minutes later."

"I read somewhere that Stalin does the same." I lowered

my voice lest the matron saints conclude we were more interesting than Africa. "Teodor told me he sent a dozen telegrams to Moscow about your situation. If he has landed in hot water, he got there defending you. He told them you were a talented young British aristocrat who considers himself a Marxist and works for the international Communist movement out of conscience, not money or fear. Moscow Centre apparently replied along the lines of *Only the proletariat has a conscience*. Teodor insisted you were doing great work reporting from Franco's side of the front. He argued that for all your loyalty and willingness to serve the cause, you weren't trained for wet jobs and couldn't be expected to carry out an assassination order. I fear he is having to explain all this in person in the Lubyanka even as we sit here amid the creature comforts of the Rock Hotel. The new *Rezident*, when he was Teodor's deputy, countersigned many of his boss's telegrams about you, which he bitterly regrets. He fears his good opinion of you will be held against him."

"How do you know these details?"

"I discovered Teodor had been recalled when I turned up for a meeting in Regent's Park—it was a stone's throw from the zoo—and I found another man sitting in his place. 'Don't be alarmed,' he said. 'I am your new *Rezident*. My predecessor has been recalled to Moscow.' He introduced himself as Gorsky. I have no idea if that's a Christian name or a family name, or for that matter a real name. The subject quickly came around to you. He knows we are old pals from Cambridge. He told me I was to come out to Gibraltar to explain the changing of the guard to you—"

"By the by, Guy, why am I meeting you in Gibraltar instead of the Swede in Biarritz as usual?"

It is quite likely I sighed at this point. "In my experience, the other shoe inevitably drops."

"What b-bloody shoe are we talking about? Has the Swede been caught? Is he dead?"

"I'm afraid it's much worse. It's right up there with a dog's breakfast. He has defected to the West."

I remember Kim gazing out at the wakes persisting in the Straits long after the passage of ships, as if to mark the channels of access and egress to the Mediterranean Sea. "I'm relieved to see you're taking this so calmly," I observed.

He turned back to me. "It's all part of the Great Game," he said. "We understood there would be occasional hard cheese when we signed on."

"Gorsky figured you'd hear about the Swede eventually so he sent me around to tell you. He thought it better if you heard it from us. There's a positive side to the bad news. According to Gorsky, the Swede sent a letter to Joe Stalin before he defected. He left behind a wife and child on the French Riviera, he left behind an assortment of parents and brothers and sisters and uncles and aunts in Soviet Russia. In his letter, the Swede reminded Stalin that he knew the identity of every single Soviet agent in Europe. He had personally worked in the field with most of them. He told Stalin that if nothing happened to his family, he would never reveal the names of the Soviet agents to Western intelligence."

Kim accepted this with a nod. "When did the Swede turn his coat?"

"Around the twelfth of this month, near as we can figure. One day he was in his rooming house in Cannes, next day he wasn't. Anybody's guess how he went over."

Kim, as always, quickly came to the heart of the problem. "How can we be certain the Swede will live up to his end of this devil's deal?" he asked.

"Well, for one thing, we're sitting here on the terrace of the Rock Hotel. Neither you nor I have been arrested."

"What if they decide to torture him?"

I thought about this. "I have never encountered the Swede. You have. I saw him once on a nearby bench feeding peanuts to pigeons when I met Otto—muscular chap with close cropped hair. Nobody you'd want to tangle with in a dark alleyway. Or a lighted alleyway, for that matter. Otto pointed him out in case the Swede and I ever needed to meet. Looking back, I can see the Swede amused Otto. He said the Swede was what the old Bolsheviks called a red meat eater. Which seemed to mean he was ready to kill, ready to be killed sort of thing."

"They say nobody can withstand torture."

"Who's *they*?"

"*They* are the authors of espionage novels."

"What do they know, sitting at desks with a view over a countryscape where the greatest threat to life and limb is a ha-ha?"

Kim had to laugh. "What does any of us know sitting here on the terrace of the Rock Hotel?"

I asked Kim the question that had been on my mind since I learned about the Swede's defection. "What would you do if you thought you'd been uncovered?"

"I'd run for it."

"You'd go live in Soviet Russia?"

"Otto seemed to think it was the nearest thing to a Shangri-La on earth. Russia would suit me if I could be sure I would be able to order books from *Bowes* and *Bowes* of Cambridge and tins of Arm & Hammer indigestion tablets from Harrods. In any case, exile in the coldest steppe of Siberia would be preferable to twenty years behind bars in Wormwood Scrubs."

"Will you go back to England once the Spanish war is over?"

"My masters at *The Times* want me to cover the war that looks to be sure to break out in Europe."

Horror of horrors, one of the matron saints materialized at my elbow. She was clutching a copy of *The Vegetarian News* open to the page with a photograph of Kim being decorated by Franco. "Please do forgive the intrusion," she said, "but I recognized you from your picture. Actually it was my friend Mrs. Crowlwithers who recognized you. In point of fact Mrs. Crowlwithers wasn't sure you were you until she noticed the head wound. You are the gentleman from *The Times* in this photo, are you not?"

"He is," I declared, thinking to put Kim on a sticky wicket. "Perhaps you could get him to autograph your copy?"

"But that's exactly why I came over!" She turned to Kim. "Might you?"

"To whom shall I mark it?"

"To *Mrs. Bayshore* would do nicely. My neighbours back in Leigh-on-Sea will accuse me of having let my imagination run riot when I tell them I actually spoke to you in person on the terrace of the Rock Hotel."

Kim fetched a fountain pen from the inside pocket of his desert jacket and wrote, in a bold hand: "To the charming Mrs. Bayshore from Essex, with high regard, H. A. R. Philby, The Rock Hotel, Gibraltar, July something or other, 1938."

"Might I be permitted a personal question, Mr. Philby?"

Kim favoured his interlocutor with a weak smile of the kind Church of England vicars regularly bestow on non-believers. "Be, be," he said.

Mrs. Bayshore was more or less breathing down his neck. "Are you by any chance a vegetarian?"

Kim winced, as if she had stirred a memory. "I was for a time when I lived in Vienna. I am sorry to have to confess to being a lapsed vegetarian, which surely aggravated my chronic indigestion."

Mrs. Bayshore lightly brushed his wrist with the tips of her fingers. The gesture was an equatorial degree of longitude short of sensual. "It is never too late to start down the straight and narrow," she confided. She threw back her head, exposing a very starched collar where her neck ought to have been, and announced in a voice that was meant to be heard across the Straits in Africa, "Vegetarian or not, you have made my day, Mr. Philby."

"And you, dear lady, have made mine," he replied.

9: LONDON, NOVEMBER, 1939

Where the Hajj Outfits His Boy for Phoney War

Mr. Rupert Herrick-Howe
Customer Service Unit
Harrods Emporium
Brompton Road
Borough of Kensington
London

The third of November, 1939

Sir,

Kindly debit my account for the items enumerated below and dispatch them posthaste to my boy Harold Philby, Hotel du Commerce, Arras, France:

One standard issue Home Guard sewing kit
One standard issue Home Guard first aid kit
Two tubes of Daggett & Ramsdell Herbal Sun-Oil
Two large-sized tubes of Johnson & Johnson unguentine burn ointment
Ear plugs of the kind employed by Royal Naval officers during gunnery practice at sea
One general issue British Infantry helmet with the words "WAR" and "REPORTER" printed in white majuscule across the front
One general issue British Infantry gas mask along with a spare Cellucotton filter
Two packets each containing twelve tins of Arm & Hammer indigestion tablets. I count on you to bill me at the reduced charge for multiple purchases of Arm & Hammer tins as advertised on the flanks of buses crossing Piccadilly Circus as recently as yesterday.
One copy of Simon & Schuster pocket book number 1 by a chap named Hilton, entitled Lost Horizon, *a favourable mention of said book having appeared in* The Times *culture section the weekend before last week.*

I would be obliged if you would include a gift card in the package with the following note: "From the Hajj, who saved you from the wrath of a furious tailor in the souk of Damascus by purchasing a soiled djellabah, *which, come to think of it, ought to fit you now."*

Y'r ser'v't
Harry St John Bridger Philby Esq.
Maida Vale

10: CALAIS, MAY 1940

Where *The Times* Special Correspondent Mr. Philby is Accused of Betraying King and Country

May something or other, 1940
Mr. Ralph Deakin, Esq.
Foreign Editor
The Times
London

My dear Mr. Deakin,

Herein, the report you requested of my time with the British Expeditionary Force in Flanders.

With the civil war ended and Franco ruling the country with an iron fist from Madrid, I quit Spain in August of '39 and made my way across the Pyrenees to an overgrown village in northern France which fancied itself an undergrown town: Arras, where the British Expeditionary Force's general staff had set up shop. The BEF's intelligence section, a starchy pride of reserve captains and colonels so freshly mobilized some of them were still attired in civilian shirts with mother-of-pearl studs and patent-leather shoes, took a dim view of my presence. They appeared alarmed by something in my curriculum vitae but as its cardboard cover had been stamped "For Eyes Only" I was unable to identify the sore point. I can only suppose, what with the Soviets having signed a non-aggression pact with Nazi Germany last year, that the intelligence chaps were put off by my being married to an Austrian Communist: Visions of me collaborating with the Red devil danced in their heads. I wound up cooling my heels for three weeks in the Hotel du Commerce waiting for accreditation—a painless interlude, I will concede, as the bar was stocked with Mr. John Walker's Scotch whisky to accommodate the ranking BEF officers billeted at the hotel. By the time I got the requisite pink slip with "Special Mission Accorded by the general staff for the Purpose of Journalism", Britain and France had honoured their treaty obligations and declared war on Germany after Hitler invaded Poland. When I managed to get permission for a junket through the beet fields of Flanders to look for the war Britain had declared, I couldn't find it for the simple reason there was none. American headline writers took to calling the eight months between our declaration of war and the blitzkrieg through Belgium and France "the Phoney War". The Germans, in an uncharacteristic display of humour, dubbed it "Sitzkrieg". The French, struck by the ludicrousness of the standoff, christened it "La drôle de guerre". The Royal Air Force pilots who dropped propaganda leaflets over Germany daily came up with the "Confetti war".

Whatever name it went by, it was a bizarre interval—110 British and French divisions, dug in along the Belgian and French borders, twiddling their thumbs, gazing across no man's land at 23 German divisions (the bulk of the German army was said to be engaged in the East), with nobody on either side firing a shot in anger.

It took me two and a half months of submitting daily requests to the press office, two floors below my own room in the hotel, before I discovered a yellow chit folded into my letterbox authorizing me to join a group of journalists being taken on a tour of the legendary Maginot Line of fortresses, behind which the French proposed to fend off the Hun if he ever attacked. We entrained for Metz at four the next morning, winding up in a third-class carriage chock-full of French conscripts in khaki greatcoats returning from leave. CBS's Bill Shirer cadged an interview with their commanding officer, a bearded chap carrying a bamboo stick tucked under his only arm (the other having been shot off in the Great War), who boasted that his men would make short work of the Hun once they reached the front. Hearing this, his junior officers cheered; the rank and file, peeling oranges, the odour of which in closed railway compartments never failed to make me queasy, continued singing their bawdy songs. At Metz's central station we were delivered into the hands of French press officers who shooed us, like schoolchildren on a day trip, into a cavalcade of Monsieur Citroën's famous traction avant *limousines repainted for the duration with brown and olive-green camouflage stripes, as if that would render them invisible to the German pilots patrolling the bridges over the Moselle in vintage Fokker biplanes, likewise painted with brown and olive-green camouflage stripes.*

Once across the Moselle, the Citroëns drove through vineyards that stretched off to the horizon, eventually pulling up at the edge of a meadow with three observation balloons tethered to stakes driven at an angle into the ground. At a field mess in a tent—alas, also painted with camouflage stripes, which had the effect of dampening our civilian appetites—a non-commissioned rating sporting one of those absurd French chef's hats had set out sandwiches of rillettes *and chilled bottles of local May wine flavoured with woodruff and pineapple slices. (Several members of our press party spoke openly of defecting to the "Frogs".) Employing my pidgin French, I managed to chat up a balloonist who'd been aloft earlier in the day. Pleasant enough fellow named Sixte something. He was a recent graduate of the French military academy Saint-Cyr and looked to be too young to have any use for a straight edge razor. I asked him if he had spotted signs of life beyond the Germans'*

Siegfried Line whilst aloft in his observation balloon. Studying the words "WAR" and "REPORTER" printed across the front of my infantry helmet with what can only be described as perplexity, he allowed as how the only thing of military interest he'd seen was a Hun observation balloon. Picture it, Mr. Deakin: The war had been going on by then for—what?—the best part of four months and the two balloonists may have been the only ones on either side of the front to catch a glimpse of the enemy. When I think back on this decidedly drôle de guerre, *I am reminded of the complicity of these balloonists, ten or so miles distant from each other, the German in all probability as young as his French counterpart (since only young men oblivious to the hazards of war volunteer to man observation balloons), the both of them using pocket mirrors to catch each other's eye with glints of sunlight before their respective ground crews pulled them in, like bloated hogs on long tethers, when night fell.*

I won't bore you with a detailed description of the Maginot fortress we visited—I expect you will have seen it in the Pathe newsreels a dozen times. Suffice it to say the evidence of flower beds and vegetable gardens on the French side didn't make it any less depressing. The troops manning the fortress, living underground as they did for months on end, had the miens of miners from the coal face—the pupils of their eyes were reduced to pin pricks, their skin was deathly pale from the absence of sunlight. Everything of consequence in the fortress transpired underground: The men ate, slept, fornicated (there were Croix Rouge *nurses seconded to the fortress's infirmary), defecated, watched cinemas in a hundred-seat auditorium; all of this in facilities blasted out of the bowels of the earth, the man-made bunkers joined by narrow passageways with steps chiselled into the stone and lighted by naked electric bulbs every several yards. It was, come to think of it, what one imagines life must be like in a submarine: The great majority of the crew live in artificial light inside the hull, only the lucky few get to climb to the conning tower and see the sea. In this case, the lucky few stationed above ground in the fortress's giant turret peered through periscopes focused on what looked to be an enemy trench system topped with sandbags. If there were Germans in the fortification a football pitch away I never caught sight of them when I was given a turn at one of the periscopes.*

Back in our Citroëns, *we were whisked off along dirt roads to an enormous underground storage facility several miles behind the front. Our French chaperones were eager to convince us that the line of invincible fortresses ordered up by their minister of war* Maginot *would never run short of supplies—we walked endless aisles between giant stacks of artillery shells, hospital beds piled one atop the other, wooden crates filled with rifle and machine gun munitions, cartons of canned food, even cases of* vin ordinaire *destined for consumption (so I supposed) by* conscrits ordinaire. *At one intersection in the vast hangar we came across a quite tall French colonel engaged in a heated argument with a quite short corporal-major. The colonel, wearing a belted leather jacket and a tanker's helmet, a cigarette bobbing on his lips, thick army stockings fitted* over *the shoe part of his knee-high boots to keep him from slipping on the ice, turned out to be the C.O. of the 507th armoured regiment, stationed well back from the Maginot Line in reserve. It developed that the colonel, one* C. de Gaulle *according to the metal name tag pinned immediately over his breast pocket, was scavenging for tank treads that had been delivered to the Maginot depot despite the fact that there were no French tanks posted* on *the Maginot Line. "Monsieur Maginot's fortresses are utterly useless," the exasperated colonel told us, much to the discomfiture of our press chaperones. "The Germans will not attack them, they'll simply go around them. The next war will be fought by tanks and won by the side that is the more mobile. To be mobile,* chers messieurs, *my tanks require treads!" The corporal-major, who had hash marks trickling down his sleeve indicating he was professional army, stood his ground, refusing to release the treads to de Gaulle without a written order, in triplicate, signed by the sector commandant. Scowling to indicate he had run out of arguments and patience, de Gaulle attached the chin strap of his tanker's helmet, formed his thumb and forefinger into a pistol and pointed it at the war medals on the corporal-major's chest. "Snap your identification tag in two," the colonel ordered, as if the pistol were real. (The tags, worn on a wrist bracelet, had a soldier's name impressed on them twice; if he were to be killed on the battlefield, half the tag was broken off and nailed to his coffin.) The bewildered corporal-major wasn't sure whether to take the colonel's fingers as a joke or a threat. He looked over at us, hoping we would clarify the situation, then, shrugging, stamped a chit and waved with the back of his hand towards the crates of tank treads. de Gaulle's men promptly loaded them onto two lorries. de Gaulle himself squeezed into the sidecar of a motorcycle and, pumping his fist in sign for the lorries to follow, sped away with his prize.*

Mind you, Mr. Deakin, phoney war is a damn sight better than the real thing. Between occasional forays into beet fields and dismal Maginot fortresses, I hung around the Hotel du Commerce, stuffing myself (on your shilling) with foie gras de Strasbourg au Porto, drinking Armagnac hors d'age, playing poker into the wee small hours. Aside from the contretemps at the underground storage facility, the only skirmishes I personally witnessed before Herr Hitler's Panzers struck were between our group of foreign correspondents in Arras and the BEF's press officers, who considered the mere mention in a dispatch of the weather over Flanders to be tantamount to treason. On one memorable occasion my Under a blazing sun *provoked the wrath of the BEF's duty censor, a reserve colonel with tufts of hair on his cheekbones that looked to be whetted with axle grease. The brass nameplate on his desk read* M. R. Protheroe, Acting Chief Censor. *"You are spying for someone, Philby," he announced huffily as he blotted out the offending phrase with a thick black marker. The reserve colonel's jowls quivered as he exhaled onto his precious censor's seal and stamped what remained of my dispatch so it could be sent from the telegrapher's Nissen shed on the roof of the Hotel du Commerce.* "Under a blazing sun *indeed!" Colonel Protheroe fumed. "Precisely what the Hun's Luftwaffe pilots must know to attack our positions in Flanders."*

"Hun's Luftwaffe pilots are rather occupied at the moment bombing Warsaw, which is roughly a thousand miles from here," I remarked.

This particular reserve colonel had the mentality of a small dog that locks its jaws on your trouser cuff. "You're working for someone beside The Times, *Philby," he persisted. "Rest assured I shall get to the bottom of this. Who employs you to provide weather information?"*

"Pravda," I said. "'Under a blazing sun' is actually a code phrase for 'The BEF are running short of Daggett and Ramsdell Herbal Sun-Oil.'"

"Your taking of a serious matter lightly has been noted against you," Colonel Protheroe declared. "Providing the Hun with weather information it can get ahold of simply by subscribing to The Times *must be seen as a betrayal of king and country."*

I recount this episode, Mr. Deakin, so you will grasp what war reporters*—to employ my sainted father's appellation—were up against whilst covering the BEF in Flanders. The high point of our sojourn in the Hotel du Commerce involved organizing a lottery on whether the "Phoney War" would end with a whimper or a bang. We had all thirty-seven journalists billeted in the hotel, along with a mixed bag of BEF ranks,* maître d's, *restaurant captains, taxi drivers, desk clerks, and telegraphers, buying into the lottery at three quid a head.*

The chaps who put their money on the bang, me amongst them, won!

On 10 May, a Friday if memory serves, the shooting war began with German Panzer divisions pushing through the Ardennes woods to bypass the Maginot Line entirely and attack Belgium and France from an unanticipated direction. In London, Prime Minister Chamberlain, having famously waved his umbrella whilst promising "peace in our time" after the Munich conference with Herr Hitler, had the good sense to resign. King George VI had the good sense to replace him with the former First Lord of the Admiralty, Winston Churchill. I had the good sense to quit the Hotel du Commerce one jump ahead of the invading boche, who in short order pierced the BEF's front and headed for the English Channel, effectively splitting the Allied armies in two. It was, as everyone now understands, the beginning of a dreadful debacle that must rank as the single worst defeat of British arms in history. We war reporters fled Arras in a municipal omnibus requisitioned by the general staff press people, who felt duty bound to personally escort us. The next days passed in a blur consisting in equal measure of dust rising from the roadways of Northern France and panic emanating from the hoards of civilians running for their lives, many on dilapidated bicycles, others pulling farm carts piled high with their worldly possessions. We drove through deserted villages acrawl with crazed dogs abandoned by their owners—they had been tied to fences and could be heard for miles howling with hunger. Our BEF lads were putting them down, one bullet to a dog. We sped across country bridges as army engineers wired explosives to the pilings. Somehow we reached Amiens, only to be roused from our beds before dawn to flee to Boulogne. That city was bedlam. Soldiers from a dozen countries bivouacked in the streets, refugees riding horses or bicycles or on foot clogged the roads leading in from the countryside. The local constabulary patrolled through the night to prevent the looting of abandoned homes. From time to time, rifle fire reverberated through the city, giving rise to rumours of German paratroopers landing in football pitches adjacent to schools. As the telegraph lines to England were down I wasn't even able to file a dispatch describing the scenes I'd witnessed, not that they would have gotten past the censor, especially if I had mentioned the weather.

Since we couldn't work, several of us hired out

the hotel's limousine and set off to play a round at the famed golf links in Le Touquet. We were waylaid en route by P. G. Wodehouse, who had a cottage thereabouts. Elated to find himself in the company of Englishmen, Pelham stood us drinks in the local café. He told us that he and his wife reckoned the Germans were civilized chaps, propaganda to the contrary notwithstanding, and had no intention of joining the exodus. Luckily for us we had stopped for a drink because word soon spread that Guderian's Panzers had reached the front nine of the links. Hearing this, we promptly abandoned any notion of golf and set off for Calais (figuring, as Collier's Weekly*'s Martha Gellhorn quipped, we could return the hotel's limousine after the war). Fact is I regretted not driving up to Touquet—imagine the scoop if I'd discovered that German commanders went to war with golf clubs in their tanks and had suspended the blitzkreig to play a round.*

In Calais I chatted up some subalterns from one of those elite units, The Queen Victoria's Rifles, I think it was. They were reconnoitering for buildings to defend in the port area. They'd been told Churchill had issued an order to hold Calais to the death and were ready to do it, except they didn't know where their general was, they weren't sure who was in command, or when their heavy equipment would be offloaded. I suppose it was then that I realized the whole shebang—the Maginot Line, Flanders, The BEF H.Q. at Arras, Amiens, Boulogne, Calais, the beaches of Dunkirk up the coast—was a colossal cock-up. Hitler had been training his Stukas and his Panzers for years whilst we brandished umbrellas. If there is an upside to the story, it's that we seem to be managing to evacuate tens of thousands of our boys off the beaches of Dunkirk, though as Churchill has pointed out, wars are not won by retreats.

I've been assigned a berth on what looks to be one of the last fishing boats out of Calais harbour—I'm typing this on my trusty Underwood portable in the cramped galley that stinks of diesel oil, actually. The French captain plans to cast off at ebb tide tonight and hopes to reach Dover before first light to avoid the Luftwaffe pilots stalking juicy targets in the channel. Hard to believe I will be in England tomorrow morning and, with any luck, in London tomorrow evening. Truth is, I feel guilty as all hell saving my own hide and leaving The Queen Victoria's Rifles behind to hold the harbour. But my guilt didn't keep me from accepting the berth when it was offered. Oddly, the Reserve Colonel M. R. Protheroe, the one who accused me of betraying king and country by describing the weather over Flanders, is a fellow passenger. "You look to be familiar," he said when he saw me backing down the ladder to the galley, my helmet with War Reporter *attached to the kit on my back and clanging against it. Colonel Protheroe appeared to have difficulty bringing me into focus. His eyes had the vacant stare I'd seen so often on shell-shocked soldiers in Spain.*

"Philby of The Times,*" I said, offering a paw. He didn't shake. I'm not even sure he noticed the gesture.*

After a long while, during which he gnawed the inside of a cheek, he inquired, "Have we met?"

"In Flanders, yes."

"Oh, dear, Flanders. Was that in the Great War or this one?"

"This one, I should think."

"I trust you'll bear with me—I recall things well enough but I am often uncertain in what order they occurred."

"News from the front being what it is, I expect there are not a few back home in the same boat," I said.

"Do you? Well, misery does appreciate company. We are off to Dover soon. I rather think the arrival will take place after the departure."

He didn't smile and I understood he wasn't attempting a joke.

Respectfully,
H. A. R. Philby

11: LONDON, JUNE 1940

Where Mr. Philby Promises to Keep a Straight Face for the Photograph on His Identity Badge

Looking out of sorts, as men will when they turn up for assignations with individuals whom they have never before set eyes upon, the Englishman wandered into the forecourt of St. Ermin's Hotel on Caxton Street near Victoria station and glanced round uncertainly. He saw me sitting in the small alcove near the curtain that led to the corridor that led to the loos, but didn't for a fleeting second entertain the possibility that his rendezvous was with me, though I was the only human in sight if one doesn't count his reflection in the mirror. I was grey-haired and elderly, not to put too fine a point on it. He checked his wristwatch, shrugged, and turned to leave. At which point I inserted two fingers between my lips and whistled—a charming trick my late brother Nigel taught me when I was twelve and has since stood me in good stead flagging down hackney carriages on rainy days. H. A. R. Philby turned back in terminal confusion. I beckoned to him with an index finger. "Do join me for tea," I called across the room. "I am Miss Maxse, your four o'clock." I was already filling a second cup with a wonderful green tea from China, the stock of which St. Ermine was unlikely to replenish if the European war spread to Asia, as I reckoned it would. "Do you take sugar, Mr. Philby?"

He settled onto the seat facing me. "I don't r-remember."

"Well, you do give satisfaction, Mr. Philby. I can't recall the last time I so discombobulated a male of the species he forgot if he took sugar with his tea."

"Ahhh, yes. Two p-please."

"Good. It has come back to you."

"I was rather expecting . . ." He let the thought slip through his fingers.

"Dear boy, do spit out what you were expecting."

"I'm not quite sure what I was expecting."

"Let me assist you in your inquiries. You weren't born yesterday. When your foreign editor at *The Times*, the very crabby Mr. Deakin, suggested someone was eager to interview you about war work, you will have figured out you were being sized up by the Secret Intelligence Service. But you were expecting someone younger."

His failure to respond was response enough.

"You were expecting a gentleman, surely," I said.

My vision is not what it used to be but I could have sworn I saw a blush tint his ruddy cheeks. "I didn't know ladies were employed by . . . whoever it is that employs you," he said.

"Other than in secretarial positions?"

"You are trying to p-put me on my b-back foot. I must admit you are succeeding."

"These days I gratefully accept whatever little successes come my way."

He sipped at his tea. "I p-presume you are a ranking officer—they would be unlikely to send a secretarial p-person to vet a prospective recruit. I didn't really think it through but I must have assumed that above a certain rank it would be like the army officer corps."

"Men's room types. Gents who pee into solid Armitage Shanks urinals, concentrating all the while at the ceiling so as not to catch a glimpse of the willy next door."

"Quite."

"Well, at least we've cleared the hurdle of your preconceptions. If you are going to come to work for us, you must learn to keep an open mind."

"Duly noted, Miss Maxse."

I am thought of as someone who doesn't smile a great deal but I suspect I might have broken the rule then with a grin. Clearly I was in charge of this conversation; it went where I steered it. "Your father seems quite keen on your joining the service," I remarked.

"In this instance, Miss Maxse, you are more familiar with my father's wishes than me."

"He has put in a word, though I will confide he wasn't the one who raised your candidacy."

"May I ask who raised my candidacy?"

"No."

"Ahhh."

Actually his candidacy had been raised by his old Trinity sidekick Guy Burgess, whom we'd lured over from the F.O. several weeks earlier. What with war raging on the Continent and the SIS frantically expanding its staff to cope, we regularly asked new recruits to suggest friends or colleagues who might be qualified for what was euphemistically called *war work*. The first name on the index card Mr. Burgess had given me was Harold Adrian Russell Philby. He was described as someone who spoke several foreign languages and knew Europe like the palm of his hand. Curious expression, that. I myself am not familiar with the palms of either of my hands. I happened to be in the Caxton Holy of Holies on the sixth floor introducing Mr. Burgess to Colonel Menzies, who had been named SIS chief on the death of Admiral Sinclair in '39, and mentioned in passing I would be vetting a Mr. Harold Philby. "Oh, you mean Kim," Colonel Menzies said. "I know his people. Westminster. Cambridge. Trinity. Good British stock. Though the paterfamilias—ha! I recollect the Admiral nicknamed him the *Hajj*—is something of a character, what?"

Normally a testimonial from the Holy of Holies is thought to be the equivalent of one foot in the door. But like my late chief, the Admiral Sinclair, God rest his soul, I was old school. Which meant Mr. Philby still had the other foot outside the door. As a matter of routine I ran his candidacy past the long noses of our MI5 cousins, who sent me a minute so succinct I am able to recite it in its entirety from memory:

From: Mr. Montague Smallwood, MI5 security subdivision
To: Miss Marjorie Maxse, MI6 recruitment subdivision
Subject: Harold Adrian Russell Philby, aka Kim
1. Nothing recorded against.

"More tea, Mr. Philby?"

"Thank you, no, Miss Maxse."

"Good. Let's talk turkey, as the Yanks say. We know all about your Cambridge escapades—your membership in the notorious Socialist Society, your canvassing for Socialist candidates in Romsey Town. We know about your motoring off to Vienna to assist refugees fleeing Nazi Germany. Good God, did you actually ride a motorcycle from England to Vienna?"

He leaned forwards. "It was a Daimler with one of their new V12 Aero engines—"

"One should avoid telling a person more than he or she can possibly grasp, Mr. Philby. That is something else you might keep in mind if you come to work for us."

"I am taking this all in, Miss Maxse."

"As I was saying, we don't hold your escapades against you. We take the broad view that those who aren't revolutionaries in their twenties have no heart, those who remain revolutionaries in their thirties have no head. Good gracious me, if we ruled out hiring staff who had a fling with Marx in their misspent youth, we should have to fight the war with the Women's Auxiliary. We know, of course, about your marriage to Miss Friedman. Rather good show on your part, I should think. Jewish damsel in distress situation. You *are* still wedded to her, are you not?"

"I am indeed. We both thought it b-best to stay wedded so long as Hitler menaced Europe."

"What is your actual relationship, apart from being wedded?"

"I beg your p-pardon?"

"Do you sleep together? Do you copulate?"

"You are disconcertingly direct, Miss Maxse. We haven't slept together since I went off to cover the war in Spain for *The Times*."

"When and where did you last see Miss Friedman?"

"In Paris. During what the papers took to calling the Phoney War. I was covering the British Expeditionary Force from Arras. Litzi—Miss Friedman—met me for b-breakfast at La Coupole. She'd come over to try and sell two small charcoals by an Italian painter named Modigliani. Our reunion was extremely civilized. She turned up with her lover. Decent sort. Journalist, I gather. Georg something or other."

"Honigmann."

"Sorry?"

"His name was Georg Honigmann."

"Ahhh. That sounds about right. He and Litzi spoke German to each other."

"That, too, sounds about right. Is he a Communist?"

"I haven't the foggiest idea, Miss Maxse. Though knowing Litzi, who is very much a Communist, he could well be."

"Are you suggesting all of her lovers have been Communists?"

"I am not suggesting anything of the sort. Surely my failure to keep track of my former lover's lovers will not be a black mark against me?"

"Are you a Communist, Mr. Philby?"

"Good Lord, no."

"It is a question I am obliged to put. We have read all the articles published by *The Times* from its special correspondent in Spain. You obviously had little sympathy for the Republican side. In one article you justified the Nationalist bombing of Barcelona docks on the grounds that Soviet supplies were off-loaded there. In another you suggested that Republican mines and not Nationalist firebombs caused the destruction of the town of Guernica."

"I must admit to being flattered by your attention to the details of my dossier."

"Whilst in Spain, you had another liaison."

"You are referring to the Canadian actress Frances Doble? We slept together. We copulated. Often, actually."

"I am relieved to hear it, Mr. Philby. Is Miss Doble a Communist?"

Mr. Philby laughed silently. "Frances is to the right of Franco, which is to say she is a royalist who looks forward to the return of Alfonso to the throne he fled when the Spanish Republic was declared in 1931."

"What is your relationship nowadays?"

"We occupy separate b-beds in separate rooms in separate hotels in separate cities in separate countries. She has decided to wait out the war in P-portugal. Intercourse of any sort, most especially sexual, is difficult under these circumstances."

"I like your spunk, Mr. Philby. You seem to have survived the Phoney War, not to mention the subsequent shooting war, in fine fettle."

"Only just muddled through. Still can't figure out why the French strung their Maginot Line along the border with Germany but stopped when they reached Belgium, leaving the northern flank of the country dreadfully exposed."

"They supposed Herr Hitler's tanks would be unable to negotiate the Ardennes Forest," I said.

"French got it terribly wrong, didn't they? B-but all that is history."

" 'What's past is prologue,' " I said. "Sorry 'bout that, I don't make a habit of quoting Shakespeare. Saw John Gielgud doing *The Tempest* the other night. The line lodged in my mind."

"Indeed, what's p-past most certainly *is* p-prologue."

"I expect it must have seemed like the end of the world to someone like yourself who witnessed the debacle."

"It was the end of the world we knew," he said. I seem to recall his looking off to one side, his eyes focused on bitter memories. "In hotels, guests stopped setting shoes outside the d-doors of their rooms to be shined whilst they slept—nobody knew if the guests, or the shoes, or the shiners of shoes would still be in town come morning."

"Between Austria and Spain and France, you will have seen more than your share of violence, Mr. Philby." He nodded in grim agreement. I changed the tone of the conversation with, "Do you have the stomach for more?"

"I abhor violence, Miss Maxse."

"That's a declaration. It's not an answer to my question."

"I am incapable of killing someone, if that's what you're driving at."

"Nobody would expect you to kill someone with your bare hands. But could you betray an agent to torture and almost certain death in order to achieve specific objectives?"

"You are asking me if ends justify means?"

"I am."

"In certain situations, certain ends justify certain means, yes."

"Well put, Mr. Philby. Welcome to the world's second-oldest profession."

"Ahhh. I shall need to give notice at *The Times*."

"I will take care of that detail for you. Consider yourself to be on gardening leave. Report to Caxton House between Broadway Buildings and this hotel Monday at seven. There will be two security men at a desk inside the door. They will be expecting you. Show them your passport, sign their ledger book. They will send you to a room where your photograph will be taken for an identity badge. Do try to keep a straight face for the photographer. I cringe when I see colleagues smiling at me from identity badges."

"I shall not make that mistake, Miss Maxse." He cleared his throat. "I hate to raise the banal question of salary—"

I took the liberty of interrupting him. "Material questions are seldom banal. Your salary will be fifty pounds a month, which you are not expected to report to Inland Revenue."

"Can you give me an idea of what I shall be doing when I come on board?"

"I should think you'll join your friend Mr. Burgess, who only recently came over to us from the F.O. He has been assigned to Section D. The D stands for Destruction. He will take you under his wing, show you the gents' room, show you where spare typing paper and carbons can be had. The two of you will join Colonel Grand's team—they are recruiting some serious talent, including Mr. Hugh Trevor-Roper, Mr. Malcolm Muggeridge, Mr. Graham Greene. You will all be brainstorming about how we might sabotage German railway lines. We're looking for weak points in the German resupply system that can be attacked from the air or from the ground by partisans. Railway bridges. Key junctions. Marshalling yards. That sort of thing. At the same time you will be learning the tricks of the trade—simple ciphers, secret writing techniques . . ."

"The art of getting lost in a crowd even in the absence of one."

"I *am* impressed, Mr. Philby. I can see you have a natural talent for intelligence work. Down the road, when you've learned the ropes, I have no doubt, what with your knowledge of the Iberian Peninsula, you'll fit nicely into counterintelligence."

I spotted a waiter in the entranceway of the forecourt and made a sign that he was to add the tea to our running tally. Philby stirred uneasily in his chair. "May I put a last question, Miss Maxse?"

"Please do."

"Is there a handbook I might read? Something along

the lines of how one becomes a Secret Intelligence Service spy?"

"Dear boy, do get a hold of Somerset Maugham's *Ashenden*. It will tell you everything you need to know and then some."

12: LONDON, DECEMBER 1940

Where Mr. Burgess Lets the Cat Out of the Bag in an Inter-office Memo

Kim old sod,

Bloody marvellous being a member of His Majesty's Secret Intelligence Service. It doesn't take long for the cockteaser crowd to suss out one has a secret life. When they ask what I mean by war work, I smile knowingly. I am the teensiest bit more forthcoming with chaps who have security clearances. I mumble something about Caxton House, and if they have the dimmest idea what that might be I name-drop Section D into the conversation, though I never say the D stands for Destruction. I have, after all, been sworn to secrecy. Beats me how you managed a straight face when they took your photograph for the identity badge. I was hard put to stifle a grin, though two or three of my absolutely closest mates have remarked upon the gleam in my eye. Christ, it's exhilarating to not be able to talk about what one does for a living! To let the cat out of the bag, espionage is an aphrodisiac. (Best keep this hush-hush lest Miss Maxse become swamped with postulants.) On top of which, we're helping win this bloody war, you and I, Kim. When I fucked one of the code breakers at Bletchley Park and he let slip the date of the German invasion of Soviet Russia, I thought I was really contributing, like you when you rode off to Vienna.

You will tell our mutual friend on the park bench it was me who got the date from the code breaker when you pass it along?

I say, Kim, do remember to burn this note immediately once you've read it.

Guy

13: LONDON, JANUARY 1941

Where the Soviet *Rezident* Gorsky Proves He is a Spy After All

My comrades in the *Rezidentura* at the Soviet Embassy could not remember a colder winter. Several had taken to joking about having been posted east to Siberia instead of west to Great Britain. The iciness gripping London City had frozen the Gentlemen's Bathing Pond on the Highgate side of Hampstead Heath. Young men in gymnasium costumes and their lady friends in woollen leggings and flaring thigh-length skirts were spending Sunday afternoon ice-skating. "Do they skate in Russia?" Sonny inquired. He was sitting on the crabgrass, his back against an old oak, his overcoat, its collar up, buttoned to the scarf around his neck, his hat balanced on a knee, his head angled towards the arctic sun.

"They do," I said, settling onto the ground next to him, my back against the same tree. I leaned towards him and lit a cigarette on the embers of the one in his mouth. For a moment our faces were quite close. I detected alcohol on his breath. "We have a park named after the late Maxim Gorky," I said. "Muskovites skate when the pond in the park freezes over. At night some hold flaming torches. The police light fires in bins on the pond's edge so the skaters can warm their hands. Old *babushkas* peddle hot wine from thermos flasks. You would like it."

"The wine?"

"The scene."

"I hope I never get to see it," Sonny said. "It would mean my cover had been blown and I'd run for it."

"It will not come to that if we are all careful," I said.

Sonny took a swig from a flask. Wiping the mouthpiece on his palm, he offered me a drink. I sniffed at it before I pushed away his hand. "Smells like real whisky," I remarked.

"Whisky it is," he confirmed. "The good stuff. B-bonded. Aged in wood kegs for ten years, so they allege on the label."

"Where do you get it? At the Soviet Embassy all we have is Russian vodka."

"State secret," he said with a humourless laugh.

"You should be careful about your consumption of alcohol," I said.

"I told you last time you raised the subject, I need my ration. Steadies my nerves. Everyone at Caxton House stashes a b-bottle in the b-bottom drawer of his desk. Nobody notices whisky on your breath because they have whisky on their breath. I should think they would notice if I *didn't* drink."

"Black market whisky is expensive. Surely you have trouble making ends meet if you're drinking most of your salary?"

"My sainted father, who has taken up residence in Great Britain for the duration despite the everlasting rain that affects his gout, slips me a hundred quid every so often."

"Might I suggest you switch to vodka? It's cheaper. And it can't be detected on your breath."

"You do take a personal interest in your agents. Can you suggest a diet to help me lose a bit of the inner tube round my waist?" Turning towards me, Sonny smirked in embarrassment. "Don't get me wrong, I do appreciate your concern, not to mention your tradecraft. Tell me something, Anatoly, is Gorsky really your name? Guy Burgess supposed it to be a pseudonym."

"State secret," I said. "But I will share it with you. Gorsky was my grandfather's family name, but not my father's and not mine. Under the Tsars, the second son was always conscripted into the army, so families with a second son farmed him out to a family without sons and the name was changed. That's how grandfather Gorsky avoided military service under the Tsar Alexander Three."

The blade of one of the skaters broke through thin ice and his left foot sank into water up to his ankle, eliciting a howl of laughter from the other skaters. In the bare branches over our heads jackdaws cawed as if in derision. I studied Sonny as he took another swig of whisky. At twenty-nine, he cut a fine figure—lean despite his claim to have an inner tube round his waist, suntanned even in winter, the livid trace of a war wound on his forehead immediately above his sunglasses. "What are you reading?" I asked, nodding at the book in his lap.

"Turgenev's *A Nest of Gentlefolk* in the Garnett translation," he said.

"I know his *Otzi i Deti*. You don't speak Russian, do you? You should learn. It's a rich language. *Otzi i Deti* means *Fathers and Sons*. Turgenev invented the term *nihilism* in that novel. I fail to comprehend how someone who believes in nothing can look himself in the mirror when he shaves. I understand a Fascist better than I understand a nihilist—at least a Fascist believes in *something*."

"I was told you'd been b-back to Moscow."

"Whoever told you that should have minded his tongue. I was visiting family."

"Didn't know you had one."

"Many things you don't know. Better that way. Compartmentalization."

"When you were in Moscow, did you see Otto?"

"No. Our paths didn't cross."

"What happened to Otto? Why was he suddenly recalled to Moscow?"

"Nothing *happened* to Otto. I heard he'd been promoted to captain and posted to the Second Chief Directorate. It's what *Rezidents* dream about. Someone mentioned he was living in a village near Moscow and commuting."

"So he's in good health?"

I nodded. "Why wouldn't he be in good health?"

"I liked Otto."

"He liked you." I cleared my throat. "What do you have for me today?"

"Something quite important, I should think. The date of the German invasion of Soviet Russia. It's scheduled for dawn on the twenty-second of June."

I always made it a point not to react when I debriefed agents. But I am afraid in this instance a whistle seeped from my lips. "Twenty-two June! That's an incredible nugget. How do you know it?"

"Guy Burgess got it from a chap who works with the code breakers at Bletchley Park. They are reading Germany's top-secret Ultra traffic."

"Be sure to convey our appreciation to Mr. Burgess. This will be enciphered and sent to Moscow before the day is out. I expect it will be brought to Comrade Stalin's attention immediately."

"There's more. They circulated an eyes-only memorandum to department heads at Caxton House. Mine let me see it. It confirmed the June date that Guy passed on to me. It mentioned the German order of battle: 4.5 million troops from the several Axis powers, 600,000 motorized vehicles and 750,000 horses are being massed along a 2,900 kilometre front for the invasion."

"Did it list the divisions by name? Did it say which were armoured?"

"I'm afraid it did, but I had all to do to memorize the numbers I gave you without the division names. I do remember the Das Reich division, if that's any help."

"If you had had that Minox camera I offered, you might have been able to photograph the page."

"I absolutely refuse to carry a spy camera into Caxton House. I won't take the risk. I don't intend to wind up watching ice-skaters in Gorky Park. Look, the security people do random body searches on p-people entering and leaving. They found one of the aerial photo analysts carrying a rolled-up nudist camp magazine the other day, the ones where the genitals are airbrushed out. The colonels who run His Majesty's Secret Intelligence Service are rather puritanical and their attitude filters down—the nudist magazine was shredded into a burn bag and the poor bastard was p-packed off to a photo recon unit in Iceland, so I heard."

"With or without the division names, this is vital information. You and your friends will have the satisfaction of knowing you are contributing to the defeat of Hitlerism in Europe."

"Will Hitler be defeated in Europe? Will the Soviet Union survive the German blitzkrieg, or will Russia get knocked off the way Belgium and France and Holland got knocked off?"

I couldn't believe he was asking the question. "Kim, Kim, we will do more than survive. We will gather our strength—the masses of tanks and planes being produced, the hordes of soldiers being prepared for battle behind the Ural Mountains. We will unleash a withering attack that will sweep the Nazi invaders back to Berlin. We will capture Hitler and parade him in chains through Red Square."

"As my dear mother would say, from your lips to God's ear."

I was rather taken aback. "I don't believe in God," I snapped. "I believe in the Red Army. I believe in Stalin."

"I have another nugget," he said. "Remember that American I told you about? The one OSS sent round to learn the ropes from us?"

"Angleton?"

"That's the one. Jim Angleton. Rather charmless chap, actually. But to give him his due, not born yesterday. Fast learner. Wouldn't surprise me to see him running their OSS in twenty years. We have become chums. We've taken to climbing to the roof to watch the German b-bombers attacking London. It's one hell of a show. Our giant search beams crisscross the night sky. Every now and then one of them p-pins a German moth to the underside of a cloud. Then our ack-ack goes to work. Small explosions, each blazing with the intensity of an igniting match head, walk their way up the beam until one bursts immediately under the fuselage. A wing snaps off, the moth tilts clumsily onto its side and slips out of the spotlight. I don't like the Hun, but all the same I couldn't help imagining desperate men clawing their way to hatches to escape the hull falling deadweight like a shot bird."

"Your sympathies are misplaced."

"Quite. Curiously, that's what Angleton said. He and I got to talking about the war. I told him I thought it would last ten years. He said no way. He said it would end in forty-four, forty-five at the latest. I asked what made him think so. When he didn't answer, I could see he wasn't going to tell me anything unless he thought I already knew it, so I took a stab in the dark—I asked him if he was talking about that new atomic d-device."

"What did he say?"

"Angleton looked at me sharply. 'How do you know about that?' he demanded. I told him it was common knowledge in my shop that our scientists had been seconded to the Americans to help them construct an atomic bomb."

"And?" I insisted.

Sonny shrugged. "Angleton appeared surprised to discover I was party to that information. He said the Germans were working on one, too. He said something about a race to use uranium-235 to trigger a chain reaction. He said the Americans were on the case and would get there first. He said they already had people identifying targets. He said the war would be over the day after the first bomb was dropped. He said the atomic bomb would give Joe Stalin second thoughts about conquering Italy and France after the European war ended."

"He actually said the bomb would give Joe Stalin second thoughts?" After a moment I murmured, "This ought to convince the doubters—"

"What doubters?"

I had spoken out of turn. When I didn't respond Sonny repeated the question. "What doubters are we talking about?"

"There are a very few comrades in Moscow who think you are too good to be true. They worry whether you are a sincere Communist and a loyal agent of the Centre. Are you, Kim? Loyal to Moscow, to Stalin, to Communism?"

"That's the last thing I expected to hear from you, Anatoly. Not after the risks I've taken. Not after all the information I've passed along to Otto and now to you."

"What made you become a Communist?"

"I read Marx. Any reading of Marx leads one to Socialism. Socialism is half the hog. I turned to Communism because it was the whole hog. It armed me for the struggle against the inequalities which have always revolted me."

"Sorry we went down this road. I don't doubt your loyalty. Others . . ."

Sonny was clearly annoyed. "I don't have to prove anything to anybody," he announced. He laughed to himself. "Except my sainted father, of course."

I laughed, too. "St John Philby. Of course."

A young man in a faded yellow duffel coat approached us. He carried a skate by its blade in one hand and an unlit cigarette in the other. "Trouble one of you gents for a light?"

"What happened to the other skate?" Sonny asked.

"Only have one skate," he said. He looked from one of us to the other. Both Sonny and I were smoking. "Match?"

"Only had one match," I said.

"Beg pardon? Are you gents refusing to give a bloke a light?"

"We are," I said.

"Well, not to over-egg the pudding but fuck the both of you," the young man said. He walked off shaking his head. I could see him leaning towards a lighted match held by a skater standing on dry land.

"Why did you do that?" Sonny asked.

"He works for me," I said. "He was holding one skate, and not two, to let me know he hadn't spotted anyone suspicious at the pond. He was telling me the coast was clear."

"B-bloody hell!" Sonny said. "You really are a spy, Anatoly!"

"What did you think this was, a game?"

"A game. Yes, I suppose I did."

14: MOSCOW, JULY 1941

Where Former Junior Lieutenant, Now Senior Lieutenant, Y. Modinskaya Visits the Near Dacha

So: It's me, Yelena Modinskaya, the intelligence analyst who interviewed London *Rezident* Teodor Stepanovich Maly moments before his execution. That was in 1938. I haven't forgotten the episode. For me, it's as if it happened yesterday. I had been assigned the Englishman's case file No. 5581 at the time and, under the supervision of my section chief in the fifth department of the second chief directorate, then Senior Lieutenant (now Captain) Gusakov, I have been working on it since. I myself was promoted to senior lieutenant last year, which made me the highest-ranking female in the second chief directorate. My maternal grandmother, who was one of the first female commissars in the glorious Red Army at the time of the revolution, would have been proud of me were she still alive.

Weather permitting, I usually walk from the flat I share with my father in a communal apartment near

Mayakovskaya Metro Station, with its remarkable fish-eye mosaics on the ceiling, down Gorky Street to my office in the Lubyanka prison. If it has snowed or it is particularly cold, say minus ten or below, I take the metro. Very occasionally I and several girlfriends have splurged on a taxi to GUM department store or the Moscow State Circus on Tsvetnoy Boulevard (which was bombed by the vile Germans on the opening day of the war, a month ago today, though our circus comrades never missed a performance). But this evening marked the first time in my life I had ever been in a Zil limousine. The two members of the Lubyanka security detachment sitting in the front were topping on the cake, as the saying has it. I was in the back between Captain Gusakov and his immediate superior, director of the fifth department of the second chief directorate, Senior Colonel P. Sudoplatov. I know it defies belief but, apart from the fact we were heading west on the Moscow Highway, none of us had any idea where we were going until we heard one of the security people mention the Near Dacha. "The Near Dacha at Kuntsevo is where Comrade Stalin spends weekends," Captain Gusakov whispered in my ear.

"Whatever you do," Senior Colonel Sudoplatov told me, "don't yield to nervousness if you should find yourself in the presence of Comrade Stalin. Nervous people are known to make him nervous, on account of he fears they may have something to be nervous about. The chief of our NKVD, Comrade Beria, is likely to be there, along with several members of the Politburo. Ignore everyone except Comrade Stalin. Look him in the eye, speak to him directly, make your case exactly as you made it to us in the Lubyanka."

Some ten or twelve minutes beyond the last of the new brick apartment buildings rising in the farm fields around Moscow, the Zil turned off onto an unmarked road that immediately plunged into a thick forest of white pines. Rounding the first bend we reached a guardhouse manned by NKVD border troops armed with automatic weapons. The driver rolled down his window and exchanged a few words with the officer, who checked a clipboard and waved us through. We passed a double perimeter chain-link fence and I thought I heard the yelping of dogs patrolling between the two fences. We passed two perfectly round clearings in the woods, each with a battery of anti-aircraft guns. The soldiers manning them had taken off their shirts and were lazing on the sandbags around the guns. Moments later we reached an oval driveway and stopped in front of a one-story green-painted dacha with unpainted wooden windows flung open as if to air out the rooms. Bedding and pillows were spread across several sills. You can laugh, no matter, but it made my heart beat more rapidly to think I was looking at the sheets on which Comrade Stalin slept. A captain of the guard opened the Zil's rear door and escorted the three of us into the dacha and through a series of large half-empty rooms, each with a great Russian ceramic tile stove in the centre. All of the rooms had walls of unpainted wood. For Comrade Stalin's sake I was glad to see this, since wood vapours are known to improve the quality of the air we breathe. We reached a double door at the end of a narrow corridor that opened onto the conference room. It was furnished with a large and thick rectangular table filled with bottles of Borjomi mineral water and plain kitchen tumblers. Comrade Beria, a small man wearing an NKVD tunic and a monocle in one eye, presided from the far end. He motioned us to the three empty seats opposite him. Several important looking comrades sat at the sides of the table. The only one I recognized was the Ukrainian N. Khrushchev, whose photograph had appeared in *Pravda* each time the city authorities inaugurated a new metro station.

A small door I had not even noticed opened in the wall behind Comrade Beria and a man appeared. He settled heavily into a seat to the left of Comrade Beria. It took a moment before the identity of the last arrival dawned on me. It was, of course, Comrade Stalin himself, though he didn't look at all like the Stalin in the photographs or paintings that hung in every office of the Lubyanka. He was wearing a military tunic that didn't conceal the stomach straining against the gold buttons of the uniform jacket. His face was pockmarked, as if from smallpox, his skin the colour of wax. His left arm, partially crippled from his revolutionist activities before 1917 (so it was generally believed), hung limply from the shoulder socket, his left hand buried inside a tunic pocket. His famous moustache had gone ash grey. His shoulders sagged with worry and I could only imagine the strain he was under dealing with the barbarous German invasion of our motherland, with tens of thousands of lives hanging on each decision. (The hourly bulletins on the radio spoke of our courageous soldiers standing their ground on the Western Front, even driving back the invaders in several sectors, but the long faces at the Lubyanka, where our comrades were better informed than the general public, told a grimmer story. There was even talk of evacuating the capital from Moscow to a city further east, but I couldn't believe it would come to that.)

Comrade Stalin nodded impatiently at Comrade Beria, who said: "Senior Colonel Sudoplatov, you initialled, Captain Gusakov, you countersigned the conclusions of Senior Lieutenant Modinskaya concerning the Englishman who was first recruited by the NKVD in 1934. Comrade Stalin is personally interested in this case file and wants to hear Senior Lieutenant Modinskaya's conclusions from the horse's mouth, as the peasants say."

Senior Colonel Sudoplatov elbowed me in the ribs. I rose to my feet and looked Comrade Stalin in the eye. "Respected Josef Vissarionovich," I began. (I had read an article in *Pravda* reporting that Comrade Stalin's collaborators were expected to address him with this more collegial title. I thought it would make a good impression if I did this without being invited.) "The Englishman is certainly an agent of the British Secret Intelligence Service, part of a diabolic scheme to penetrate Moscow Centre and feed us disinformation to distort our worldview and impede our ability to combat the enemies of the Soviet state."

"Evidence," Comrade Beria snapped. "Proof."

"I shall begin with the Englishman's roots," I said. "His father, Harry St John Philby, is on record, in interviews published in obscure bulletins and local newspapers, as favouring what he calls a Christian solution to the German problem, thus freeing the British and French and Germans to combat what he considers to be the principal adversary, the Soviet Union. It is extremely unlikely the son would stray so far from the paternal mould that he would work as a secret agent for this principal adversary." I removed a recent telegram from case file 5581 and read it aloud: "This cable from the London *Rezident* to Moscow Centre is dated 24 December 1940: *Sonny*—" I glanced quickly at respected Josef Vissarionovich and interjected, "Sonny is the Englishman's cryptonym."

Respected Josef Vissarionovich muttered, "I am not an imbecile, Senior Lieutenant Modinskaya."

"It was not my intention to suggest—"

"Read the telegram."

"Sonny has been recruited by the British Secret Intelligence Service. He has been assigned to Section D for Destruction, a unit with the mission of identifying weak points in the German resupply system." I looked up at respected Josef Vissarionovich. "It strains credibility to believe that our supposed agent, recruited in 1934, then had the good fortune to stumble into employment with the infamous *Times* to cover the civil war in Spain from Franco's side, after which, in 1940, this same agent was supposedly recruited by the Secret Intelligence Service, which has a reputation for running one of the most competent intelligence operations in the world. It defies credibility that SIS is staffed with imbeciles who didn't notice that state secrets were being leaked to Moscow. I must insist that the Englishman's rise within the ranks of SIS—despite his Cambridge University Socialist activities, despite his marriage to a woman widely known to be a member of the Austrian Communist Party—has been implausibly rapid. If we are to swallow Philby's most recent report, dated 18 July 1941, he has been assigned to the elite counter-intelligence unit run by the Colonel Felix Cowgill and known to the few insiders who are aware of its existence as Section Five of Six, the Six standing for MI6, which is the administrative designation of the Secret Intelligence Service. According to Philby, Section Five has focused on penetrating German and Italian espionage organizations and feeding them disinformation that would reach the German High Command, even Hitler himself. I suggest that if they are able to penetrate the German and Italian espionage organizations, they have the capability to penetrate our espionage service. I suggest that Philby's supposed recruitment by Moscow Centre in 1934 is at the heart of this penetration."

Comrade Beria muttered something in an undertone to respected Josef Vissarionovich, who pursed his lips and shrugged. Comrade Beria said aloud, "The business of the roots is pure conjecture."

Thinking back, I marvel at my audacity. "Who among us knows a son who has strayed far from his father's roots?" I asked.

Respected Josef Vissarionovich snorted. "I know one. Me. My father was a shoemaker who spent most of his wages on alcohol. It would surprise me to discover he knew the meaning of the word *proletariat*." Respected Josef Vissarionovich waved his good hand in my direction. "You surely have more concrete points to make, Senior Lieutenant Modinskaya."

"I do," I agreed.

"She does," Captain Gusakov said anxiously. "For God's sake, make them," he instructed me.

"*God's sake* has seldom been invoked in this room," Comrade Beria said from the head of the table. Respected Josef Vissarionovich almost smiled.

"In 1934, the London *Rezident*, Teodor Stepanovich Maly, cryptonym *Mann*, begged Moscow Centre for permission to contact the Englishman and, when this authorization was reluctantly granted, he recruited him on a bench in one of London's great parks. Upon his recall to Moscow, Maly confessed to being a German agent. He was sentenced to the highest measure of punishment. I interviewed him moments before his execution. He said nothing to dissuade me that the Englishman was also an agent of a foreign power. It should be noted here that the London *Rezidentura* was a cesspool of treason. Maly's predecessor, Ignaty Reif, cryptonym *Marr*, was shot as a foreign agent. Anatoly Gorsky, cryptonym *Kapp*, Maly's successor who countersigned many of the *Rezident*'s telegrams to Moscow Centre defending the Englishman, was recalled to Moscow last year and is the object of an ongoing investigation—there is a strong suspicion that he, like the two London *Rezidents* before him, is a foreign agent. Given Gorsky's obstinate defence of the Englishman's failure to assassinate Franco, I would not be surprised if the investigation produces criminal charges and a confession."

Respected Josef Vissarionovich regarded Comrade Beria. "Who ordered the Englishman to assassinate Franco?"

"It wasn't so much an order as a suggestion," Comrade

Beria explained. "I heard you mention one night that the only thing that could save the situation in Spain was the death of Franco. I took it upon myself to pass along your comment—"

"How could a journalist trained to gather intelligence be expected to execute a wet job?" respected Josef Vissarionovich demanded.

Comrade Beria looked flustered. "I can say he was not expected to assassinate Franco himself, only identify breaches in his security so that more skilled operatives might organize the thing."

I felt the ground move under my feet. The Englishman's failure to make the slightest effort to eliminate Franco was a pillar of my case against him. "There is still more evidence, respected Josef Vissarionovich," I said. I am afraid my voice was unsteady. I kept myself from trembling by placing both palms on the flat of the table.

Respected Josef Vissarionovich frowned. "You appear nervous," he observed.

"I am only exhausted," I said. "I have been up most of the night going over my report."

Was it my imagination or did respected Josef Vissarionovich's moustache twitch like that of a cat toying with a mouse? "Go on," he said.

"When the Englishman first claimed to have been recruited by SIS seven months ago, we put one question to him: 'Give us the names of the SIS agents in the Soviet Union.' Soon thereafter he responded"—I glanced around the table for the first time; several of the participants averted their eyes from mine—"that there were no SIS agents operating in the Soviet Union. No British agents? No British networks? What can we make of this reply in light of the thousands who have confessed to being British agents and suffered the highest measure of punishment for their treachery?"

I turned back to respected Josef Vissarionovich. He was uncapping a sealed bottle of Borjomi and carefully filling a glass with mineral water. He raised his moustache with a finger of his left hand and took a sip, then delicately patting dry his lips on the back of a cuff, looked over at Comrade Beria and inclined his head to one side. Apparently it was a gesture Comrade Beria recognized. "Is that it, Senior Lieutenant Modinskaya?" he called across the table.

"There is also the revealing matter of the Englishman's lifestyle," I said. "According to the London *Rezident*, Sonny is drinking heavily. He seems to have an endless supply of black market whisky at £4 a bottle, which, given his consumption, comes to roughly £20 a week, all this on a supposed salary of £50 a month. On top of that he spends heavily at a public house, The Duke of York in Jermyn Street. And he keeps up his membership in the gentlemen's club called the Athenaeum, where he is said to dine occasionally. The question must be posed: Where does the money come from? I suggest the possibility—I would go so far as to say the *probability*—that the Englishman is being paid twice or three times the £50 he claimed because he is an SIS disinformation agent. Living several lives and several lies would also account for the heavy drinking."

Stalin waved his crippled arm in the air, as if to say he was not bowled over by the points I was making.

I took a deep breath. "Which brings me to Alexander Orlov—"

"Cryptonym the *Swede*," respected Josef Vissarionovich interjected. Clearly he was familiar with the contents of case file 5581.

"The Swede, who was the Englishman's field controller when Sonny was able to cross the Spanish border into France for debriefings, defected to the Americans three years ago this month. Despite this, the Englishman has not been arrested. Nor have his two close friends from Cambridge, cryptonyms *Maiden* and *Orphan*, who were, on the Englishman's suggestion, recruited by our service. Which leads one to suspect that all three could be British moles feeding us disinformation."

Respected Josef Vissarionovich asked, "Did you know the Swede personally?"

"I never met him, respected—"

He cut me off. "I have. I know him from the revolution. He is a Jew—Feldbin, if my memory is correct—but I never held that against him. There are also good Jews. Feliks Dzerzhinsky recruited the Swede as a Chekist and brought him around to meet me. When I went down to Stalingrad to stiffen our resistance against the Whites, the Swede was one of the Chekists I relied on. We rounded up the weak-kneed commanders who had retreated and bound them hand and foot and pushed them into the Volga from a barge. Our commanders stopped retreating after that. To mark the occasion, the Swede and some of his Chekist friends gave me a fine-looking Italian Beretta. I still have it—I keep it in a drawer next to my bed. The Swede and I crossed paths from time to time over the years. If they cross again, I will have him shot for treason. But it can be said he was a man of iron, a man of honour. When he went over to the Americans he sent me a letter through Beria saying if I didn't touch his family he wouldn't touch mine, my family being our agents he handled in Europe. I haven't touched a hair on the heads of his people. Which explains why the Englishman—your Sonny, along with the two others, Maiden and Orphan—are still at liberty."

N. Khrushchev raised a finger, as a child will in a classroom. "I remember the Swede from the period of the suppression of the Kulaks in the Ukraine," he said. "Broad shoulders. Military-style haircut. A Bolshevik through and through. Nobody dreamt he would one day go over to the enemy."

"Respected Josef Vissarionovich, even if the Swede did not betray to the West the identity of the Englishman and our other agents, he would have passed on to them the *product*, which is to say the details that the Englishman provided to Moscow Centre. I myself have studied the product as if I didn't know where it came from—intelligence reports on German armaments reaching Franco, on German instructors teaching Franco's pilots to fly the newest Messerschmitt 109s, on the installation in the Heinkel 111 of a new bomb sight. Even a child could have narrowed the source down to a dozen or so British journalists covering the war from the Nationalist side, then narrowed it further to which cities, at which point you would be able to identify the supposed Soviet agent. Harold Philby in Salamanca. If I can do this in Moscow, it is unthinkable that the vaunted

British Secret Intelligence Service could not reach the same conclusion in London. There is only one plausible explanation for their failure to arrest Sonny: He is an SIS disinformation agent."

I noticed respected Josef Vissarionovich glancing surreptitiously at the palm of his right hand as he packed tobacco into the bowl of a pipe. It occurred to me that he was employing an old ruse that bureaucrats used when they wanted you to think they were talking extemporaneously and not from notes. "The Englishman informed us that the Hitlerian invasion of the motherland would take place at dawn on the twenty-second of June," he said. "He furthermore told us that 4.5 million troops of the Axis powers, 600,000 motorized vehicles and 750,000 horses would invade along a 2,900 kilometre front. His information was precise."

"Respected Josef Vissarionovich, it is clearly in England's interest to pass on to us the date of the Hitlerian invasion so that we are better able to resist the invaders, so that we and the loathsome Germans exhaust each other in endless battles, which has been the eternal British dream since the Soviet state was created."

"Respected Senior Lieutenant Yelena Modinskaya," Josef Vissarionovich said, his voice reduced to a gruff whisper and dripping with what can only be described as sarcasm, "I was informed you were an intelligence analyst. I was not informed you were an authority on international affairs as well, and specialize in the motivation of capitalist governments." He jammed the pipe between his teeth and leaned towards Comrade Beria, who held a lighted match over the bowl. Respected Josef Vissarionovich's head disappeared behind a cloud of tobacco smoke as he told the others at the table, "Contrary to the naïve view of Senior Lieutenant Modinskaya, it was in the British interest to have the Hitlerian war machine crush the Soviet Union the way it crushed Belgium and Holland and France. It is well known that the English upper class, which is the governing class, is secretly pro-German and not so secretly anti-Jewish. With the Soviet Union crushed, Hitler would have his hands full managing the conquered countries of Europe and extracting their resources—petrol from the Caucasus, grain from the Ukraine. There would be no reason for him to invade England. He and the English upper class would quickly reach an understanding. The British Fascist Mosley would become prime minister. King Edward, who honeymooned in Germany after he abdicated in order to marry that American divorcée Simpson, would be recalled to the throne. Senior Lieutenant Modinskaya completely misreads the value of the warning we received from the Englishman. There can be only one explanation for misreading it to that extent: She is determined to discredit the agent Sonny. Which raises the suspicion that she herself could be a foreign agent." Respected Josef Vissarionovich turned back to me. "Tell us frankly: For whom do you work? The Germans or the English?"

I had difficulty finding my voice. "I work for the Communist dream," I finally managed. "I work for the Soviet Union. I work for you, respected Josef Vissarionovich."

Respected Josef Vissarionovich expressed amusement as if at a private joke. Comrade Beria and N. Khrushchev laughed along with him as if privy to the joke. The others around the table joined in, though I doubt they understood what they were laughing at.

"The Englishman passed on other secrets that attest to his being a legitimate Soviet agent," respected Josef Vissarionovich continued. "He informed us that the Americans, with the collaboration of British physicists, are attempting to split the atom in the expectation of building an atomic bomb by 1944 or '45. He told us the British had broken German's top-secret Ultra code, which is how they knew the details of Hitler's plans to invade the Soviet motherland. He told us about a secret British device installed along their coast called radar—it looks like a giant bedspring and emits radio waves that can provide warning of German bomber attacks in time to scramble fighter squadrons and defend the targets. He passed on to us what the British knew of the German order of battle, of their losses in men and materiel in the Polish and French campaigns, of the flawed armour on their *Panzerkampfwagen* One, of the heavier armour that limits the mobility and autonomy of the *Panzerkampfwagen* Two."

"Respected Josef Vissarionovich," I said, my trembling voice rising to no more than a murmur, "it is self-serving for Britain to provide us with information on German military deficiencies. After the defeat of the British Expeditionary Force in Flanders, after the humiliating retreat from Dunkirk, London's nightmare is that we will make a separate peace with the Hitlerians if you, respected Josef Vissarionovich, conclude the English are too weak to defend their island against a German invasion."

Respected Josef Vissarionovich said, "Comrades, we are fortunate to have in our midst someone who is not only an authority on international affairs but one of the world's leading experts on strategic military theory."

N. Khrushchev snickered. "We should count our blessings."

Respected Josef Vissarionovich looked at Captain Gusakov, sitting to my left. "You, Gusakov, signed off on Modinskaya's conclusions."

With an effort Captain Gusakov pushed himself to his feet. "Comrade Stalin, it is an exaggeration to say I signed off on her conclusions. My countersignature means I verified that her report accurately quoted telegrams and conversations and events presented in case file 5581. Her conclusions are her own affair."

"You accuse me of *exaggerating*?" respected Josef Vissarionovich demanded.

"I choose my words without thinking—"

"Perhaps you signed off on Modinskaya's conclusions without thinking." Respected Josef Vissarionovich turned to Senior Colonel Sudoplatov, who likewise rose stiffly to his feet. The room was so quiet I could hear respected Josef Vissarionovich sucking on the stem of his pipe. "You, Sudoplatov, signed off on Gusakov's work, putting your initial 'S' on the upper right-hand corner of each page of Modinskaya's conclusions."

Senior Colonel Sudoplatov cleared his noticeably dry throat. "I initialled Modinskaya's reports that bore Captain Gusakov's countersignature. I can state that it was one of hundreds of documents that crossed my desk on any given day. My initial in no way indicates support for her actual conclusions, only that the techniques of examining case file 5581 were authenticated by the countersignature of an experienced NKVD officer."

"And *my* desk," respected Josef Vissarionovich said with a snarl. "Does it occur to you that *thousands* of documents pass across it each and every day?"

Senior Colonel Sudoplatov bowed his head. "With all respect, Comrade Stalin, it was not my intention to suggest otherwise."

And then something curious occurred that I cannot explain, I can only recount. To Senior Colonel Sudoplatov's mortification, he began hiccupping—stifled gasps that made it sound as if he were choking on a bone in his throat. Stalin stared at the comrade colonel almost sympathetically. "Stop that," he said in a voice that was not devoid of benevolence. And Senior Colonel Sudoplatov did. He stopped hiccupping on the spot.

Respected Josef Vissarionovich waited a moment to be sure the hiccups had ceased. Then he said: "When I sign my initial 'S' on the upper right-hand corner of a page, Sudoplatov, it indicates I agree with the contents." Respected Josef Vissarionovich leaned forwards and tapped the bowl of his pipe on the desk to emphasize the point he was making. "Permit me to give you an example. The last thing every night Comrade Beria brings around is the list of wreckers and traitors to be shot the next morning. I occasionally draw a line though the name of someone I know has rendered exceptional service to the revolution and the motherland. When I sign an 'S' on the upper right-hand corner of the page, it signifies I agree with the executions."

Respected Josef Vissarionovich fell back into his chair and turned his attention to Comrade Beria. "For my money, they are all in this together. Which implies they must sink or swim together. If Modinskaya wants us to conclude that a valuable intelligence operative is a Western disinformation agent, one has to ask what is behind this interpretation. If Gusakov countersigns her conclusions, if Sudoplatov initials them in the upper right-hand corner . . ."

Respected Josef Vissarionovich shrugged as if to say he had little choice in the matter at hand and finished his thought in what I took to be Georgian. Comrade Beria nodded carefully. "I am of the same opinion, Comrade Stalin. It has the stench of a wrecking conspiracy."

The trip back to town passed in the silence associated with tombs. The two security agents, who had chatted and laughed on the way out, uttered not a word. Summer darkness, which is saturated with dampness in Moscow that is thought to be excellent for the complexion of women, had settled over the city. Distant bursts of red illuminated the horizon—the Hitlerians were bombing munitions factories—but the explosions were too far away to be heard. The streets had become deserted, air raid blinds had been pulled over apartment windows by the time we reached the avenue behind the Lubyanka. The giant building, which had been home to an insurance company before the glorious revolution, so the story goes, hovered over us, blotting out the sky and its stars. The driver passed the main entrance with the ornate double doors leading to the great court by which we normally entered and left. Further along the avenue the Zil pulled up in front of smaller metal doors and the driver claxoned twice. With a grinding noise the metal doors swung open and the Zil, its headlights dimmed, drove into the courtyard used to bring in prisoners. Captain Gusakov leaned forwards. "You have mistaken the doors," he said.

The driver, who had an open peasant's face, turned in his seat. "There has been no mistake, comrade officers," he assured us. He looked genuinely embarrassed. "We thought you understood—you have all been arrested."

15: MOSCOW, JANUARY 1942

Where Former Senior Lieutenant Y. Modinskaya Refuses a Last Cigarette

"The trick is to turn the recording volume to five. When you speak into the microphone the needle should jump, but not into the red zone. If it jumps into the red zone, you have set the recording volume too high."

"When I need your help, prisoner Modinskaya, I will ask for it. [Pause] Testing one, two, three. It appears to be working now. I shall begin the interrogation."

"Yes, by all means do. We don't want to keep the comrades in the crypt waiting."

"You need not take that tone. This is an ordeal for me, too."

"I understand how you must feel. I was on your side of the tape machine on one memorable occasion, in this very room as a matter of fact."

"There is a new regulation since your time—condemned prisoners are to be offered a last cigarette. Here, take one—"

"I don't smoke."

"So that I am not reprimanded, can you confirm on tape that I offered the cigarette and you refused."

"You offered a cigarette. I refused."

"All right, let's begin. Interrogation of state criminal number SH seven nought seven one nought eight. [Pause] Prisoner Modinskaya, do you wish to register any complaints about your treatment since your arrest?"

"These leg irons are biting into my ankles, which are swollen and infected."

"Leg irons, wrist irons are obligatory for condemned prisoners. [Pause] Do you know where you are?"

"So, you waste your breath on silly questions. I am disillusioned but not disorientated. I recognized this room the moment they brought me here from the cellblock. I recognized its narrowness, its bareness, the high ceiling, the straight-backed wooden chair you might find in any honest Soviet kitchen. I recognized the three-legged stool on which I was instructed to sit. I recognized first light the colour of ash and the weight of lead oozing through a slit of a window high in the wall. If the room reeks of an unpleasant but unidentifiable odour, I would be the last person in the world to know it, my nasal passages having been blocked when one of the jailers broke my nose the night of my arrest. To answer your question: I am on one of the lower floors of the Lubyanka prison where they interrogate state criminals. I even recognize the scream of the friction brakes when trolley cars stop below us in Dzerzhinsky Square. [Pause] Dear God, if only all the screams that reached my ears in this building came from friction brakes."

"Prisoner Modinskaya, the comrade guards have observed you talking to the wall of your cell. I remind you that talking in the cellblock is a grave breach of rules with serious consequences."

"In the Lubyanka, prisoners in need of a sympathetic ear often end up talking to a wall. If the wall were to reply I could understand your concern—that would constitute a conversation. Until now the wall in my cell, no doubt aware of your rules, has remained silent."

"Prisoner Modinskaya, you have been found guilty of being a British agent and condemned by a special tribunal to the highest measure of punishment. You are to be shot immediately after this interrogation terminates."

"The garments I was wearing the night of my arrest have been reduced to rags. I will need suitable clothing."

"Suitable clothing?"

"A dress. There is a long grey one in the cupboard of the flat I share with my father. It has a modest velvet collar that buttons to the neck and long sleeves with lace cuffs. I will also need clean undergarments, clean stockings."

"I don't understand. The dress must be suitable for what?"

"Are you dimwitted?"

"A prisoner in your delicate situation should be wary of insulting a Chekist."

"As the condemned prisoner Maly once remarked, someone minutes away from having a large-calibre bullet shot into the nape of the neck doesn't lose sleep over the insulting of a Chekist. [Pause] The clothing must be suitable for a funeral."

"There will be no funeral. Executed prisoners are buried in a common grave."

"You cannot execute prisoners in January. Impossible to prepare common graves when the ground is frozen."

"This is First Secretary Stalin's Union of Soviet Socialist Republics, not Chiang Kai-shek's China. Our workers are equipped with earth-moving machines that are capable of excavating ditches in the fields behind Novodevichy cemetery in the coldest of winters."

"I hope to God they don't mix the men with the women in this common grave of yours. Imagine being forced to lie for eternity next to some man, one you don't even know at that. [Pause] I was a virgin the night of my arrest but the comrade interrogators put an end to that with a vodka bottle. They punched my breasts with their fists, all the while yelling that I must come clean. 'Only sign the confession and your troubles will be over,' they shouted over and over. 'Confess to what?' I asked. I was never ordered by Trotskyists to assassinate respected Josef Vissarionovich. I was never instructed to wreck bread production by throwing glass fragments into sacks of flour. I was never recruited by the British Secret Intelligence Service to discredit the Englishman. 'I would certainly sign your paper if I were guilty of these crimes,' I told them. [Pause] I don't think they heard me."

"Prisoner Modinskaya, do you recall what rank you held before your arrest?"

"I was a senior lieutenant in the fifth department of the NKVD's second chief directorate, reporting, like yourself, to Captain Gusakov."

"The late Captain Gusakov. A special tribunal convicted him of being a British agent. He was executed the day before yesterday."

"So it *was* Captain Gusakov I heard being dragged down the passageway snivelling like a child, begging for mercy between sobs."

"He didn't make life easier for the comrades in the crypt."

"The comrades in the crypt didn't make death easier for Captain Gusakov."

"Prisoner Modinskaya, do you know who I am?"

"Everyone in the second chief directorate knows who you are. You're Nina Petrovna, the post room slut who slept her way into the fifth department secretariat and wound up working as a research assistant for then senior lieutenant Gusakov when I was promoted to intelligence analyst. You were legendary for submitting summaries of interrogations that were utterly illiterate. We used to read them aloud in the corridor for entertainment when you were not there."

"You are absolutely determined to make things hard on yourself."

"As I am scheduled for execution when this interrogation terminates, I don't see how I can make things harder on myself."

"Comrade Beria himself initiated this interview in the hope that you would do what you have refused to do during the five months of your formal interrogation—confess to being an agent of the British Secret Intelligence Service, explain why they are so intent on discrediting the

Englishman. Your immediate superior, the Captain Gusakov, confessed. His immediate superior, the late Colonel Sudoplatov—"

"Late! Has he been executed, too?"

"The Colonel Sudoplatov went to the crypt, it must be said, with a measure of dignity, walking on his own two feet, refusing, like you, a last cigarette on the grounds that inhaling tobacco fumes could damage his lungs."

"Who would have suspected Senior Colonel Sudoplatov of having a sense of humour?"

"I have his signed confession if you care to see it. He named you and Gusakov as agents of the British SIS. He said all three of you had been instructed by your controller, a second secretary at the British embassy in Moscow, to leave no stone unturned in your efforts to discredit the Englishman."

"There is no point to showing me the colonel's confession. I am no longer able to read. My right eye cannot focus, my left eye is so bruised I see black spots when I open it."

"If you had confessed, your interrogators would not have been obliged to treat you as a hostile witness. You can still confess, prisoner Modinskaya. I can promise you your sentence will be reviewed at the highest level, taking your years of party work and your confession into account. [Pause] Please be so kind as to explain why you refuse to confess."

"I don't confess because I am not guilty of being a British agent. I don't confess because I refuse to stain Communism by giving false evidence against myself. I don't confess because I am convinced the Englishman is an

SIS disinformation agent. As a Communist, as a party member since my graduation from the NKVD academy, as a dedicated Stalinist, I have an obligation to expose the Englishman so that our state organs will not be infected by the manure he disseminates."

"Can you put forward a single instance of disinformation that the Englishman passed on to Moscow Centre?"

"We asked him for the names of British agents working for Her Majesty's Secret Intelligence Service in the Soviet Union. He responded there were none. Not one. He said the SIS was underfunded by its parent organization, the Foreign Office. He said in any case SIS was focused on Hitler's Germany and Mussolini's Italy, and not the Soviet Union."

"How can you be sure this is false?"

"How can I be sure this is false? Surely you and I are living on different planets. Both Captain Gusakov and Senior Colonel Sudoplatov have been executed, and I have been condemned to death, all of us guilty of being British spies. As our Soviet system of justice is infallible, it means the Englishman was lying when he claimed the British ran no agents in the Soviet Union."

"Do you admit, then, to being a British agent? Be careful how you answer. You are in an awkward position. If you claim your condemnation as a British spy was a mistake, if you convince us that you and Captain Gukasov and Senior Colonel Sudoplatov are not British agents, the Englishman will have been telling the truth. Which means your effort to discredit him is tantamount to wrecking, and every Soviet child knows the punishment for wrecking. On the other hand if you admit to being a British agent, it would mean you were right all along when you said the Englishman was lying to us when he claimed the SIS had no spy network in the Soviet Union. But being right about the Englishman cannot help you once you admit to being a British agent."

"I am lost no matter which way I turn."

"Your only hope of salvation is to put your trust in Comrade Stalin and his organ of state security, for which you recently worked. Neither Comrade Stalin nor his People's Commissariat for Internal Affairs are capable of making mistakes. You must trust our judgement, which is inspired by Comrade Stalin's perception of reality. We have come to the conclusion, after meticulous examination of the Englishman's bona fides—I believe you are familiar with the contents of case file number 5581—that the agent known by the cryptonym *Sonny* is true in his allegiance to international Communism and the Soviet Union; that he has been since his recruitment by our London *Rezident* in 1934; that the secrets he has conveyed to his various handlers are genuine, most recently the date of the dastardly Nazi attack on our motherland."

"I need time to think . . ."

"I tell you frankly, prisoner Modinskaya, one woman speaking to another, in your shoes I would be terrorized at the prospect of imminent execution."

"I am beyond terror, comrade interrogator. I remember when the comrade guards, thickset men wearing stained leather aprons over their NKVD uniforms, came up from the crypt to collect the prisoner I had interrogated. They were smoking fat cigarettes and laughing nervously. These same men have made guest appearances in my nightmares ever since."

"The tape is reaching the end of the reel. My time with you is almost up."

"Don't go, for God's sake."

"The interview can only continue if I obtain a confession."

"What good would the confession of an innocent comrade do you?"

"Once we have your confession in hand, innocence or guilt is beside the point."

"My innocence *is* the point."

"What can I say to convince you otherwise, to overcome your pigheadedness? Listen . . . [Pause] Do you hear footsteps in the corridor? It can only be the comrades coming up from the crypt to collect you."

"Ohhh, I *am* frightened. [Pause] I must talk to you as long as possible."

"Prisoner Modinskaya, it was Comrade Stalin himself who exposed the diabolical scheme to discredit Sonny. It was Comrade Stalin himself who unmasked the traitors. Surely you don't give the same weight to your delusions of innocence as Comrade Stalin's unshakeable belief in your guilt."

"I [inaudible]."

"You must speak louder."

"I [inaudible]."

"Someone has inserted a key in the door."

"Oh God, yes. You are surely right. I must be guilty if

respected Josef Vissarionovich believes I am guilty. How could it be otherwise? To think we shot Teodor Stepanovich Maly without giving him a last cigarette and he was telling the truth about the Englishman's being a genuine Soviet agent. I confess. I confess to not being a virgin. I confess the Trotskyists ordered me to assassinate respected Josef Vissarionovich. I confess to wrecking bread production by throwing glass fragments into sacks of flour."

"And the Englishman?"

"Yes, yes, most of all the Englishman. I confess to being in the employ of the British Secret Intelligence Service. I confess to slandering the Englishman in order to discredit a genuine Soviet agent reporting to us from the heart of British darkness—"

16: LONDON, JULY 1945

Where the Hajj Writes the Third Act of an Espionage Drama

Dear Colonel Menzies provided the shoulder I leaned on when my father, the Admiral Sinclair, passed on in December of '39. Oh, if only he had lived to see this day: Hitler and Mussolini dead, the Nazis delivering their unconditional surrender, the world war that ravaged Europe over and done. Here in London, some four weeks after the German capitulation, groups of young gentlemen and ladies still wander the streets singing "Kiss Me Goodnight, Sergeant Major", which father often hummed to himself as he shaved.

It was Colonel Stewart Menzies, Old Etonian, Royal Horse Guard with a DSO in his lapel for gallantry at Ypres, who became chief of His Majesty's Secret Intelligence Service upon father's untimely demise. I am persuaded it was an appointment universally cheered (with the possible exception of Colonel Vivian, a belt-and-braces veteran of the Indian Police Service and father's second deputy, who had to settle for the counter-intelligence portfolio). In those first difficult months, poor Colonel Menzies was treated as an irksome stepchild by his masters in the Foreign Office who were, in the Admiral's words, prisoners of a nineteenth-century mindset that considered espionage (as opposed to diplomacy) to be an inconsequential tool in the Great Game, that age-old rivalry between Russia and Britain and France for control of the Hindu Kush. Espionage can be said to have come into its own after Munich, when even the Philistines in the F.O. thought it could be useful in predicting and containing Hitler's ambitions in Europe.

Like the Admiral before him, Colonel Menzies took the F.O.'s hostility in stride. He was the soul of kindness as he and I scurried around Hampstead and Kensington so I could identify the dead letterboxes that father had serviced himself the day before his death. Back at Caxton House, I'd deciphered the index cards father had carried around in his breast pocket (I am the only one able to make heads or tails of his handwriting) listing his espionage agents, one agent to a card: there was a hodgepodge of foreign embassy cipher and post room clerks, two South American ambassadors, a Norwegian freighter captain, a Brazilian matinee idol, a handful of Swedish and Spanish businessmen, a Lebanese money changer, an Indian pretending to be a maharajah, the madam of what we English call a bawdy house, a Jewish diamond merchant with associates in South Africa, Bechuanaland, and Holland. Oh, I mustn't overlook the Liechtenstein princess who claimed to be in touch with her royal cousins in the various Slavic kingdoms of Europe, God knows how. As I recall it, Colonel Menzies, whose straightforward gaze betrayed a certain innocence of spirit, looked up from his note-taking soon after father's death. "It goes without saying, Miss Sinclair, you *will* stay on—you are, after all, our institutional memory. Who can be trusted to take minutes of top-secret meetings if not you?"

In truth, I was only too relieved to submit to Colonel Menzies' entreaties. Mind, I still didn't receive an honorarium, but thanks to my father's flag-rank pension I was able to make ends meet without too much difficulty. And I didn't fancy myself living out the days Providence left me preparing tea and crumpets for Temperance Society spinsters in Camden Town. "I shall be only too pleased to keep my nose to the grindstone," I'd informed the Colonel. And I had, through the chaotic weeks of the blitz when SIS was expanding exponentially and we were issued sidearms to repel German paratroopers who might land on the roof of Caxton House; through the exhilarating months following the Normandy invasion when the red arrows on the giant war map marking the progress of our armies inched closer to Berlin; through these last several days when blood, sweat, and tears gave way to the exuberance of church bells ringing in every borough and shire.

Colonel Menzies' prickly voice broke into my remembrance of things past. "Miss Sinclair," he growled, his cherubic face in the doorway of my cubicle, "I shall be requiring your services this afternoon. That chap your father called the Hajj seems to be coming by at four."

My institutional memory rose to the occasion. "You must mean the Arabist St John Philby," I said.

"That's the one. Let's hope he has combed the lice out of his beard, what? Could you fetch the minutes of the meeting we had with him in '34 so I can stir my memory?"

It didn't take me long to locate the minutes in the steel filing cabinet the security people had insisted on installing in my cubicle. I brought it up to the colonel's topside parlour immediately. He had changed the décor since father's day. The thick curtain the Admiral favoured had been replaced by venetian blinds, albeit closed day and night; a mixed bag of kings and queens eavesdropped from the walls in the place of Wellington's generals; a large electricity-powered wall clock thunderously ticked off the seconds where once father's nautical chronometer had delicately chimed watches at sea. "I expect this is what you are looking for," I said, giving the typescript of the minutes in question to the colonel.

He read it on the diagonal, as we say in the espionage trade. "Seems to be a gap near the end," he announced. I handed him my original shorthand notes of the minutes. Half a page had been blacked out.

"Who did that?" He demanded.

"Father."

"Why?"

"I don't know, really. I suppose he didn't want to leave a paper trail."

He plucked the telephone off its hook. "Mrs. Mortimer, kindly ask Captain Knox downstairs in science to drop what he's doing and come by."

Moments later there was a rap on the door. "Come," Colonel Menzies called.

"Sir?"

"What do you make of this, Knox?" Colonel Menzies asked, holding out my shorthand notes of the minutes.

"Why, it's been blacked out by a thick marker, hasn't it?"

"I can see that, man. Are you able to make out what's under the black marker?"

"I should think so."

"How will you do it?"

"I expect I shall hold the paper up to a very bright light and photograph it, then work on the printing of the negative to bring out the writing a bit more on each positive."

"How long will it take?"

"I should have it ready for Miss Sinclair to type up by the time you return from lunch."

"By the by, what is your clearance, Knox?"

"I am cleared to read anything the prime minister can read, sir."

"I am not convinced that he is cleared to read this bit."

"I take your meaning, Colonel. I shall make no effort to decipher the shorthand under the black marker."

"Good man, Knox."

Knox was true to his word. Here is the last part of the minutes. I've italicized the half page that father had blacked out:

The Hajj: The future is perceptible to those who are not fearful of gazing into the crystal ball. Europe is heading for another Great War. Soviet Russia, with its limitless manpower, with Stalin's ruthless thirst for conquest, will emerge from it to dominate Europe. The Soviets, keen to recover lost territories, will dress up old Tsarist appetites in Communist ideology. Revolutionary movements financed and encouraged by the Soviets, and ultimately loyal to the Soviets, will spring up in the most unlikely places. The empire will be at risk. India will be the first to go.

Colonel Menzies: What would you have us do, St John, that we're not already doing?

Colonel Vivian: Can we suppose you have something up your sleeve?

The Hajj: Be a damn fool turning up here if I didn't.

Father: Could you tell us about it?

The Hajj: I shall have to kill you all immediately if I do. [General laughter]

Father: You haven't interrupted your exploration of Arabia's Empty Quarter to hold back on us, old boy. Do spit it out.

The Hajj: We must dangle an Englishman under their Soviet noses and entice them into recruiting him. Not just any Englishman but someone from the upper class, someone with a smart school tie, someone who the Russians think can worm his way into the Establishment. You see, we don't have to penetrate Moscow Centre, we need only let Moscow Centre think it has penetrated our Secret Intelligence Service. Then we can feed them foolscap until the cows come home, along with the occasional real secret that they are able to verify. There is no end to the possibilities that will open to us. We can get into Stalin's brain and do his thinking for him, we can manipulate his decisions. If we succeed, Stalin's NKVD will become a wholly owned subsidiary of our SIS.

Father: I presume you have a candidate in mind.

The Hajj: I do, actually. My boy, Kim. He was made for the Great Game. I had him flirt with Communism at Cambridge to establish his Marxist credentials. When he came down from university, I packed him off to Vienna to spout clichés about the Homo Sovieticus *rising to historical challenges whilst he himself participated in the inevitable Communist mutiny against Dollfuss. He contacted me for permission to marry one of Moscow Centre's local agents and bring her to safety in London. Not surprisingly, the Russians went for the bait. Swallowed it hook, line and sinker, you might say. The Soviet NKVD recruited my boy on a bench in Regent's Park one month ago.*

Father: St John, do I understand you to be telling us that your boy Kim is a Soviet agent?

The Hajj: They think he is. We must let the Russians go on believing they have an agent who can work his way up in the Foreign Office or on Fleet Street. With time they will come to trust him. At some point—after, say, he has made a reputation for himself as a diplomat or a journalist—you might recruit him into His Majesty's Secret Intelligence Service. The Russians in Moscow Centre will break open bottles of bubbly, which is an amusing way of celebrating, actually—the one time I drank Soviet champagne it was flatter than stale beer. Think of the possibilities, man. Think of the disinformation we can feed them, think of what we can learn simply from the questions his Soviet handlers ask? We'll be able to figure out what they don't know.

Colonel Menzies: Outrageous, what?

Colonel Vivian: Rather boggles the mind.

Father: Outrageous, indeed. But filled with the potential

to influence the way the Soviets see the world. Can we agree that this meeting never took place?

The Hajj: What meeting?

St John Philby turned up at Colonel Menzies' door on the hour. He was still wearing scuffed tennis plimsolls but the rest of his attire was straight from the flea market on Portobello Road: dark, pinstriped, threadbare, double-breasted with a frayed Westminster school tie knotted to the Adam's apple, and the tip of what I took to be a Cellucotton gas mask filter spilling from his breast pocket.

"You look fit," Colonel Menzies remarked, greeting the Hajj at the door of the Holy of Holies, shaking his hand and pulling him into the room at the same time. "You will remember Colonel Vivian," he added. "He still minds our counter-intelligence shop, which ought to be right up your alley, what?"

"Great day," Colonel Vivian remarked as he poured claret into three small glasses and offered one to the visitor.

"Great day for those who can't see beyond the tip of their nose," St John said. He carefully set his glass on the low table, lowered himself smack centre onto the couch, and reached down to undo his laces. "Ask me, our troubles are only just beginning."

"How so?" Colonel Menzies inquired.

"Zhukov's army beat us to Berlin. Red Army took Warsaw and Budapest and Sofia and Prague. I don't see Stalin bringing his boys home any time soon. What with the Americans abandoning the European theatre to concentrate on the Nips, nothing stands between the twelve-million-man Red Army and the English Channel. Uncle Joe may be tempted to organize a victory parade that finishes up on the French beaches facing our white cliffs of Dover."

"We have been dealing with that eventuality," Colonel Vivian said. "We've had your boy feeding them bogus information designed to ruin Stalin's appetite—aerodromes in Britain and Ireland crammed with B-29 bombers, the bombers armed with that new atomic explosive device the Americans tested in the New Mexico desert yesterday, even a list of five hundred Soviet cities we plan to obliterate if the balloon goes up."

Philby senior sank back into the cushions of the couch. "I take it my boy has earned his keep here."

Colonel Menzies beamed. "Kim was born to be a spy. He took to espionage like the proverbial fish to water. I don't know how he keeps the various storylines straight in his head, but he does. I can tell you that despite his young years, he has become a rising star in Section Five, an expert in counter-intelligence. We had him in charge of our Iberian operation for most of the war."

Colonel Vivian said, "The Americans were so impressed with your boy they seconded one of their bright OSS recruits fresh from Yale to learn counter-intelligence at his feet. Chap name of Jesus Angleton."

Colonel Menzies wagged a finger. "His name was James Angleton. Jesus was his middle name."

"Whichever," Colonel Vivian muttered.

The old animosity between the two colonels was never far from the surface.

Colonel Menzies ignored his deputy. "You will get a kick out of the latest, St John. Once the end of the war came in sight, we opened a small Soviet Russia counter-intelligence operation. Change of focus, what? Called it Section Nine. Decided to put Kim at the helm of this new tender, too."

"Russians probably couldn't believe their good fortune when Kim let his handler know about this assignment," Colonel Vivian said. "Seen from Moscow, they will think they have their mole running our anti-Soviet operation."

"Do the Yanks know about Kim being a double agent?"

"I should think he qualifies as a triple agent," Colonel Vivian remarked.

Again Colonel Menzies took no notice of his chief of counter-intelligence. "Not counting Kim, only the three of us in this room"—Colonel Menzies noticed me, sitting off to one side taking notes on a clipboard—"or should I say the four of us, yes, with Miss Sinclair here, only the four of us know the real story."

Colonel Vivian, restive, helped himself to more claret. "Wasn't always smooth sailing, mind you. In the late thirties Moscow Centre had an obstinate female analyst who was convinced your boy was feeding them disinformation."

Colonel Menzies finished the story for him. "It was touch and go for a time. The analyst presented her conclusions to several constituencies in Moscow Centre, raising doubts about your boy's loyalty to the Soviets. She was eventually discredited, we're not sure why, we're not sure by whom. The only thing we know is that at some point she was convicted of attempting to assassinate Stalin and shot."

"All of which brings me to the third act," the Hajj said.

"The third act? Dear fellow, with a bit of good fortune we can keep this show on the road indefinitely," Colonel Vivian said.

"I have given this a great deal of thought," Philby senior said. "We should not count on the Russians being eternally duped. If the NKVD is anything like your Secret Intelligence Service, there will be a new generation of analysts coming up through the ranks. One of them will want to make a name for himself. What better way than to suss out a British agent. He will analyse all of Kim's telegrams, beginning with 1934 when he told the then *Rezident*, the one who was later summoned back to Moscow and shot, that he had gone through my private papers and found no evidence I was working for the Secret Intelligence Service."

"That was true," Colonel Vivian observed.

"It was true enough to pass muster," the Hajj agreed. "But a careful analysis will reveal that most of the so-called secrets my boy passed on either served British interests—as when he informed Stalin of the date Hitler had chosen for the German invasion of Soviet Russia—or were patently false. Take this business of the aerodromes in Britain and Ireland being crammed with B-29 bombers armed with that new-fangled atomic thingamabob. The Russians will eventually figure out it was not true. And an analyst worth his salt will raise the possibility that my boy knew it wasn't true when he passed the information on to his handler, which would suggest he is a double agent."

"Oughtn't that to be triple agent?" Colonel Vivian interjected.

Both Colonel Menzies and Mr. Philby looked intently

at Colonel Vivian, who scratched at his cheek in discomfiture. Colonel Menzies turned back to the Hajj. "Do finish your thought, St John."

"I was saying, when enough doubts are raised, the scales will tilt against my boy and the suspicion that he is a double agent—yes, I think *double agent* is the more accurate term—will begin to set in."

"What you're telling us is quite unsettling," Colonel Menzies allowed. "Can we preempt?"

"We can and we should," the Hajj said. "I should think the shelf life of an agent leading two lives is roughly ten years. Kim came on board your shop in 1940. If my hunch is right, we can continue on as we are for another five years."

"What then?" asked Colonel Vivian.

"Around about 1950, we might arrange for my boy to be exposed as a long-time Soviet agent."

The colonels stared at the Hajj, speechless.

"Am I to understand you to be suggesting—" Colonel Vivian sputtered.

"Surely you are pulling our leg?" Colonel Menzies said.

I could see that Mr. Philby seemed quite pleased with himself. "I have never been more serious," he declared. "It ought to be simple enough. The Americans could break out phrases from old encrypted Soviet diplomatic telegrams indicating that one of their agents inside the F.O., whilst serving in the British Embassy in Washington, visited his pregnant wife in New York at weekends. That will lead directly to Kim's old Cambridge sidekick Donald Maclean—"

"You would have us expose Maclean!" Colonel Vivian exclaimed.

"He is, after all, a genuine Soviet agent," the Hajj reminded his listeners.

"Fair point," Colonel Menzies murmured.

"My boy," Philby senior went on, "would in the course of his counter-intelligence activities discover that the Americans were closing in on Maclean. He could dispatch Guy Burgess to warn Maclean to run for it. If Kim could manage to frighten Burgess, perhaps he would lose his nerve and run for it with Maclean. We would be rid of two Soviet spies without the awkwardness of bringing evidence against them in a public trial. When the two surfaced in Moscow, the Americans would zero in on my boy—he was, after all, a Cambridge comrade of theirs since the early thirties. Surely someone would recollect it was Burgess who put forward Kim's name for recruitment into SIS. And how else could Maclean have been warned to flee if not by Kim?"

The colonels were hanging on the Hajj's words as if he were recounting the plot of a spy novel. "Then what?" Colonel Vivian demanded a bit breathlessly.

"You would have to sack Kim, of course. He would be put through the wringer by your interrogators, but he would deny everything. 'Me, a long-time Soviet penetration agent? Ludicrous!' Any evidence against my boy—operations of his that turned sour, agents he ran who were rounded up by the Russians—could be written off as mere coincidences. Given the American qualms, Kim would have to be put to pasture. Perhaps he could go back to journalism. Yes, why not? A journalist covering the Middle East, which he knows well, from, say, Beirut. A bit of time would need to pass for the Russians to digest all of this. One fine day you could come up with the single detail—a witness who swears Kim tried to recruit her as a Soviet spy, something along those lines—that makes the case against Kim airtight. He would be given the choice of admitting his treachery and doubling back against the Soviets, or going to prison for the rest of his life. At which point he, too, would run for it. The Russians will have an exfiltration plan in place for just such an eventuality. My boy would surface in Moscow, where he would be given a hero's reception. He would be welcomed into the Heart of Darkness, Moscow Centre in the Lubyanka. The Russians would be fools not to use Kim's skills. He would become a senior Soviet intelligence officer, consulted on past and current operations, asked to vet prospective penetration agents, invited to give his opinion on potential targets."

The two colonels melted back into their seats, incapable of human speech. Each stared at his shoes with Delphic intensity. The silence lasted an eternity. Colonel Vivian was the first to find his voice. "You obviously assume Kim would go along with this scenario," he said. He raised his voice at the end of the sentence, transforming it into a question.

The Hajj favoured the colonels with one of his crooked smiles. "My boy lives for the Great Game. He is keen to be an important player in it. And he does what his sainted father tells him to do. Always has, always will."

Both colonels sat there shaking their heads. Colonel Menzies said, "What you are suggesting, St John, is out of the realm of possibility."

"My sentiments precisely," Colonel Vivian agreed with unaccustomed vehemence.

The Hajj reached down and began tying up the laces of his plimsolls. "Why, pray tell, is it out of the realm of possibility?"

"To begin with," Colonel Menzies said, his voice reduced to an edgy scratch, his Horse Guard whiskers ruffled by the whiff of a plausible answer to the question he was posing, "who would believe it?"

EPILOGUE: BEIRUT, JANUARY 1963

Where the Englishman Flees to Soviet Russia with Ten Tins of Arm & Hammer Indigestion Tablets in His Pockets

At midnight, the Russian freighter *Dolmatova* quietly winched in its lines from the bollards on a Beirut pier and slipped out of the harbour. Only later did British intelligence agents in the Lebanese capital notice that the freighter had sailed without taking on a cargo or waiting for an ebb tide. As the bow pitched onto the first sea swell, the ship's only passenger, an Englishman, climbed the ladder to the flag bags aft of the bridge. A deckhand wearing dirty overalls and a thick oilskin was raising a large hammer-and-sickle ensign—snapping in the wind like gunshots, it seemed to confer Soviet citizenship on the Englishman as it made its way up the halyard to the yardarm.

The passenger looked back over the stern at the lights of the Lebanese capital. In his mind's eye, they appeared to be stammering in Morse code on the receding horizon, much the way he stammered when he spoke. He wondered what message they might be sending. Squinting, he thought he could make out the dimmer lights of the Druze village on a hillside above Beirut where his father had lived out his last days in a modest cottage. The Englishman had driven up most weekends, and they had spent countless hours taking in the sun on wooden reclining chairs in the small garden, talking about how the Great Game might play out. When the end came the Englishman had buried his father in a Muslim graveyard below the village, marking the site, as Muslims did, with a small stone. As there was no name engraved on the stone, nobody would know where St John was buried now that his boy had left.

The Englishman, a Middle East correspondent for two London newspapers, *The Observer* and *The Economist*, had fled Beirut one jump ahead of the British agents come to arrest him as a Soviet spy. He left the city with the clothes on his back, two thick woollen sweaters worn one over the other, a spare pair of reading glasses, ten small tins of Arm & Hammer indigestion tablets and the much thumbed copy of Simon & Schuster's pocket book number 1, James Hilton's *Lost Horizon*, that his father had had sent from Harrods in 1939 to replace the hardcover edition he'd lost during the Spanish Civil War. The Englishman had used both the hardcover and the paperback edition of *Lost Horizon* for enciphering purposes (page number, line number, letter number) when he'd communicated with his Soviet controllers. He expected to keep in touch with his father's friends in London the same way after he reached Moscow.

As a spy, the Englishman had had a bloody good run. He'd managed to lead a double life—or should that be triple?—for the better part of two decades. His career had come to an abrupt halt in the early 1950s when Her Majesty's Secret Intelligence Service seconded him to Washington as the British liaison with the CIA. American code breakers were in the process of exposing Donald Maclean, the Englishman's chum since their undergraduate days at Cambridge University, as a Soviet agent. The Englishman had immediately come under suspicion and been expelled from America, then grilled for months by SIS interrogators who had thrown every botched intelligence operation, every blown agent in his face. He'd shrugged until his shoulders hurt, denying everything. As they had no smoking gun, they couldn't bring charges against him without a confession. SIS had been obliged to fire him, since the Americans refused to talk to their British cousins while this particular Englishman was on their payroll. After a decent interval he had gone back to the career he'd begun in Spain during the Civil War: journalism. Which is how he wound up as a Middle East correspondent in Beirut.

As the lights of the Lebanese capital vanished into the penumbra where land met sea, the Englishman turned to gaze ahead over the fall of salt spray on the fo'c's'le, trying to imagine the life that awaited him in the Soviet *Shangri-La*.

Would the Russians swallow the scenario that his sainted father had concocted?

Would they believe Her Majesty's Secret Intelligence Service had turned up in Beirut with the last piece of the puzzle; hard evidence that he was in fact a long-time Soviet penetration agent?

Would Moscow Centre welcome him into the Heart of Darkness as a senior Soviet intelligence officer?

Would he be allowed to order books from *Bowes & Bowes* of Cambridge and tins of Arm & Hammer indigestion tablets from Harrods?

Would the Great Game the Englishman was so keen on playing have a third act?

For spies and rock climbers, was there really no way out except up?

CODA: A TRUE SPY STORY

Where the Author of *Young Philby* Explains Why the Idea That Kim Philby Might have been a Double Agent—Or Should That be Triple?—is Not Far-Fetched.

I spent the winter of 2000 in Jerusalem doing research for a novel set in the Middle East. One evening I had dinner with my great friend Zev Birger, the head of the Jerusalem Book Fair at the time. He had been instrumental in introducing me to then retired prime minister, now president of Israel, Shimon Peres, with whom I eventually collaborated on a book of conversations. Zev, who was said to know everyone important in Israel, asked me out of the blue if there was anyone in the country I wanted to meet that I hadn't met. I told him that as a matter of fact there was. It was the long-time mayor of Jerusalem, Teddy Kollek, by then retired.

The next morning Zev phoned to say he had arranged a rendezvous. At noon on 31 January 2000 I turned up in Teddy Kollek's office at the Jerusalem Foundation on Rivka Street. Mr. Kollek, a heavy man, then eighty-nine, who smoked thin cigars, waved me to a seat across the desk from him and asked why I wanted to see him. He regarded me through professorial half-glasses that had slipped down along his nose. I explained that I was familiar with his biography: He'd grown up in Vienna and had been active in Socialist circles there in the early 1930s. I was curious to know if Mr. Kollek had come across a young Cambridge graduate in Vienna named Kim Philby. Mr. Kollek said that everyone in the leftist community in Vienna had been acquainted with Philby in those days, that he himself knew him by sight. I asked if Mr. Kollek had known Litzi Friedman as well. Yes, he said, he'd known Litzi well enough to say hello to her; in Vienna, he continued, everyone knew she was a Communist and many assumed she was some sort of Soviet agent. I asked if Mr. Kollek was aware that Philby and the Friedman woman had gotten married in Vienna after the right-wing Chancellor Dollfuss suppressed the Socialists and Communists in 1934. Again he said yes, it was common knowledge that Philby had married Litzi to get her a British passport. And then, to my surprise, he added that it had been widely assumed Litzi Friedman must have recruited Philby as a Soviet agent.

Unprompted, Mr. Kollek began telling me another story:

When the Jewish state was born in 1948, the Mossad, Israel's CIA, was eager to contact the new American Central Intelligence Agency, but the CIA people, believing that the Mossad could have been infiltrated by Soviet agents posing as Jewish refugees, kept the Israelis at arm's length. After repeated requests, the Americans finally relented and agreed to a first tentative meeting. It was Teddy Kollek, working for the Mossad, who was dispatched to a certain room in the Statler Hotel in Washington to make contact. The person representing the CIA at that initial meeting turned out to be none other than its legendary counter-intelligence chief, James Jesus Angleton.

A word about James Angleton: Fresh out of Yale University in the early 1940s, he'd joined the American wartime intelligence organization, the Office of Strategic Services, and been posted to London to learn counter-intelligence from His Majesty's Secret Intelligence Service. It was the older and more experienced Kim Philby, a rising star in the SIS, who took the young American under his wing. The two became fast friends, bunking together on beds in the SIS building during the German blitz, climbing to the roof to watch the German bombers raiding London. After the war in Europe ended, Angleton moved on to direct OSS operations in Italy and when President Truman created the Central Intelligence Agency in the late 1940s, Angleton became its counter-intelligence chief.

When Teddy Kollek and Angleton met in the Statler, they hit it off and became good friends. In Mr. Kollek's words, they had a close relationship. Mr. Kollek brought Angleton, whose hobby was growing orchids, rare Israeli orchids from a farm that belonged to the Rothschilds and dined with Angleton and his wife, Cicely, at their Washington home. And of course they regularly collaborated on intelligence matters.

Fast forward to 1952: With the Cold War in full swing, Mr. Kollek came to Washington to see his friend Angleton at the CIA buildings, old World War II barracks on the

Reflecting Pool. "I was walking towards Angleton's office," Kollek told me when I interviewed him in Jerusalem, "when suddenly I spotted a familiar face at the other end of the hallway. There was no mistake about it. I burst into Angleton's office and said, 'Jim, you'll never guess whom I saw in the hallway. It was Kim Philby!' And I told him about Vienna and the marriage to Litzi Friedman and the suspicion that Philby may have been recruited by her as a Soviet agent. And I said, 'Once a Communist, always a Communist.' "

Startled, I asked Mr. Kollek if those had been his exact words. "Yes," he said. "I told him, 'Once a Communist, always a Communist.' "

I asked if Angleton had reacted. "No, Jim never reacted to anything. The subject was dropped and never raised again."

When Mr. Kollek spotted Philby at the end of the hallway, he was serving in Washington as liaison between the Brits and their American counterparts at the CIA and FBI. Kim met with his old pal from London, Jim Angleton, almost daily. The two regularly lunched together at a Georgetown watering hole on Fridays.

"What happened after you told Angleton about Philby and Vienna?" I asked.

I have this memory of Mr. Kollek concentrating on the ash threatening to drop off the end of his cigar. "Your guess is as good as mine," he replied.

My guess is at the heart of *Young Philby*.

In the course of Angleton's long career, which ended when he was fired by CIA Director Colby in 1975, the counter-intelligence chief was obsessed with the possibility of Soviet penetration. CIA employees who spoke fluent Russian or had Russian or Polish-sounding names fell under a cloud. Lie detector tests were administered left and right; not everyone passed. Careers were ruined by Angleton's shadow of a doubt. Would-be defectors were turned away for fear they might be Soviet disinformation agents. Ultimately the CIA's entire Soviet Russia division was gutted and its operations against the Soviet Union crippled because of Angleton's obsession with Soviet penetration. Whether Angleton learned about Philby's suspicious past (Cambridge Socialist Society, Vienna, Litzi Friedman) from Teddy Kollek, or knew it already, it is unthinkable that he would have permitted Philby to set foot inside the CIA's sanctum unless . . .

Unless he had personally *turned* Philby, or Philby had been a British agent feeding disinformation to Moscow all along. In the end, the best way to penetrate the Soviet Heart of Darkness would be to make Moscow Centre think it had penetrated Western intelligence agencies. At which point the British and Americans, in the words of my character *The Hajj*, could feed the Soviets disinformation until the cows came home.

When Donald Maclean, on the point of being exposed as a Soviet agent, fled to Moscow (along with Guy Burgess, who apparently lost his nerve at the last moment and went with him), Kim Philby's cover was blown. Forced by SIS to resign in July of 1951, he ended up working as Middle East correspondent for two London newspapers, *The Observer* and *The Economist*, in Beirut. After he, in turn, fled to the

Soviet Union in 1963, Angleton let drop hints to his CIA colleagues that there was more to the Philby story than met the eye. The suggestion was obviously self-serving. But was there more?

Teddy Kollek died on 2 January 2007.

The mystery of Philby's ultimate loyalty lives on.

Also by Robert Littell

THE STALIN EPIGRAM

'A wonderful and compelling read about power, poetry, love, literature, terror and Russia'
Simon Sebag Montefiore

'A tremendous atmosphere of despairing suspense is created immediately and sustained almost unbearably until the final pages'
Guardian

ISBN 9780715640739 eBook also available

Moscow, 1934. As thousands of peasant farmers starve under Stalin's regime, Osip Mandelstam, perhaps the greatest Russian poet of the twentieth century, defies the Kremlin with a few short, audacious lines of verse – a searing indictment of Stalin secretly recited to a handful of friends and fellow artists.

When a transcript of his work falls into the hands of the secret police, the poet is taken from his home to Lubyanka prison under accusations of counter-revolutionary activities, which carry the highest penalty. His fate – as well as the fates of those close to him – is cast into bleak uncertainty.

Duckworth Overlook
90-93 Cowcross Street
London EC1M 6BF
info@duckworth-publishers.co.uk